MELT THE ICE

CALGARY MOUNTIES

BOOK 2

ALLISON A ANDREWS

AAW Publishing

Published by AAW Publishing

Cover design and artwork by Magnrarts

Chapter Image by Gorodenkoff

ABOUT THE AUTHOR

Allison A. Andrews is a romance author, wife, and mum based in Brisbane, Australia.
A lifelong book lover with a vivid imagination, she turned her passion for storytelling into swoon-worthy novels filled with men who don't need to be taught how to be human, strong women, and unforgettable stories.

www.aawpublishing.com

ALSO BY ALLISON A. ANDREWS & ANTOINETTE W. MAY

Order of the Dragon Trilogy (Paranormal Romance)

#1 Illusions

#2 Blood Memories

#3 Phoenix Rising

Circle of Friends Series (Contemporary Romance)

The Winning Ticket

Chasing Horizons

Dance With Me

Pieces of Us

Calgary Mounties

(Contemporary Hockey Romance)

On Thin Ice

Melt The Ice

Coming Home For Christmas Anthology

From Snow to Surf (Circle of Friends and Calgary Mounties Crossover)

Dark Desires (Contemporary Spicy Romance)

(Writing as Antoinette W. May)

Reckless (Intro Novella)

Ravage

Ruin

CONTENTS

AUTHOR'S NOTE

Whilst this book is generally humourous and light hearted, there are some subjects - while handled with respect - that some readers may find upsetting, such as past death of a parent, parent with alcoholism and workplace sexism.

Please protect your peace and proceed with caution should you be sensitive towards these subjects.

To everyone who's ever fallen for someone they absolutely shouldn't... Love is always worth the risk.

SPOTIFY PLAYLIST

Scan the QR code here to be taken to the official Spotify playlist for Melt The Ice.

Chapter One

WELCOME TO THE MOUNTIES

Alanna

I stare at the clock on the wall, trying to keep my leg from jiggling while rubbing the pendant on my necklace between my fingers. Whether it's from nerves or frustration, I can't quite tell. I've been waiting in this hallway for twenty minutes without seeing a single other person, which seems a little odd.

The hall is lined with framed jerseys and trophy cabinets, and I've read the newspaper article on the wall in front of me several times now - about the back to back Stanley Cup finals a few years ago - so the admiration has somewhat dimmed. I guess it's exciting that I've come to work for an NHL team who are clearly impressive... but right now, I just want to get out of this hallway.

Just as I stifle yet another sigh, wishing I'd brought my phone with me, a woman opens a door further down the hall and bustles towards me, her high heels clicking loudly on the concrete floor.

"Alanna? I'm so sorry to keep you waiting," Felicity Clare says, smiling apologetically as she reaches me.

The head of Human Resources is impeccably dressed in a pale pink fitted dress, without a single hair out of place. I don't think I've ever been that put together in my life. She's been my main point of contact for the last few weeks while we've been organizing my move here, and she's been lovely, so at least I know she isn't as intimidating as she appears.

"It's okay," I reply, getting to my feet and shaking the hand she extends towards me.

"I just had a meeting run over, but I thought Trevor would have been here to get you started." She checks her watch before moving towards the closed door across from where I've been sitting, and raises her hand to knock.

"Trevor? I thought I was meeting with Ted?"

She stops with her hand a fraction of an inch away from the door, and turns to look at me again. "Didn't anyone tell you?"

A prickle of unease runs down my spine. "Tell me what?"

She grimaces and lets her hand drop to her side.

"Ted retired last week. Today is Trevor's first day as the head trainer."

Stunned, I manage to keep the disappointment from my face, impressed with my self control even while my stomach sinks.

"Oh... That's a shame. I was really looking forward to working with him."

That's putting it mildly. Ted Rogers pioneered several practices in sports medicine amongst professional sports teams and is a legend in our field. I'd met him at an international conference last year and he'd really pushed for me to make the move to Calgary in Canada from my home in Auckland, going out of his way to interview me several times. And not once did he mention he was retiring.

Felicity gives me a sympathetic smile and knocks finally.

"So Trevor... Is that the Trevor who was on the panel of people interviewing me at the final stage?" I ask, rubbing my pendant again and praying she says no.

"Yes. It's good you met him already, at least it won't be such a shock."

Fabulous.

The door opens, and Trevor appears.

"Yes, Felicity?"

Glad to see he's been sitting in this office the entire time I've been waiting in the hallway for our meeting.

The man looks to be in his mid-fifties, with a receding hairline. He obviously keeps in shape, if his muscular arms are anything to go by. But it's the annoyed look on his face that really stands out. It's the same one that was on his face during my final interview.

The same interview where he had expressly told me that he didn't think women had a place working as trainers on men's professional sports team. Because according to him, he's seen how these men can treat women.

I believe his exact words were "women have no place in this industry, it makes the players uncomfortable. There's too much temptation there."

Which is a load of bullshit. I've worked exclusively with male athletes since I was eighteen and have never had a single issue in the eight years since.

So I highly doubt his attitude has anything to do with protecting my delicate feminine self, and all about the fact that women belong in the kitchen only.

"Alanna Jameson is here for her induction," Felicity replies, her smile looking a little strained.

"Oh." He flicks his gaze my way, and his scowl deepens.

I didn't think it was possible for him to look more annoyed, but apparently I was wrong.

He steps aside, and I follow Felicity into the small room, taking a seat at the table when he waves his hand in that direction. Felicity takes the seat beside me, turning her body slightly to face me.

"It's so good to have you here with us, Alanna, finally. How was your flight? Is the hotel okay?" Felicity asks.

Her warm smile is a stark contrast to the cynical expression on Trevor's face as he takes a seat opposite me.

I avoid looking at the new head trainer and keep my eyes on the bubbly blonde instead. "Yeah, it was good. Long. But I guess pretty much anywhere feels far away when you're flying from New Zealand," I reply, returning her smile with one of my own.

"Yeah, what was it, fourteen hours to Vancouver?" Felicity shudders and I give a little chuckle.

"Yeah. And then that last hour or so to Calgary was the kicker. I passed out pretty early last night. And the hotel is great, by the way."

"Good. Let me know if you need any help with finding a place. But from what I've witnessed so far, you strike me as the type of woman who gets things done, so I'm sure you'll have that sorted in no time."

"Thank you. I've already got a few places lined up to check out."

She grins, pointing at me. "I knew I was right about you."

Trevor clears his throat, and we both glance his way. "Now that we've got that out of the way, shall we start discussing your induction information? I don't have all day."

Felicity frowns at him before returning her smiling eyes to mine. "Of course. I know how precious your time is, Trevor."

I don't miss the the trace of sarcasm in her tone, and it makes me wonder if he has a problem with female trainers, or women working for a sports team in general.

Felicity pulls a binder out from the giant handbag she'd deposited on the floor, handing it to me. "So, this is the employee manual. You can read that in your own time. And I'll take you for a tour of the arena a little later. Some of the players are around already, but most of the ones from out of town are still back home until training camp starts next week."

I nod, eager to get right into my new role.

"I've assigned your players already," Trevor says, cutting Felicity off when she goes to continue speaking.

Felicity closes her mouth with a raised brow, leaving the floor open for Trevor to take over. He hands Felicity a list, and she scans it quietly before passing it to me. She avoids looking at Trevor, who watches us both with a steely glint in his eye. I have no idea what's going on, but I have a feeling some sort of power move is being pulled here.

"These five are good guys who have been with us for several seasons. They are all dedicated to their training, so you shouldn't have a problem with any of them."

"Oh... Only five?" I know that there are three assistant trainers and assumed that the twenty-three hockey players would be spread across the three of us, with Trevor running the show.

Maybe he's still keeping some himself?

"Yes. As the youngest trainer and the least experienced, I didn't want to overwhelm you with too many players."

I try not to react to that obvious insult. I was the most senior of the assistant trainers at my old job back home, with eight professional rugby players I was personally responsible for. I was also told that I was the only assistant trainer with a masters degree in sports medicine here at the Mounties.

This has nothing to do with my age, and everything to do with the lack of a male appendage dangling between my legs.

Felicity clearly agrees, judging by the way she purses her lips while she watches the exchange between the two of us.

I don't bother arguing, though. I refuse to play his games,

and can tell he's just waiting for me to say or do something he can use against me.

I've been through too much to get this job to let some old guy with an inferiority complex get in my way.

"Thanks so much for thinking of me, Trevor. I'm sure once I've settled in, I'll be able to take on more of the players. Especially the more complex cases, given my background."

I watch the way his jaw works while he grinds his teeth, clearly wanting to say more but knowing there's only so far he can go with HR in the room.

Point one, Alanna.

"Well, for now, you'll be working with the rookies over at our practice arena," Trevor says, a smirk playing across his lips. "It's the start of training camp next week. The general manager and coaching staff will be deciding who goes to the Mounties and who's going down to the Cowboys, the AHL team. They have their own training staff, but we've got enough training staff here at the moment, so you can go help them out. I'm sure the five guys on your list will be fine to travel over to you for their training, in the meantime."

Fabulous. So he's sticking me with the less experienced players and making it difficult for the veterans to see me, in the hopes that they will request one of the other trainers.

Point one, Trevor.

Once the unpleasantries are out of the way, Trevor makes an excuse to leave, keen to point out just how busy he is, leaving Felicity to give me the tour.

"He'll warm up once you've been here a little longer," she says, and I huff a laugh.

"No he won't, but it's fine. I've worked for men's sports teams since I was eighteen, and he won't be the last guy I come across that thinks I shouldn't be swimming in the deep end of the pool."

We get to our feet and I follow her through the door leading into the gym next door.

"So, in here is the training room. Your new home away from home during the season... Once you're back from the practice arena. We've got the best of everything in here, but if there is any equipment you think might be needed, just let Trevor know and he can arrange it for the team."

Yeah, like he's going to listen to me.

I'm pretty sure she knows she's dreaming with that statement, but hey, gotta pretend my new boss isn't a giant dickhead, right?

Giving her a smile, I let my eyes wander around the room to give it a brief look and see a few guys over on the mats, stretching.

Professional hockey players are some of the fittest athletes around, so it's not surprising that they are already hard at work, despite it still being the off-season.

"Oh, Lincoln. Good, you can be one of the first to meet our new trainer, Alanna Jameson. She's assigned to you," Felicity says, and a tall, very good looking blond man grins at me as he gets to his feet.

"Hey! Was wondering when the new trainer was arriving. Welcome to the Mounties," Lincoln says, coming over to shake my hand.

"Nice to meet you," I reply, and he cocks his head to the side.

"Aussie?"

I laugh. "Close. Kiwi."

He winces. "Ah, sorry. Is that like calling me an American?"

"We claim each other when we're overseas," I say, grinning while I wiggle my hand in front of me - the international sign for 'sort of'.

The guy he was talking to comes over to join us, and sticks his hand out. "Welcome, Alanna. I'm Seth."

Lincoln grins while I shake Seth's hand. "He's our captain, and recently married an Aussie. Hence my recognizing the accent. Well... not quite recognizing it... You know what, I'm rambling. She's Aussie, you're a Kiwi, and they are both completely different." He clamps his mouth shut and grins at me.

I chuckle, shaking my head.

Okay, so Lincoln is clearly very eager to please. Kind of like a giant golden retriever.

I'm also introduced to Michael, Riley and Anders. Lincoln and Riley are both on my list of players, so it's good to put faces to names.

Jet lag is starting to get the better of me as Felicity walks me around the rest of the spaces and introduces me to a few other staff members.

"I should let you go and get some sleep," Felicity says, as I discreetly cover the latest yawn.

"I want to say I'm fine, but I'm definitely fading," I reply with a smile, and she laughs.

"Well, go get a good nights sleep. You'll need it. Things are about to start ramping up now, and if you're as thorough as I think you are, I know you're going to want to hit the ground running tomorrow."

Good to see she's worked out I'm a workaholic already.

JUST SLUGGISH

Dean

I've always found the first week of training camp to be a struggle. But after a month spent eating and drinking my way around Italy, this week is particularly painful.

"Man, what the hell was that? It was like playing with a college kid after a bender out there." Ollie Matthews, one of our veteran forwards, skates up beside me as I make my way towards the player tunnel after practice.

"Just sluggish. It's not like anyone else was in their top form out there," I reply, shaking my head.

It's a shitty response, but I'm not in the mood to be reminded that my game has definitely slipped. I grew complacent last season, comfortable in my spot in the NHL with my stats for shutouts the highest in the league. And that arrogance carried into the off-season. I kept up with my workouts, but I didn't see a single hour of ice time while I was away, and now I'm paying for it.

Every muscle in my body is screaming at me, and my goalie coach, Oscar, looked unimpressed with my efforts. I definitely need to get back in shape fast. Especially after seeing how quick our newest rookie goalie, Mark, is.

There's a whisper of unease at the back of my mind at the memory of Mark blocking shot after shot all week.

Cursing my stupidity, I ignore the usual banter amongst my teammates as I strip off my jersey and pads.

"You're particularly quiet today," Lincoln comments, dropping down onto the bench beside me.

"Just processing the fact that I should have done way less eating and a lot more skating over the summer," I reply, grimacing.

I know he's spent the time since our captain's wedding during the summer doing daily intense workouts and practicing his slapshots, and it showed during practice. He's at the top of his game right now, guaranteeing his place on the first line with Seth and Riley once again.

If my performance today is anything to go off, I'll be lucky to be the second string goalie this season.

Vowing to spend the next few weeks dedicating myself fully to getting back on top, I finish stripping off my goalie gear and head for the training room to get in a workout while my muscles are still warmed up. My trainer, Simon, already has the squat rack loaded up for me when I enter the room, and I eye it with a sigh.

This is going to hurt like hell.

"Hey, Dean. How was Italy?" Simon asks as soon as I make my way over.

We've been working together for five years now, and I'm glad I didn't lose him in the reshuffle when Ted retired unexpectedly.

"Good, man. Did you get any time off?" I position myself under the bar and get counting, hoping he'll keep talking to distract me from the screaming in my thighs.

I really hate squats.

The older I get, the more my body protests the strain

hockey puts on me, but I can't give it up. I'm not sure what I'd do with myself if I wasn't playing, and at thirty-one, I'm one of the highest-paid goalies in the league.

"I had a week off. Was meant to be longer, but then Ted retiring threw things right off," Simon says as he stands back with his arms crossed, assessing my form.

I get through the first twelve reps and back out of position, shaking my legs out.

"Yeah, I heard about that. What happened?"

He shrugs. "I think something happened with his wife's health. It was all hush hush, but it would take a lot for Ted to leave the Mounties."

I grab my drink bottle and squirt some water into my mouth. "What's happening with Trevor's spot?"

"Ted had hired a new assistant trainer, so it worked out well, I guess. Probably a bit of a shock for her, though. Apparently no one told her about Ted until she arrived for her induction. Would suck thinking your coming to work for a legend and then... not..."

It's the most diplomatic reply he can give in the situation, I guess. It's no secret how much of a dick Trevor is.

"Wait, we're getting a female trainer?" I ask.

"Yeah. About time, too."

"Yeah, it is," I reply, impressed that the Mounties have decided to join the small number of teams with female trainers on staff. "When does she start?"

"She started two weeks ago, actually. She's been over at the practice arena with the new kids, so you probably wouldn't have seen her."

"Right. I knew O'Malley and the others were travelling over there each day, but I didn't know why. Seems a little odd."

Simon sighs as he nods back towards the rack, and I get back into position.

"Pretty sure there's a bit of friction between her and Trevor, and he's pulling some sort of power move," he says, keeping his voice low so that only I can hear him.

I grunt in response as I work through the rest of my set. It doesn't surprise me, but it is disappointing. We finally get a female trainer and she's forced to work with Trevor. Hopefully he doesn't scare her off. We need more female trainers in the NHL.

"She's been doing most of the heavy lifting over there, so I'm hoping to show her tomorrow that we do work as a team here, despite how it seems."

I can just imagine the sort of shitty tasks Trevor had her doing. I've seen how he speaks to the female staff members in other departments, so I have no doubt he's got his boxers in a twist about having a female trainer on staff.

"Anyway, enough about that. What'd you get up to while you were away?" he asks, once I've finished my second set.

I shrug. "Oh, you know. Visiting the parents, eating way too much pizza and pasta."

Simon chuckles. "And, I'm guessing, making a few friends of the female variety."

I force a smirk. "Maybe."

Despite my reputation as a ladies man, I actually didn't hook up with anyone while I was over there. My parents are both getting on in years, so I spent most of my time with them in their Roman apartment, or with my former teammates from when I lived there in my teens. On previous visits, I'd had a regular 'friends with benefits' deal with one of my former high school friends, but she's now happily married, and I've started to realize that all these casual relationships are leaving me drained. Maybe it's from watching my teammates start to settle down, or the fact that I'm not getting any younger, but I'm beginning to think there's more to life than hockey and casual sex. Never thought I'd feel that way, but here we are.

After finishing with my weights routine, Simon begrudgingly agrees to let me run outside, rather than hitting the treadmill for my cool down. I find the treadmill tedious, but he usually forces me to use it, arguing it is better on my knees and keeps my pace steady. Guess he's taking pity on me today.

Once I return from my run, I hit the showers, standing under the hot water for longer than usual in the hopes it will help my aching muscles.

I'm one of the last to leave, feeling no need to rush home to my empty apartment. Another new development I'm not sure how to process. I'm normally a fan of my own company, but I know that time alone is just going to lead to me beating myself up for growing complacent with my training in the off-season.

So instead of going down to the players parking lot to my truck, I make my way out the front door of the arena, heading for my favourite coffee shop at the hotel down the street.

Chapter Three

HAD YOU PEGGED AS A LATTE GIRL

Alanna

It's been a long two weeks, with only one day off since I started, and today I finish work late for the fifth day in a row. It's been a whirlwind trying to wrap my head around all the hockey terminology while getting to know my regular players. I've spent the two weeks out at the practice arena, running around doing the grunt work for the Cowboys training staff. I've counted a ridiculous amount of strapping tape and bandages, set up multiple training stations for trainers less qualified than myself, and dealt with eighteen-year-old hockey players with massive egos. And I did it all with a smile on my face, not showing an ounce of frustration at what feels like a giant slap in the face. At least the head trainer for the Cowboys, Colin, is much nicer than Trevor, who I've only dealt with via email since my induction. Emails filled with attitude and thinly veiled sexism.

If it wasn't a step down, I'd be looking to transfer to work under Colin, but I'm determined to make this work.

My five veteran players from the Mounties, Lincoln, Riley, Timo, Max and Ollie, have all travelled over to the practice arena daily for their treatments and dryland training, thwarting Trevor's efforts to get them to request a different trainer. All five of them seem really approachable and dedicated to their training, each taking my suggestions on board without any pushback. It's also given me the opportunity to build a rapport with them without interference. I've learned that Lincoln hates ice baths, Riley despises running, Max is a giant flirt, Ollie is a sweetheart, and Timo hates pretty much all people. And they've all learned that, while I may have breasts, I'm a hard ass who will put them through their paces and push them to their limits.

Tomorrow is the start of what I'm told is an intensive couple of weeks as the team prepares for the pre-season games starting in a few days, and I desperately need a good night's sleep ahead of finally starting at the main arena. Trevor has run out of ways to keep me away from the Mounties, and I am itching to get into my regular job. Due to the long hours, the jet lag has taken longer than I thought it would to calm down, and I still have so much paperwork to get through before tomorrow morning, so I make a beeline for the coffee shop attached to the hotel.

The fresh smell of coffee welcomes me as I push the door open, and my gaze immediately falls on an extremely good looking man standing at the counter, chatting to the server as he hands over his credit card. I've always had a thing for the tall, dark and handsome type, and this one has just the right amount of facial hair to give him a slightly rugged look. He's got to be at least six-foot-four and is clearly in good shape. His muscular legs are clad in dark blue jeans, and his arms strain the seams of his black t-shirt. A backwards baseball cap completes the look and does all sorts of things to my insides.

Despite the tiredness I'm feeling, a little flutter occurs in my belly when he turns my way and runs his appreciative gaze over me. His eyes are the most intense blue I've ever seen, and I nervously run a hand through my long red hair. It's an unconscious habit whenever I leave it down, which is rare. But my messy bun had been giving me a headache earlier, so I'd released it from my hair-tie and haven't bothered doing anything with it, and it now hangs in loose waves down to my lower back.

Reaching for the pendant around my neck that I never take off, I rub it between my fingers as I give the man a shy smile, and he steps aside for me to give my order to the young guy behind the counter.

"Americano please," I say, and the kid nods, pressing buttons on the register.

"Ooff, I had you pegged as a latte girl," Mr tall, dark and handsome comments while I tap my phone over the pay machine.

I raise an eyebrow, turning to face him. "Oh really? Let me guess. With some fancy alternative milk?"

He smiles, his eyes lighting up at my teasing tone. "Oat milk, of course."

We step aside, and he leans casually against the counter. It's obvious he's comfortable in his own skin, and definitely knows he's hot.

I wish I didn't find that so damn attractive, but sadly, I'm a sucker for cocky guys. Although usually it takes more than an appreciative look for me to warm up to them. But after two weeks of speaking to only the people I work with, it seems I'm desperate for some non-work related company.

"I had no idea I presented as an oat milk latte kind of girl. All this time I've been drinking the hard stuff. I've clearly been missing out," I zing back.

The smile turns into a full blown grin, and he opens his mouth to reply when the barista places his drink in front of him. "Here's your oat milk latte, Dean."

A laugh bursts from me, and I cover my mouth when he lifts the takeaway cup to his lips to take a sip.

"It could have been beautiful between us," he says with a smirk.

"Yeah. Such a shame you can't handle the strong stuff," I reply as my own coffee is placed in front of me.

He laughs and holds out his hand. "Dean."

"Alanna." I place my hand in his, and he squeezes gently as he shakes it.

"Kiwi?"

I nod. "Very good. Most people immediately guess Australian. Or South African, for some weird reason."

We move away from the counter, and when he takes a seat at a table, he waves his hand for me to join him.

I hesitate for a moment, before deciding it can't hurt to flirt with him a little longer. It's really hard to say no to those pretty blue eyes, after all.

"So, what brings you to Calgary?" he asks.

"I needed a fresh start. So I came for a new job."

"That's cool. What do you do?"

I bite my lip while I consider my response. I've already worked out this town is hockey mad, so I've been avoiding wearing my team polo shirt outside of the arena while I'm staying nearby, changing into jeans and a hoodie each time I leave.

"Let's not talk about boring things like work. It's so cliche, right? To talk about our jobs like it's the most exciting thing about us?"

The last thing I want is to bring attention to the fact that I'm going to be up close and personal with the city's heroes. And as for needing a fresh start... That's definitely not something I plan to get into with the only person I've met outside of the Mounties since I arrived here.

He cocks his head to the side, studying me for a moment. "Well, now I'm just convinced you're a spy."

I laugh, shaking my head. "Nothing that exciting, I promise. Just... I've always worked way too much, and I'd kind of like to talk about other stuff with a new friend."

He nods. "I get it. Okay. I promise not to talk about work. So... what do you like to do for fun?"

"I'm a runner. But I also like reading. And travel... when I get the time."

He places a hand to his chest. "It's like looking in a mirror. Those are all my favourite things, too."

I smirk and raise an eyebrow. "What a coincidence. We must be soulmates."

He shoots me a cheeky grin, and we spend the next twenty minutes chatting about the books we're both reading, and he is obviously a shameless flirt. So far, he's complimented my hair, my smile and my laugh, but done it so subtly that it hasn't felt forced or creepy.

I finish my coffee, nursing the cup for a little longer because I'm not quite ready to leave. It's rare for me to entertain guys like this. I usually shut them down and get on with my day, too busy for dating or relationships. But there's just something about Dean that has me wanting to keep him talking. After spending so many years hanging out almost exclusively with athletes, it's rare that I get a chance to talk about things outside of sport, and it's nice to talk about other topics for a change.

But there's only so long I can pretend to drink from an empty cup.

"I guess I should probably head up to my room. I've got a big day tomorrow, so I should try and have a decent sleep to ward off the last of the jet lag," I say, reluctantly getting to my feet.

He stands, downing the rest of his coffee and taking both our cups to the bin near the counter.

I linger, still unable to walk away for some reason.

"This is probably a little forward, but... Would you like to have dinner with me tonight?" he asks, flashing a cute little grin when he rejoins me.

"Dinner?"

I shouldn't. I really need to get a good night's sleep. And I have so many files to review.

I bite my lip, fiddling with my pendant once again while staring at him as he smiles at me, silently asking me to say yes.

Chapter Four

JUST DINNER

Dean

I don't think I've ever been more grateful for my need for evening caffeine, but I'm certainly thanking the coffee gods today.

I've always had a thing for redheads, and Alanna is hot as hell. She's at least a foot shorter than me, with long, deep red hair and green eyes, and a fit, curvy body that I'd love to feel pressed up against me. And as luck would have it, she's from out of town and doesn't appear to recognize me. It's so refreshing not having a woman fawn all over me just because of what I do for a living that I don't want this time with her to end.

"Dinner?"

I can see the indecision in her expression as she grips her necklace like a lifeline.

Watching as she bites her lip, I turn on the charming smile. "Yeah. I really like talking to you, and you know, you don't know anyone in town, so..." I raise an eyebrow.

She hesitates a moment longer, then nods. "Okay. But I *can't* have a late night. So you have to promise it's just dinner," she says, pointing her finger at me with a small smile.

"Of course! I'm a gentleman, after all. Just dinner. I promise."

She excuses herself to get ready, reappearing half an hour later in the lobby of the hotel dressed in a fresh pair of jeans and a tight, green sweater that clings to her curves and makes her eyes appear even greener. Wearing minimal makeup and sneakers, it's obvious that she leans more towards comfort over the latest fashion trends, and I have to admit, I love it. Most of the women I've dated over the years have spent hours in front of the mirror ahead of dates, coming out looking nothing like their natural selves, even though they were all beautiful without the makeup and skimpy clothes.

She reminds me a lot of Kylie, Seth's wife, and her cousin Adele. They are both two of the most down to earth women I've ever met, and I wonder idly if they'd all become friends if something were to happen between us.

Jesus, Dean. You've talked to the woman for twenty minutes. Calm down.

But it's hard to ignore my attraction to Alanna. She's like a breath of fresh air that I didn't know I needed.

"So... Where to?" she asks, sliding her hands into her back pockets as she rocks from one foot to the other.

Sensing her nerves, I keep a healthy distance between our bodies, waving my hand for her to go ahead of me through the lobby doors.

"I thought we could hit up the steakhouse down the road? I mean, Calgary is known for its beef." I swallow hard, suddenly realizing she may not be a fan of steak. "Unless you're vegan?"

Probably should have asked before I assumed I knew best.

She smiles over her shoulder. "Nope, I love meat. Sounds good."

I breathe a sigh of relief, and we make our way up the street at a leisurely pace. The sun is still high on the horizon, bathing the city in golden light, and Alanna comments on how strange it is to have this much light in the evening. Guess it gets darker earlier in the summer in New Zealand.

"I think I kind of love it here, though. It reminds me of home a little. Everyone seems friendly, and it's around the same number of people" she says, and I nod.

"Yeah. It's a welcome relief after the constant bustle of Rome. I feel like it's easier to connect with people in a city this size."

"You've been to Rome?" I can hear the awe in her tone as I nod.

"Yeah. I have family there. I was just in Italy for a month."

She sighs, her expression growing a little dreamy. "I'd love to go one day. I've been to a few places in Europe, but haven't made it to Italy yet."

Over dinner, we chat about our travels and the places we'd love to go. I've never felt such a fast connection with anyone before, finding her so easy to talk to.

"Why do you love travel so much? I mean, I know why I do, but I'm always interested in what drives others' wanderlust," she asks, after I wax lyrical about my time in Spain a few years ago.

I blink, struck by the profoundness of her question. No other woman has ever tried to get to know me on a deeper level before, simply wanting to get close to me due to my job and bank balance.

"I just enjoy fully immersing myself in other cultures. I love learning how others live and what drives them. Oh, and the food, of course," I add with a grin.

She laughs, and it's such a pretty sound that I find myself wanting to hear it more.

A lot more.

After dinner, we make our way back to the hotel. I'm determined to keep my promise to her for an early night, feeling like I need to prove that I'm not just trying to get her into bed. But she surprises me by asking if I'd like to have a drink in the hotel bar before she has to head to bed.

But one drink becomes two.

Two drinks leads to four.

And by the time nine o'clock rolls around, we're both a little tipsy.

Erasing all distance between us on the leather seat of the booth we've claimed as our own, I reach to push a loose strand of hair behind her ear before cupping her cheek.

"I've had a really nice night. Thank you for agreeing to have dinner with me."

She bites her lower lip as her eyes scan my face. "Thank you for asking." Her voice has grown husky, although I can't tell if it's because of the alcohol or my proximity.

But there's no mistaking the heat in her gaze as she holds mine without looking away.

I clear my throat. "I should probably let you get to bed. I promised you it would just be dinner, and we've already moved on to drinks."

She's quiet, continuing to search my face with those big green eyes.

My god she's beautiful.

"Or... You could come up for one more drink?"

Well... How could any man possibly resist an invitation like that?

Light is streaming through the window as I let out a groan. It takes me a moment to work out where I am. The pillows feel too soft, the mattress too firm, and a slight dip in the mattress tells me that I'm not alone in this bed.

Cracking one eye open, the first thing I see is hair the deepest red I've ever seen splayed across the pillow beside me. Hair that, only hours ago, had been wrapped around my fist.

We probably shouldn't have slept together, but it would have been rude to turn her down when she'd shyly asked if I wanted to come up for another drink...

She told me she never jumps into bed with guys, and I could tell she'd surprised herself when she'd asked the question.

A more honourable guy would have just gotten her number and called it a night, not wanting her to do something she'd regret the next day. But there is just something about this woman that draws me in. She's unlike any woman I've spent time with before.

We went all night, and passed out only an hour before sunrise.

While it was one of the best nights of my life, I'm a little disappointed in myself for having such a late night when I'd just vowed to dedicate myself to my training.

I slip out of her bed slowly and she stirs, but doesn't wake.

Normally, I'd be grateful, keen to avoid any awkward morning-after chit-chat, but this time, I have to fight to keep myself from waking her to kiss her goodbye.

I don't normally date, preferring to keep things casual, but I already can't wait to see her again. The banter between us last night had been fun, and she's clearly off the charts smart. I have no idea what she does for a living - we'd both expertly avoided talking about either of our jobs, which was refreshing. I'm going to guess she does something in the medical profession though, based on our conversations last night. We'd somehow gotten onto recovery after injury, and she'd passionately launched into the correct methods for easing back into movement as soon as possible. It had been hot, and I suspect it's what led to little Dean doing all the thinking from then onwards.

I tug on my pants and scribble her a note with my phone number before leaving, hoping she'll call.

I don't have time to go home, but her hotel is just down the street for from the arena, so it's an easy five minute walk.

Heading for the locker room, I nod to a few of my teammates through the window of the gym. Guess I'm not the only one getting in early this morning.

"Hey, buddy. You're in early," Lincoln says, giving me a nod as I walk in the door.

He's sitting in front of his open locker, already in his practice jersey, taping up his stick.

"Hey. Yeah, after the last week's shitty effort, I thought I'd better whip my ass into shape," I joke, bumping fists with Ollie, before taking a seat in front of my locker.

Seth wanders in next, and the four of us chat about our summer breaks while I get suited up. While I've been back for two weeks, I haven't really had much of a chance to catch up with any of them properly, as training camp started immediately and everyone has been so busy. I was a groomsmen for Seth when he married Kylie in Tahiti, right before I headed to Italy, so he gives me a brief rundown on the honeymoon, where they spent the next few weeks island hopping on a private yacht.

Sounds sickeningly perfect.

"Did you hear about Adele and Ben?" Ollie asks me.

I raise an eyebrow while Lincoln goes eerily still beside me. "No, what happened?"

"They broke up at the reception."

"I left early the next day so didn't see anyone after the reception," I reply with a shrug.

Interesting. I've kind of had a thing for Kylie's cousin for awhile, which I'm sure is why Ollie is smirking at me now that she appears to no longer be engaged. Maybe if I hadn't just had the night of my life with a stunning redhead, I'd be plotting a way to comfort Adele, but now I'm just hoping she's okay.

I open my mouth to ask just that, but the door of the locker room flies open, banging loudly against the wall behind it.

"Thomas! O'Malley!" Lincoln and I both spin around to look at our general manager, Alistair, as he marches into the room, with Coach Stephens trailing behind him.

I've been here for five minutes. What could I possibly have done to be on his shit list already?

"Yeah?" Lincoln asks, flicking a wary look my way.

"We've got a new trainer," Stephens says, his tone weary as he stops in the middle of the room.

Alistair nods and crosses his arms, his lips pursed while he glares at us both for some unknown reason.

"Yeah, I know. I've been working with her already," Lincoln replies, raising an eyebrow in my direction once again.

Like I have any clue why Alistair is glaring at us both, while Stephens just looks like he wishes he was anywhere but here.

Alistair gives a curt nod. "Ah, so you know."

"Know what?" I ask.

"That she's a woman."

"Can you catch me up here? Why does it seem like you're pissed at us?" Lincoln voices both of our confusion.

"I shouldn't need to remind you both, but given your previous transgressions, I thought it bears mentioning. It's against team policy for any fraternization between players and staff."

Ah. Now it all makes sense.

And I'm pissed.

Alistair has only been with the team for two seasons, and the stout General Manager has already proved to be an asshole with a chip on his shoulder. His animosity is usually saved for

Lincoln for some unknown reason, which is weird, because Lincoln is a popular player amongst the team and the fans alike.

So this is the first time I've been on the receiving end of Alistair's bullshit.

I don't like it.

Doing my best to keep from snapping at the man who holds my career in the palm of his hand, I sit back in my seat, crossing my arms. "With all due respect, I've not even met her yet. Isn't it a bit presumptive to come in here and accuse us of doing something with her when we haven't done anything wrong?"

"And disrespectful to her, too," Seth adds.

Lincoln and I exchange a glance before giving him a nod. Our captain might not speak a hell of a lot, but he calls out bullshit when he see's it. And this whole thing reeks of bullshit.

Stephens mutters something that sounds a lot like "I warned you," under his breath, and Alistair shoots him a glare.

"I'm protecting her," he barks back.

"From us? We've never done anything with any of the staff." I level him with a glare, the tentative hold on my patience coming very close to snapping. "Except him," I say, pointing at Ollie. "But he's married to one of them, so that doesn't count."

Ollie rolls his eyes and throws up his middle finger. He's been married to our marketing manager, Sarah, forever. They both grew up in Calgary, and they've been together since college. They did the long distance thing while she was an assistant in the marketing department here before he was traded here from Toronto years ago. It wasn't like the team could insist they break up, so they are the exception to the fraternization rule.

Stephens clears his throat. "Might I suggest we leave it at that, Alistair?"

Alistair continues to stare Lincoln and me down for

another moment before turning on his heel and marching back out the door.

Stephens sighs, shrugging at us before following him. Alistair is his boss, too, so it's not like he can say much.

"Well... It's good to see he's just as much of a dick as ever," Lincoln mutters once they're safely out of earshot.

"I don't know why he lumped me into all of that," I grumble, grabbing my stick and standing up.

"Because you have a reputation with the ladies," Ollie replies, no doubt still annoyed I dragged him into the conversation.

"Yeah, but none of them worked for the team. And every single one of them has been a fully consenting adult." I bend to straighten my pads. "And besides, I'm turning over a new leaf."

Lincoln scoffs as he gets to his feet. "Yeah, okay."

I raise an eyebrow. "You're one to talk, O'Malley."

"I'll have you know, after that whole reporter debacle last season, I haven't slept with anyone except-" he stops abruptly, clamping his mouth shut.

"Well... Now I just want to know who you were about to say," I reply with a smirk.

A reporter he'd jumped into bed with went full blown stalker on him last season, breaking into his apartment and making herself very comfortable in his bed. Determined to never settle down, I guess it was only a matter of time before one of his trysts went south. Although the way he's blushing makes it obvious he's slept with someone we know since then.

He shakes his head. "No one. I have slept with no one. Let's go. I need to get warmed up."

The rest of us laugh at his obvious deflection before following him out of the room and head for the ice. It's no business of mine, and everyone is entitled to their secrets, so I don't bother giving him a hard time.

The whole conversation with Alistair had been strange, but I have zero intention of sleeping with anyone right now. Except for a certain redhead, who I really hope calls me later.

After we finish our rather gruelling practice, I collapse onto the bench in front of my locker, aching all over once again. Thankfully, I'd blocked most of the guys shots, but I definitely need a decent sleep tonight to make sure I'm at my full strength tomorrow for our final practice before preseason games start.

I peel off my gear and change into my athletic shorts and Mounties t-shirt. Once I'm no longer weighed down by my goalie pads, I dig my phone out of my duffle bag. Sadly, there is no message from Alanna, and disappointment settles in my belly. I hadn't considered that she might not want to see me again, and the idea of not hearing from her makes me feel a little off balance. I've never not heard from someone the next day. This is just the first time that I've really wanted to.

Shoving my emotions aside, I make my way towards the gym for a cool down before I hit the showers. Whistling to myself as I pull my headphones over my ears, I come to an abrupt halt when I enter the gym, coming face to face with Alanna.

She looks up from where she's setting up some work stations near the mats, her eyes widening as her gaze falls on me. She looks different dressed in an oversized Mounties polo shirt and black athletic tights. Still hot as hell, though.

Well... Fuck.

The woman I slept with last night is the new athletic trainer... The one I can't get out of my head. And the one I've just been told is one-hundred percent off limits.

"Um... Hi," she says slowly.

"Hey... So... This is awkward..." I look around to make sure we're the only ones in the gym.

"Yeah... You work here?" She eyes me warily as I remain in the doorway.

"So... about that..."

Her eyes widen further as I point to the team photo on the wall. The one from when we won the Stanley Cup up a few years ago. I'm standing in the middle, holding it above my head with Seth and Lincoln on either side of me at centre ice, the three of us soaked with sweat and grinning like maniacs.

"Shit... You're on the team?" she murmurs, once again gripping her pendant as she stares at me.

"Yeah." I rub the back of my neck as I slide my other hand into my pocket, not sure what to say or where to look.

"Why didn't you say anything?" she hisses, her eyes darting to the hall behind me.

"Why didn't you?!" I shoot back.

"Because I didn't know if you were a massive fan of the team like everyone else in this town. I didn't want to have to think about whether that was why you were talking to me."

I cross my arms, smirking. "And you wondered why I didn't tell you? Exact same reason. Do you know how many women - and a few men - try to get into our pants the second they work out we're hockey players?"

She clenches her jaw. "Well, it would have had the exact opposite effect on me. I don't date athletes."

Despite the tension, I can't help but laugh. "You saw me naked and didn't work out that I'm a professional athlete?"

"It's not like you had "Property of Calgary Mounties" tattooed on your chest, Dean. For all I knew, you just spent way too much time in the gym."

I smirk. "Nope, just super ripped from all the training I do while having rubber discs shot at me for a living."

She opens her mouth to say something, but clamps her mouth shut again when Lincoln and Riley wander in for their session with her.

I stay where I am for a moment before turning on my heel and heading back out of the room, snapping my headphones down over my ears.

So much for cooling down... I need to go for a run.

A really fucking long one.

Chapter Five

I'M SUCH AN IDIOT

Alanna

Of all the mistakes I've ever made in my life, this has got to take the cake.

After taking Lincoln and Riley through their new training regime, I spend the rest of the day avoiding any further interactions with Dean. Not that it was hard to do, because he practically bolted once his teammates appeared.

Why oh why did I choose now to break my 'no sex on the first date' rule?! Probably because he was super charming and hot as hell. And god, the things that man can do with his tongue.

No, Alanna! We aren't going to think about last night ever again.

Yeah, like that's an option. The memory of last night and the many many orgasms he gave me is going to haunt me for the rest of my life. When I'd woken up this morning and found his note, I'd been grinning from ear to ear, excited he wanted to see me again.

But that had all come crashing down when, an hour into my first day in my rightful role, I came face to face with him in the gym and realized I'd inadvertently slept with one of the players on the team.

And not just any player, but their star goalie. And one of the highest paid in the league, from what I've learned today through my subtle questions while Lincoln was complaining in his ice bath.

For fuck's sake.

I can just hear my brother's voice in my head now, reminding me how stupid it is to get involved with professional athletes. Like I needed reminding, after our upbringing.

When I make it back to the hotel, I ask the concierge if I can get some fresh sheets, needing to eradicate any reminder of the night we spent *not* sleeping in my bed.

Once the bed is made, I shower and collapse on top of the covers, staring at the ceiling while continuing to silently berate myself for my poor life choices. But despite my better judgement, I can't let go of the desire to see him again. Even taking out how good the sex had been - the best I've ever had - I'd really enjoyed getting to know him last night. He was charming and funny, and clearly intelligent. We'd talked about books we both enjoyed, places we've travelled, hobbies we enjoy. Everything except the one thing we should have talked about, apparently.

Like what we both did for a living.

And who we worked for.

After a night spent tossing and turning while cursing my idiocy, I drag myself back into work. In my previous job, I was always the first to arrive, but it appears these hockey players get started far earlier than rugby players, because there are already a few of the guys in the gym, doing their workouts before morning skate.

I'm still learning all the terminology when it comes to this sport, and I'm yet to set foot on the ice. Which is probably a good thing, because I'm not a fan of falling over. The shoes I had to buy are supposed to keep me from slipping on the ice, but I'm dubious about this. Ice skating isn't a huge sport where I'm from, and I've never even attempted it... Lord only knows why I thought working for an ice hockey team was a good idea, but I'm here now, so I guess I better work it out soon.

Trevor has assigned me the super fun task of taking this year's draft picks through a series of exercises for the morning, before they hit the ice for a final time with the veterans. Some of them I've already been working with over at the Cowboys, and not all of them are on the team yet. A few of the younger ones are off to college in a few weeks, while others will find out after training camp if they are on the Mounties or Cowboys. But all of them are new to dealing with the level of fitness expected in the NHL, so it's an interesting few hours. I thought I'd seen the last of them after leaving the practice arena, and some have been resistant to the training plan I put together for them. But one look from Seth when he swung by to check on them had them keeping their grumblings to themselves.

"Cocky little shits," Riley mutters under his breath when he stops by, taking a seat next to me on the treatment table I'm sitting on while I watch the rookies go through their various workouts.

He must have caught one of the college kids grumbling on his way over to me.

I snort. "Nothing I'm not used to. It's always the new recruits who think they know more than the trainers, until they wind up injured doing something stupid."

He chuckles, crossing his arms. "How's your first few weeks been?"

I shrug, watching as one of the youngest of the guys attempts the stretches I've given him to help with his groin pain, his face contorting into a grimace that he tries valiantly to hide. "Okay. Adjusting to the different way of doing things. And actually having a decent budget for state of the art equipment. That's a welcome change."

"Not a lot of money in rugby?" Riley asks, sounding surprised.

A laugh slips out as I shake my head. "Ah, no. I mean, they obviously have money, but the money that is thrown at those teams is nothing compared to the NHL. That's why I wanted to get in with a North American sports team. You guys take sport to a whole new level here, and the resources are amazing."

We chat a little longer before he heads off to get suited up for practice, and I finish with the younger players before heading out to the bench to get things ready for morning skate. It's freezing in the arena, and I zip my team jacket up to just under my chin before lining the water bottles up along the top of the barrier, which I have been told is called the boards.

"Alanna, I need you to go and count the supplies once you're done here," Trevor barks from the players tunnel, not bothering to come and speak to me properly.

"Oh. Okay. I actually did that last night," I reply.

I'd used it as a way to hide from Dean before he left, hanging back in the storage room tucked away behind the gym.

He raises an eyebrow and crosses his arms. "It needs to be done daily."

Like hell it does. It's obviously yet another power move, but there's no point arguing with him.

Just suck it up, Alanna. You wanted this, remember?

. . .

Two hours later, I've recounted all the supplies again, rolled a pile of bandages and am just going through my notes on my laptop when the door opens and Dean appears.

I freeze, watching warily as he walks in and shuts the door behind him.

"So... We should probably talk about what happened," he says.

"And hello to you, too," I reply, crossing my arms.

He sighs, rubbing the back of his neck. "Sorry. Look, if I'd known-"

"No, I get it. It's the same for me," I say, cutting him off.

I don't really want to hear him reject me, even though we both know it needs to happen.

"The GM read Lincoln and me the riot act yesterday, telling us we had to keep our dicks to ourselves with the new female trainer. Which I had every intention of doing. Except it turns out..."

"You'd already slipped and fallen into the new trainer?" I finish for him, trying to keep the mood light even as a little prickle of unease works it's way up my spine.

He chuckles. "Yeah. I guess Lincoln and I both have a reputation, although it felt a little rude."

I raise an eyebrow. "I'm not really sure how to feel about that."

He shrugs, scratching the back of his neck. "No, I thought that was pretty shitty, too."

"Which part?" I ask, studying him closely.

"The part where he just assumed you'd be set upon by the team because you're female," he replies, eyeing me slowly with a slight frown.

Like he senses a trap.

"Oh," I say, casually. "So not the part where you've got such a bad reputation with women that your boss spoke to you about it?"

Of course he's a player. I'm such a fucking idiot.

His mouth drops open for a moment as he stares at me, wide-eyed, before shaking his head. "No, that's-I don't have a bad reputation with women!"

"Well you've obviously been with enough women for your boss to comment, Dean." I give up on my laptop and sit back in my chair, crossing my arms and raising my chin to stare him down. "So I was just, what? Another notch on your bedpost? Were you even going to answer the phone if I called you? If the number you left was even your number, of course."

He returns to gaping at me, and I can practically see the wheels turning in his mind. "I had every intention of seeing you again. We had a great time," he sputters, raking a hand through his hair. "Or at least, I thought we did."

He almost sounds like he means it...

"Yes, it was great," I concede with a sigh, before shaking my head to glare at him again. "But now it turns out I slept with a guy who just hooks up with every woman he meets." The disgust I feel with myself practically drips from my voice. "I'm such an idiot."

He shakes his head, his eyes wide. "No, it wasn't like that. I really liked-I mean *like* you. And I really did want to see you again. But we obviously can't, so I don't know why we're even arguing about this."

"We're not arguing. You're a player and I'm an idiot. What's there to argue about?" I shrug, feigning indifference that I definitely don't feel.

He throws his hands up. "I'm *not* a player!" He stops, letting his arms drop to his side, his jaw clenched. "Look, whatever. I came in here to tell you we obviously can't do anything like that again, and I've done that, so yeah. Talk to you later."

He turns and wrenches the door open, storming out and letting it slam shut behind him.

Well... That went well.

Grumbling under my breath, I turn back to my computer. I barely have a chance to attempt to read through Lincoln's file when there's another knock on the door.

Seriously?

"What?!" I snap, expecting Dean to reappear, ready to try to defend himself some more.

Instead, it's Lincoln stepping through the door, his eyes wide as he freezes in place. "Um... hi?"

I cringe. "Shit, sorry O'Malley. I thought you were someone else."

He raises an eyebrow as he gives me a cheeky grin. "Nope, just little old me."

It's obvious he saw Dean stomp out of here, but I'm grateful he doesn't say anything else. The last thing I need is for anyone to work out something happened between us.

Not that it's going to be a problem moving forward.

Because I'm never sleeping with that man again.

Chapter Six

CAN YOU MOVE?

Dean

ONE YEAR LATER

I've never been particularly superstitious, but ten years into my NHL career I've got a pretty good routine going before each game - run through my reflex drills, stretch, stretch some more, even more stretching... And, most importantly, ignore my teammates antics by putting my noise cancelling headphones on and getting into the zone.

But today is the season opening game and my headphones have run out of charge. I've also forgotten to pack my backup pair in my backpack, and when I realize, my mood immediately sours.

Then Alanna walks into the room, her face like a thundercloud, with Trevor right behind her, and I have to force myself not to care about why she looks so upset. We've both been doing our best to stay out of each other's way since she started with the team, with varying levels of success. There have been a few moments where I've caught myself checking her out, and had to remind myself that nothing can ever happen there.

Not that it would, because she hates me. I'm ashamed to

admit how many times I've lain in bed at night with that final conversation playing over and over in my head. I'd put it down to it being because it was the only time a woman has outright rejected me... But I know it's because, despite everything, she is still the only woman that I want.

Which fucking sucks.

Rolling my shoulders, I look away, attempting to get my head back in the zone. And that's when Lincoln and Adele's golden retriever, Milo, starts running circles around me while I bend into a hip flexor stretch.

Everything just goes downhill from there.

Milo is cute and all, but this whole dog mascot thing has been bugging me ever since they started doing it last season. They'd decided we needed to be like the other teams and have a fluffy ambassador to play into the whole family friendly vibe. Which is all fun and games, but as far as I'm concerned, a golden retriever doesn't belong in the players' tunnel. Or the fucking locker room.

Adele leaps into action to get Milo under control after Lincoln waves her over, but a few moments of barking and tail chasing is more than enough time to fuck with my head.

I bite my tongue when Adele clips Milo's leash on, shooting me an apologetic smile before ushering the dog out of the room.

It was a real surprise when Adele and Lincoln became a thing last year at the beginning of the season, and it still feels weird seeing them together. The team pays her to film content for Milo's social media accounts - yes, he has a whole damn account with millions of followers, work that one out - and the logical part of me knows she's just doing her job.

But it still takes all my self control not to snap at her.

However, I strongly suspect that watching Trevor talk down to Alanna is what tipped the scales firmly into the 'I'm fucked' category. The guy has been on a serious power trip ever since he became the head trainer, with most of his ego laser focused on Alanna. I'm pretty sure he's threatened by the fact that she is so damn good at her job.

Not that I've been watching, or anything.

Because she's strictly off limits.

And she hates me.

When we hit the ice for warm-ups, my reflexes are off by a second with every shot sent my way, and I just barely catch the pucks that don't manage to slip by me.

After last year's rocky start in training camp, I turned things around and clawed my way back to the top again, and I'm determined to stay here. But something is definitely not right tonight, and I can't tell what it is. Or how to fix it.

Seth skates over to check if I'm okay, and I say yes, lying through my teeth.

I don't know what to tell him. Conscious of the thousands of eyes on me when the game starts, I try to put the weirdness out of my mind and get in the zone.

When the puck drops, a little voice whispers in my ear that something is going to go very wrong, but I ignore it, keeping my eyes trained on the little black disc.

Pieter, one of our defensemen, steals it from Tampa's winger and sends it flying back towards the other end of the ice, where Lincoln intercepts it and flicks it over to Seth.

They are two of our fastest forwards, along with Riley, who is also on their line, and they are usually an unstoppable force when they're all on the ice together. There's a reason the three of them are amongst the highest paid players in the league.

Even with the puck down the other end, I don't allow myself to relax. Hockey is a fast-paced game, and anything can change from one second to the next. I'm one of the most experienced goalies in the league, but that means nothing when there are dozens of guys just waiting for me to fuck up so they can take my spot. We picked up a talented rookie, Mark, last year, fresh out of college, and he's already played more games than any of the previous second string goalies prior to him. Coach Stephens has obviously seen what I have - a young player with a bright future ahead of him and a drive to prove himself.

It's the first time I've felt threatened, and while I've tried to be supportive of Mark, it's set my teeth on edge every time I've been on the bench and watched him block more shots than I had in the game prior.

Having the fans muttering that I'm past my prime also isn't helping.

Fuck, maybe it's not the change to my routine that has me off tonight? Maybe I'm just a washed-up has-been?

It's this moment of doubt that pulls me out of the game, undoing every attempt I've made since I arrived at the arena to get my head right.

Seth takes a shot, and the puck ricochets off the post behind Tampa's goalie. Their centre seizes the opportunity, shooting off with it and streaking down the ice towards me. Pieter and the other defenceman on the ice, Michael, take off after him, but they aren't able to catch up. Riley gets in front of him, but the scrappy little guy just zips around him.

I get in position, ready for whatever this guy is going to try, silently cursing Pieter and Michael for not being faster. We won the Stanley Cup last season, but I wonder how much longer we're going to be on top. We're an aging group, with more guys over thirty than any of the other teams. I used to think that was a good thing, but seeing how slow they are off the mark right now has me questioning all of that.

No matter how many years I've been doing this, seeing grown men skate at full speed right for me will always come with a healthy dose of anxiety. And while I've always shut that fear out, attempting to thrive on it instead, something about tonight makes that a lot harder.

Swallowing hard, I keep my eyes on the puck, anticipating which way he's going to go. I've spent the last few days studying the moves of all the guys on this team, so I know he favours slap shots, and I'm ready for it.

What I'm not ready for is Tampa's other winger, who comes out of nowhere to my left. Instead of taking the shot himself, the centre passes the puck to him, and he spins to take the shot. Pieter has finally made it down here, and the puck hits his skate, sending it across to the other side, where Lincoln is waiting.

I let out a small sigh of relief, but my muscles remain locked in place as I watch their centre and Lincoln scramble to take possession of the puck, both trying to dig it out from the boards with their sticks while shoving each other out of the way. One of Tampa's defencemen smashes into Lincoln, pinning him to the boards and giving them the chance to steal the puck. Their centre spins my way again, and I clench my jaw, preparing myself for his next attempt. The other winger is parked right in front of me, jostling with Michael as he tries to block their centre from getting a clear shot.

And in that split second, the Tampa player in front of me loses his balance.

People fall all the time in hockey - kind of hard not to when you're sliding around a slippery surface with knives attached to your feet.

But he's closer to me than I'd realized, and as he comes

down, his body turns at an odd angle, and he lands right on top of me.

A blinding pain screams through my hip as I do the splits with one hundred and fifty pounds of pure muscle on top of me. I'm limber and the splits are just one of my regular moves, but I don't normally have someone pushing me down. I feel something pop and I can't stop the bellow that comes out of my mouth.

The ref's whistle goes off, and Michael yanks the guy off me, shoving him hard. "What the fuck, man?! Get the fuck off our goalie!"

It's an unwritten law that you don't mess with the goalie, and while a fight breaks out in front of me, Simon comes sliding across the ice to check on me.

I'm fighting the urge to vomit inside my mask as pain radiates from my hip to my groin, and I know there's no way I'm going to be finishing this game.

"Can you move?" Simon asks, keeping his face close to my ear so that no one can read his lips on the thousand and one cameras that are no doubt zooming in on where I'm lying on the ice.

I shake my head, not wanting to risk speaking in case I end up screaming again. But I know without a doubt, it's going to be a few weeks off the ice.

And that's a few weeks where Mark will continue to show that my time between the pipes will soon come to an end.

Chapter Seven

BRING MEN LIKE YOU TO THEIR KNEES

Alanna

As soon as the meeting starts, I know today is going to suck.

"I'm sorry, Alanna. Are we boring you?" Trevor glares at me from the head of the table.

We've been sitting in the training room for exactly five minutes, and there is not enough coffee in the world to help me with the exhaustion I'm dealing with right now.

I shake my head, covering my mouth as I stifle another yawn. "Sorry, I was up late reviewing my files and-"

He cuts me off. "I don't want to hear excuses. You should have been more prepared."

I bite my tongue, hard, to keep from snapping back at the arrogant asshole. He has had it in for me ever since I started last year, and is showing no signs of letting up.

"Now, where were we?" Trevor leans down and grabs a file from the stack beside him.

The four of us are sitting on chairs in a circle in the middle of the training room, each gripping takeaway coffee cups from the cafe down the road. Well, except Trevor. Pretty sure he survives purely off the negative energy that he produces.

"We've got Dean back in today after a week of rest. As you

know, the injury to his hip has him out of action for a few weeks. Simon, he's one of your players, so I'll leave him with you for his recovery," Trevor says, reading through the paperwork in front of him.

I shake off the memory of the way my heart had leapt into my throat when Dean went down last week. When I'd watched them stretcher him out, I knew that would hurt his ego far more than any physical injury.

Despite my concern, I couldn't be seen worrying about him. He's not one of my guys, and we have barely had anything to do with each other since he stormed out of my office a year ago. As far as everyone else in the organization believes, Dean and I don't even know each other.

Simon clears his throat. "Actually, Trevor, I can't. Dayna is scheduled for her cesarean tomorrow, remember? I'm on paternity leave for the next few weeks."

Trevor sighs, rubbing his temple. "Right. Yeah, I forgot. Okay..." He shuffles through the papers in front of him.

I'm surprised that he doesn't tell Simon what an inconvenience it is for his wife to have a baby right at the start of the season. I guess those sorts of snide remarks are just for me.

After a few more moments of dithering, Trevor sighs, his scowl deepening. I reach to play with my pendant as I send a silent prayer out into the universe. *Please don't say my name. Please don't say my name.*

He thrusts the paperwork at me. "Try not to stay up all night with this one, Alanna."

Fuckity fuck, fuck, fuck.

I really hate this man. But the Mounties sponsored my visa, and if I quit, I'm pretty sure I'll have to be on the next flight back to Auckland. And I really don't want to go back to New Zealand.

I open the file and scan the notes from the team doctor,

swallowing hard. I know I'm the most qualified when it comes to the more complex injuries, but working with Dean is not something I had on my bingo card for this year.

Or ever.

"It says here Nicholas recommended two weeks' rest before we start treatment?" The notes from the team doctor make it appear that this is a very strict requirement.

Trevor rolls his eyes. "It's not up to you to question the timeline, Alanna. Just get him well enough to get back on the ice."

I bite back the growl of frustration clawing its way up my throat. This type of old school 'suck it up and push through the pain' mentality is why so many athletes end up with lifelong pain. They've changed how they do things now, favouring player recovery over getting them playing at all costs. But Trevor is old school and refuses to change. Despite the fact that Nicholas is his boss, Trevor rarely takes notice of the doctor's assessments. I'm surprised Nicholas hasn't pulled rank, but it feels like Trevor is untouchable most of the time, which grinds my gears to no end. I'd hoped after Alistair was fired midway through last season, that things might change under the new general manager. But no such luck.

I really wish Ted hadn't retired.

Simon glances my way with a lopsided smile, and I grimace in response to the unspoken apology while remaining silent. While it would be good if one of the guys actually called Trevor out on his shitty behaviour, this is the reality of working in a male dominated industry. I've had to develop a thick skin and just learn to let it roll off my back. The rugby team I worked with back home had been the same, and I knew coming here would be no different.

Doesn't make it suck any less, though.

The meeting continues as we each give an overview of

where our players are at. Simon's guys are spread out amongst the rest of us, and I've now got seven guys I'm responsible for amongst the twenty-three current players. It's still less than Simon and Joel normally have, and we all know Trevor has done this on purpose, deciding to take some of the players himself rather than split them evenly between Joel and me.

"Arrogant asshole," Joel mutters to me as we gather our things together at the end of the meeting.

I shrug, because there's really nothing I can do about it.

I've learned to keep my head down when it comes to making comments about colleagues. Too many people are ready to throw you to the wolves, hoping to claw their way to the top. While I'm friendly with my colleagues, I've kept them all at arm's length since I arrived, just wanting to work my way up quietly.

Dean isn't due to come in for a few hours, and I push aside the nerves at having to deal with him one on one.

I head for the treatment room to meet Lincoln. The charismatic forward is my favourite player on the team, and it's always fun when I work with him.

"Hey Red," he says with a cheeky grin when I walk through the door.

He's sitting on the treatment table in my section, wearing a black henley and athletic shorts, his legs swinging back and forth while he waits for me.

Seth shakes his head from where he's doing some stretches on a mat in the corner while he waits for Joel. "That's the least original name I've ever heard, Linc."

Seth doesn't talk a lot, but he'll never miss a chance to chirp at his best friend.

"What? It's suits her! You know, because of the hair?" Lincoln replies, winking at me as he waves his hand towards my hair, which is currently piled high on top of my head in my signature messy bun.

"Save the flirting, O'Malley. You're not going to be able to talk your way out of me working on that calf."

He grimaces. "Take pity on me, Jameson. I've been a good boy and done all my stretches." His blond hair flops over one eye as he tries to give me his best puppy dog face.

I give him a pointed look. "In that case, it won't hurt when I work on it."

He sighs. "You take far too much joy in inflicting pain, Red."

"You're on to me, Lincoln. It's all about being able to bring men like you to their knees."

Seth chuckles but doesn't say anything as Lincoln opens and closes his mouth in dismay. It takes a lot to silence Lincoln, and I lift a finger to draw an imaginary tally in the air. He narrows his eyes, but the twitch of his lips gives away his amusement.

We enjoy ribbing each other, although I think he is still trying to work out how to deal with a woman who doesn't fall all over herself for a chance to get close to him. He's attractive, there's no doubt about that. But even if he wasn't happily shacked up with his girlfriend, he's not my type.

No, apparently my type is six-foot-four goalies with ruggedly handsome good looks and a really grumpy attitude. Although he wasn't grumpy when we met. I don't know what happened to that version of Dean, but he's been stomping around like a bear with a sore head for the last year... I don't want to claim it's because of our night together, but it's definitely hard not to feel partly responsible for his mood.

Lincoln begrudgingly lies face down on the table, and I get to work on his calf. I know he's been doing the exercises I've given him, but the way he jumps when I press down on the muscle tells me he's still got some areas we need to work on.

"Jesus, Alanna. Have mercy," he whimpers, pressing his fist to his mouth.

"You're such a baby," I reply, shaking my head while I continue pushing down on the trigger point.

"And you're a big bully," he counters.

"O'Malley, you're really not doing yourself any favours. The more you complain, the harder she's going to go," Michael calls out from across the room.

"Shut it, Jenson," Lincoln growls before letting out another yelp when I push down harder.

Michael sniggers. "Told you."

I shake my head while they all keep giving each other a hard time, and I continue working to release the tension running down Lincoln's calf. The guys on the team are all close, and I get along with all of them, with the exception of Dean, who I just avoid. They work hard to keep the team at the top of the ladder, and I've watched them throw their bodies on the line daily to keep that position.

I spend the next fifteen minutes working on Lincoln's calf and up into his glute, shaking my head each time he complains.

"You coming with us tonight Alanna?" Riley asks when he enters the room.

Lincoln's head pops up, and he turns to give me a pleading look. "Is my turn over now? Is that why Butler's in here?"

I smirk. "Yes, you big baby. Riley, you're up. And yeah, I'll be at trivia tonight."

"You guys do trivia?" Lincoln hops off the table, wincing as his foot hits the ground.

I narrow my eyes as I watch him walk, and the smile on his face seems a little too big. Probably hoping I didn't notice the way he favours his left leg.

Riley sits on the table, sliding back so his feet dangle just off the ground. "Yep. Alanna is a genius. She knows everything!"

I shrug. "I just know a bunch of useless facts, that's all. Comes with the photographic memory."

Riley shakes his head. "Nope, don't sell yourself short like that. Tierney says you guys won the last two weeks because of you."

The team's crazy schedule means Riley doesn't always get to come along to the trivia night. I don't travel for every away game - I somehow almost always seem to get the short straw, getting left with the injured players while the other trainers are on the road with the team. So I've attended every trivia session for the last month with Riley's sister, Tierney, who also happens to by my roommate.

"I wanna come," Lincoln says.

"You guys are welcome to come along. But we take it seriously, O'Malley. So no clowning around." Riley levels his friend with a pointed look.

"Seth will keep me in line."

Seth sighs, shaking his head. "That's Adele's job. I have never been able to keep you in line once in the thirty years we've known each other."

Lincoln grins. "True," he concedes, before turning back to Riley. "Can we bring the girls?"

"If it means you might actually take it seriously, sure. Kylie and Adele are always welcome." Riley nods towards me. "You'll like Kylie, she's an Aussie."

I laugh. "I'm not sure if you're aware, but that's like me saying to you that you'll get along with Michael because he's from the US."

Riley grimaces. "Sorry, buddy," he says, thickening his Canadian accent.

"Hey!" Michael lifts his head from Simon's table.

"Relax," I tell him waving him off. "I didn't say there was anything wrong with that. It's just, while Australia and New Zealand are neighbours, it doesn't mean we all automatically get along."

Lincoln slings his arm around my shoulders. "Yeah, but Kylie is awesome. You'll love her. And she was only complaining the other day that she never gets to do anything fun anymore because she's puking non-stop since Seth knocked her up."

Seth blushes at the mention of his wife's pregnancy. The team is super excited to have a baby Davidson on the way. I've seen his wife a few times, but we've never spoken. On the few occasions I've attended work events, I've stuck close to Riley and Tierney, avoiding socializing with the WAGs. The wives and girlfriends of the players are all stunning, and some of them are pretty terrifying - like Anders' wife, Bethany. While he's not one of my assigned players, he's another one of my favourites. But Bethany is some sort of influencer, and seems a little bitchy whenever I've seen her interact with the others. I still can't work out why they're together, because Anders is super friendly. While I've heard that Kylie and Adele are nice, I've just found it easier to keep to myself, still finding it difficult to make many friends outside of the team.

I open my mouth to reply to Lincoln when Dean limps into the room, wincing each time he puts his left leg forward.

"Hey man! I thought you weren't coming in til later?" Lincoln steps away from me to clap Dean on the shoulder.

"Couldn't handle sitting around at home anymore," Dean grumbles, not quite meeting Lincoln's eye.

We've perfected the art of avoiding each other unless absolutely necessary, and he doesn't look my way as he continues on towards the spare treatment table in the centre of the room.

I swallow hard, almost strangling myself when I twist my necklace between my fingers while I wait for the moment when someone informs him that Simon won't be the one helping him.

"Shouldn't you still be resting?" Riley asks, flinching when I return to my task of stretching his right arm out to the side to assess his shoulder.

"No." It appears being injured has made the grumpy goalie downright cantankerous.

He's a solid wall of muscle and still one of the most attractive men I've ever laid eyes on. But right now, that gorgeous face is contorted into a scowl, with no trace of humour.

"Simon, work your magic, man. I need to get back out there." He keeps his head down while his teammates exchange concerned looks.

"Actually, Dean, Alanna's going to be taking care of you."

Dean stops in his tracks and finally looks up, shooting Simon an incredulous look. "What? Why?"

Ouch. I continue assessing Riley's range of movement while I eavesdrop, hoping he doesn't make a scene.

"Dayna's having the baby tomorrow, so I'll be off on paternity leave for a few weeks." Simon smiles while nodding over at me. "But Alanna is way better than me anyway, so she'll have you up and running in no time."

Dean swings around to look at me and shakes his head. "No." He turns back to Simon.

I'm sorry, what?

"Excuse me?" I say, my mouth hanging open.

He scowls at me over his shoulder. "Nothing personal, but it needs to be Simon."

Not personal, my ass.

I cross my arms. "Simon? Who's about to have a baby and therefore isn't available to cater to your every whim?"

His scowl grows darker as he meets my gaze properly for the first time.

Lincoln clears his throat. "Bud, Alanna is awesome. You'll be fine." Dean grunts in response, and Lincoln lets out a long, low whistle. "Keep it up, Dean, and she's going to inflict so much pain on you."

Dean opens his mouth to reply, but Seth speaks up first. "Dean, pull your head in. That was rude, and you owe Alanna an apology."

I continue to stare at the grumpy goalie, waiting for him to crack a smile. Or something close, at least.

But he just keeps on scowling.

And I'm now very aware that the player who needs my help the most is about to become even more frustrating than he already is.

Chapter Eight

CAN'T HANDLE A FEMALE TRAINER?

Dean

I honestly didn't mean to be a rude asshole, but I have no idea how to explain that I can't have Alanna working on me. Even without our history, if I stray from my usual patterns now, it's going to fuck everything up even worse. I've already missed three games because of this fucking hip injury, and having to sit back and watch while Mark and Connor - my temporary replacement they called up from our AHL team - make all the saves has me on edge. Now Simon's off for god knows how long because his wife decided it would be a great idea to have a baby right at the beginning of the season, and I have to get used to a new trainer? One who I have seen naked and I'm constantly wishing for a repeated tumble between the sheets with?

The logical part of my brain knows that it's not the universe working against me and that women can fall pregnant whenever they want. But I'm not feeling particularly logical right now.

"Can we work something out with Dayna that I can just have you for like the next two weeks?" I practically beg Simon, avoiding meeting Alanna's gaze, although I can feel her glare burning a hole into the side of my head.

Simon raises an eyebrow. "Ah... I seriously doubt that. She's already angry with me for coming to work today and not helping her get everything sorted out around the house. And if you think it's only going to take two weeks for that injury to settle, you're not going to handle reality well."

"What is your problem, Thomas? Can't handle a female trainer?" Alanna is practically shooting laser beams at me with her eyes now.

Is she for real right now? Has she completely forgotten what happened between us?

I sigh. "No, I have absolutely no problem with the fact that you're a woman. I love women, ask any of these guys. It's just..."

Fuck, why are we having this conversation in front of half the team and training staff? And why is she giving me a hard time?! Surely this is uncomfortable for her, too?

"He's superstitious," Lincoln says, his eyes twinkling with amusement.

Sure... Let's go with that.

"Shut up, O'Malley," I say through clenched teeth.

Alanna shakes her head. "Seriously? So you think that if I work on you instead of Simon, you'll what? Be even more broken?"

Without thinking, I shift uncomfortably on my feet and pain shoots through my hip and into my groin. I fail at hiding the grimace that plays across my face.

"Why are athletes such idiots?" she asks, sounding exasperated.

"Hey!" Lincoln looks insulted.

"She's got a point, O'Malley. Dean, I get it. But Alanna is seriously the best out of all the trainers, and she also has the most experience with injuries like yours. So suck it up, big guy." Simon nods towards the chair in the corner. "Sit down and stop being a pain in the ass."

I grumble under my breath but limp towards the chair. I'm

not sure how much longer I could have handled standing, anyway.

Our team doctor, Nicholas, has insisted I need at least two weeks of rest before I start working with the athletic training staff to get myself back into shape. But I can't handle sitting around anymore. Every missed game is just another reminder that I'm past my prime.

Alanna eyes me warily as she returns to working on Riley's shoulder, and I can tell she's assessing my movements. I know she's good at her job. She's developed a reputation for taking zero shit from anyone, which I've admired from afar. But now that I'm in her sights from a training standpoint, I'm not sure I'm going to like that attitude so much.

I stare down at my phone, avoiding looking at anyone else as I doom scroll through social media.

"Dean, you should come to trivia with us tonight. No use sitting around home feeling sorry for yourself," Riley says.

I look up. "What?"

Lincoln sniggers. "Trivia. We're all going."

I lift an eyebrow. "You actually know the answers at trivia, O'Malley?"

He glowers at me as Seth shakes his head. "Stop sniping at each other, the pair of you. Dean, you should come. Kylie and I can swing by and pick you up on the way."

I shrug. "I guess. Not like I have anything else to do."

Everyone continues talking amongst themselves, so I go back to staring at my phone as a text message comes through.

ANASTASIA

Hey you. Up for a visitor tonight?

I scowl at the screen. I've basically ripped myself in half and this woman is asking if I'm up for sex? Un-fucking-believable.

DEAN

Out of commission for awhile, sorry. You're going to have to hit one of the other guys up.

I'm aware that I have a bit of a reputation with the group of women that hang around the team. In previous seasons, I had no problem admitting that I'm up for consensual, casual sex with the professional husband chasers. I am a red-blooded professional athlete, after all. But ever since that night with Alanna, the only action I've had is with my own hand, because I've been unable to erase the memory of how good it was between us that night. The two occasions I attempted to push those feelings aside when talking to a woman who was making it clear she was interested, Alanna had noticed the flirting and I felt like a piece of shit when I'd noted her raised eyebrow, so nothing happened.

Anastasia is in the group of women that hang around with Anders' wife, Bethany. Of all the WAGs, Bethany is the least liked due to her snooty attitude and the obvious way she uses her husband's fame to get attention. If Anders wasn't such a good friend, I'd be asking him what the fuck he sees in her. Her friends are all the same, and Anastasia has been hitting me up since she broke up with one of the AHL guys over the summer. I'm starting to think she's lined me up as the one that's finally going to put a ring on her finger. While we hooked up once a few years ago, I am definitely not interested in going back for seconds, let alone proposing to her.

I have no problems with commitment, and if I meet the right woman one day, I'll happily walk down that aisle. But it won't be with a woman who can barely take the time to learn about my interests outside of making her moan.

ANASTASIA

I could kiss your boo-boo better?

Fuck me, this woman clearly isn't great at hearing no. And it's more than a fucking boo-boo.

I grit my teeth as I bash out my response.

DEAN

Not gonna happen.

I ignore the reply that comes through, pocketing my phone again before returning to glaring at Alanna and Riley. How long does it take to work on a slightly sore shoulder? If I'm going to get back out on the ice, I need to get started on my rehab, and he's taking forever.

"Dude, you need to lighten up. I get this sucks, but glaring holes in the side of Butler's head is not going to get you anywhere," Lincoln says, clapping a hand on my shoulder.

I shrug him off. "I'm fine."

"No, you're not. You've been a grouchy asshole for months and now you're like ten times worse." Lincoln crosses his arms. "Adele said you even stopped trying to get her to dump me and give you a shot. So clearly you are broken."

I glare at him. Which does nothing other than prove his point.

It still blows my mind that Adele went and fell head over heels for my idiot friend. They are clearly made for each other, though. She keeps him in line, and he worships the ground she walks on. That doesn't stop me from bugging the shit out of Lincoln by constantly flirting with her in front of him, though. It's pretty much the only fun I have these days.

Mustering up a smirk, I shrug as I tear my gaze away from Alanna and Riley. "I'm just waiting for the next time you fuck up, and then I'll swoop on in and remind her who the real MVP is."

Lincoln chuckles. "There's the dickhead I know and love." His expression shifts. "Seriously, though. You need to take it easy. You don't want to make the injury worse and be out of commission even longer."

"Thanks Dad," I retort.

Seth joins us, shaking his head again. "You know he's right. You never would have considered going against doctor's orders before. So tap back into that common sense part of your brain and take it easy."

I don't bother responding, sick of having everyone tell me how stupid I am for wanting to get back out there sooner rather than later.

They don't get it. None of them have some rookie breathing down their neck, just waiting for them to fuck up.

"Right, Dean. You're up," Alanna calls out, stepping back so Riley can hop off the table.

Her eyes narrow as she watches me use the arms of the chair to push myself up with a barely concealed groan. Her expression darkens further when I limp towards the table.

"You are pushing yourself too hard," she mutters once I finally plonk my ass down.

"No such thing," I retort.

Her eyes flare but she doesn't fire back, instead moving to grab a file from the desk behind her. She flicks through it, scanning the words that I'm sure are about me. "You had a corticosteroid injection yesterday?" I nod, and she frowns, shutting the file and looking at me again. "And you're still limping like that?"

I shrug. "They said it might not make it completely stop hurting straight away."

"Which means you should still be resting," she says, seemingly unable to keep from telling me off.

"I can't rest anymore, I'm going fucking nuts sitting at home. So work your magic, Miss 'Best of the Trainers'." I was going for charming, but it just comes off as dickish, and she does not look impressed.

"Fine. Let's get you started on some exercises, Mr 'I refuse to listen'."

And then she proceeds to make me wish I'd stayed home after all.

When I get home, I collapse onto the couch and glare at the wall.

What an absolute clusterfuck. I've spent the last thirteen months trying to keep my distance from that woman and get her out of my head. Now I'm injured and have to deal with her on a daily basis - with her hands all over my body while she helps me with my rehab - and try not to think about the last time we touched each other.

My phone rings as I'm wondering why the universe hates me, and I look down to see 'Mom' appear on the screen. With a sigh, I drag my finger across the screen.

"Hey Mom," I say, trying not to sound grumpy.

A slight stab of homesickness hits me as I imagine her sitting in the living room of the apartment she shares with my father in Rome.

"Just checking in to see if you're actually resting," she says, proving that she knows me far too well, even though we live half a world away from each other these days.

"I'm fine."

"That wasn't what I asked, kiddo."

I sigh, pinching the bridge of my nose. "I'm working with the training staff to get back on the ice as soon as possible."

"So, in other words, no, you're not resting, and instead pushing yourself far too hard," she replies, the frustration in her tone more than evident.

"I promise I'm following doctor's orders," I say, lying through my teeth.

"Dean Alexander Thomas. I know when you're lying to me. Because you suck at it."

My mother has never been one to beat around the bush, which I'm usually grateful for. Just not when it's directed at me.

"How's Dad?" I ask, hoping to divert the conversation.

"Busy, as always. And don't change the subject."

This woman has spent far too long in Italy, where the mama's rule the household and bring their sons to task constantly. When they aren't babying the shit out of them. At least she didn't pick up that trait, because that wouldn't bode well for either of us.

Sighing, I shake my head, forgetting for a moment that she can't see me. "Mom, I promise, I'm getting the best advice there is. And there's no way my trainer is going to let me get away with pushing myself too hard."

"Pfft, Simon has always just let you call the shots, I doubt he's being firm with you now."

"It's not Simon. He's on paternity leave. It's Alanna, one of the other trainers."

She's quiet for a moment. "A female trainer? Well, I guess working in a male dominated industry, she'd have to be tough as nails. Good. I hope she forces you to take it easy."

Tough as nails isn't even close to the right description for Alanna. I'll be lucky if I'm back on the ice in a month with how bossy she is. And it sucks that I find that so hot while also being infuriated as all hell that her bossiness is now turned on me.

Mom finally calms down and we talk a little longer about

what she's been up to since her and Dad were here during the off season. Once we hang up, I let my head fall back against the top of the couch, staring at the ceiling as I return to cursing the world for my current bad luck.

Chapter Nine

DO YOU EVEN OWN A DRESS?

Alanna

Dean clearly regretted his stubbornness when I put him through a series of exercises that would have no doubt hurt. I was probably a little cruel, but I had a point to prove. And that point was that maybe, just maybe, the goalie should still be resting.

He'd barely been able to look at me by the time the session was done. I don't know how much of that was because of the pain I'd made him endure, or because of our complicated history. I'm pretty sure he was ready to go completely postal when I handed him a walking stick, though. But when he could hardly walk, he had no other choice but to take it and hobble on out of the room.

The rest of the day is fairly uneventful, and after I finish restocking the supply room, I head home to get ready to go out with everyone, trying not to think about the fact that I now have to see Dean outside of work because Riley went and invited him to trivia.

Nice work, Butler.

I can't be mad at him, though. No one knows anything

about what happened with Dean and me, so why would they think it was weird to invite him out with us?

When I walk through the door of our small bungalow style rental, I find Tierney standing in front of the mirror that she propped up in the living area when she moved in - the only place we'd had room for it.

"Wow! You're getting all fancy?" I ask, dropping my backpack on the floor inside the hall closet.

She's dressed in tight black jeans with a low-cut red top that looks amazing with her long, wavy blonde hair. She's a former dancer turned personal trainer, so she pretty much looks good in anything, but this is definitely more dressed up than I was expecting for a night down at the local pub playing trivia.

She spins around to look at me, her cheeks immediately going pink as she bites her lip. "Um, well... Riley called and said he invited a few of the guys along..."

Understanding dawns on me, and I chuckle. "And one of those guys is Michael?"

Her blush grows more pronounced as she nods slightly.

She's had a thing for Michael ever since she moved to Calgary from Vancouver six months ago, after she broke up with her ex, a former teammate of Riley's when he played there. Riley had been so excited that his baby sister was moving here and thought she'd live with him. But she wasn't interested in living with her over-protective big brother. So when she found out I was looking for someone to move in after my last housemate moved out, she appeared in my life like a whirlwind and has become my best friend in the process.

She'd met Michael her first night here and has been lusting after him ever since. But Riley laid down the law before she arrived - telling the entire team (including the support staff) that his sister was off limits after her ex smashed her confidence apart. Given that Riley is one of the most respected players on the Mounties, they all listened, including Michael. But Tierney is determined to get him to see her as more than just Riley's younger sister, and puts a lot of effort into her appearance whenever he's around.

"You know the poor guy is trying so hard to respect Riley's wishes, right? Are you purposely trying to make it difficult?" I kick my shoes off, throwing them into the closet and slamming it shut before anything can come tumbling back out. "Really need to sort through that," I mutter, before turning back to look at her with my hands on my hips.

Tierney ignores my remark about the overstuffed hall closet and sighs. "I didn't ask Riley to lay down that stupid law, and I refuse to live my life doing whatever he thinks is right for me. If he doesn't want me around hockey players, then maybe he should have picked a different career."

"I get it. I'd kick my brother's butt if he tried to tell me who I should date, but Riley is just trying to look out for you. It's no excuse, but he did basically raise you."

She groans and flops down on the couch. "Yeah, but now I'm twenty-four. No more raising needed. And I never asked him to take the dad role. I just want my brother to be my brother and let me date whoever the hell I want. I will win this silent war, Lahney. You're just lucky your brother is half a world away."

I hide my smile, knowing that will just make things worse for her. She's two years younger than me, but sometimes she feels so much younger when she's complaining about her big brother bossing her around. My own brother would never dream of trying to tell me who I could date, even if we lived in the same hemisphere. But I'm also far more formidable than sweet Tierney.

"Come on, you can help me work out what to wear," I say,

knowing that getting to dress me will distract her from her troubles.

She bounces back up and races into my room like an excited puppy. “Yes! I have been dreaming of this day! Can I please throw out all the boring clothes while I’m in your closet?”

I laugh silently as I follow her at a more reasonable pace. “No.”

She pouts as she pulls the doors of my small closet open and stares at my very modest clothing selection. “There is nothing in here I can work with, Lahney.”

I shrug. “All I do is work and sleep, so why bother buying clothes I’ll never wear?”

Tierney frowns. “You know you’re only twenty-six, right? Not some old lady? You have more than enough chances to come out with me and the guys from work.”

I screw my nose up. “Pass. You know how much I hate going out.”

Besides, the last guy I struck up a conversation with - and consequently went against my usual nature and slept with - ended up being the goalie of the team I work for. Not keen to have that happen twice, thank you very much.

She waves her hand in my direction. “Whatever. We’re going to my closet. Yours is too sad.” She grabs my hand and drags me back out the door, crossing the hall towards her own room.

When she’d first moved in, I had been in the main bedroom, but one look at how much stuff she had told me she needed the space more than me. I’d barely used a fraction of the giant walk-in robe, but now it’s overflowing with clothes and shoes. I avoid coming in here because all I want to do is sort it all out and make it look less like a tornado ripped through it.

She starts rummaging through the clothes, yanking out a

black dress and holding it up with far too much sparkle in her eyes.

"No. No dresses," I tell her firmly, and she sighs in disgust.

"You have an absolutely gorgeous figure and I hate that you hide it behind all of... that." She waves her hand up and down my body.

I look down at my workout tights and Mounties polo. "This is what I have to wear for work."

"Except you also dress like that when you're not working. Do you even own a dress?"

"Yes," I reply defensively, crossing my arms.

"In this country?"

I sigh. "No."

She nods in triumph. "My point exactly."

"I'm not wearing a dress to trivia. I have no interest in trying to look good for any of these guys."

Well, maybe one of them, but we can't go there again.

I hastily push the thought aside. "I will allow a nice top and that's it."

She groans, but gives in, producing a dark green halter top. I run a suspicious eye over it, but eventually figure it'll cover all the important bits. And I'll be wearing a jumper over it, anyway. It might only be October, but it's already getting cold, and I had regretted not taking one to work this morning.

Half an hour later, I'm showered and dressed in my favourite jeans and Tierney's top, and suffering through having my make-up done. Seriously, this is all far too much effort for a night at the pub with my colleagues.

Once she's deemed my appearance acceptable, we walk the few hundred metres up the street to Buck's Bar. The guys have all been coming here for years, as Buck makes sure that no one bothers them, or he will ban them for life.

When we enter, I scan the room, looking for any familiar

faces. Spotting Riley and Michael sitting at a long table, we weave our way through the rapidly filling room. They'd only started the trivia nights a few months ago, but it has proven very popular, and now we have to book a table ahead of time to make sure we can actually get in.

"Hey," I say, taking a seat next to Riley.

He nods at me, doing his best to hide the way he watches Tierney slide into the seat beside Michael across the table.

Michael smiles at her, his eyes drifting over her before snapping back up to her face, a blush creeping up his neck. He turns to look at me, his eyes wide as he avoids Riley's pointed glare.

Poor Michael.

We're saved from the awkwardness when Lincoln and Adele arrive a moment later. They really are such a striking couple. At six foot two, Lincoln is probably one of the hottest guys on the team, all blond, Norse-god like, with the typical hockey player body - not an ounce of body fat on him. And his girlfriend is equally stunning, with long brown hair, tanned skin, pretty brown eyes and a face that wouldn't look out of place on the cover of a magazine. When Seth arrives a few minutes later along with his wife, Kylie, the hot factor goes through the roof. The captain of the Mounties is the dark to Lincoln's light. He's slightly taller at six-foot-four, and is the epitome of tall, dark and handsome with his shaggy brown hair, blue eyes and tanned skin. And his wife, Adele's Australian cousin, could be her slightly curvier twin with emerald green eyes that sparkle with humour.

Add in Tierney beside me, and I kind of feel like I stand out, with my deep red hair and pale skin.

I'm remembering now why I've avoided getting to know any of the players' partners. They are all confident in ways I could never imagine being.

Chapter Ten

BREED THEM TOUGHER DOWN UNDER

Alanna

"Where's Dean?" Lincoln asks when Seth drops into the seat beside me.

"Hop-Along is just in the bathroom," Kylie replies for her husband as she rounds the table to give Adele a hug.

Hearing her thick Australian accent gives me a slight pang of nostalgia. While Aussies and Kiwis might act like rivals on our home turf, when we travel, we claim those cousins as our own.

"Don't let him hear you calling him that. He'll throw a major tantrum," Adele says, shaking her head.

"What are you talking about? I've been calling him that the entire car ride." Kylie gives her cousin a wicked grin before taking the seat across from Seth.

Seth shakes his head. "Yeah. I could see Dean's expression in the mirror and he was *not* happy."

Kylie shrugs. "Well, what else is new? He's a grumpy asshole most of the time these days."

Dean arrives, scowling as he hears the last of Kylie's words. She doesn't look bothered in the slightest when he glares at her. I'm surprised to see the walking stick in his hand. I'd figured he was going to ditch it and continue to be a stubborn idiot about his injury.

"Nice," he says, moving to sit across from me.

I shift in my seat, avoiding meeting his gaze.

Kylie grins and pats him on the shoulder. "Whilst it was said with love, you have been incredibly grouchy for months now, and you know it. So either cheer the fuck up, or accept that I will call you out on it."

Okay, I like her.

"Are we waiting for anyone else?" Adele asks, cutting in before Dean can respond.

"Yeah, Ollie and Sarah are coming, too," Michael says, speaking for the first time since I sat down, while Dean continues glaring at his captain's wife.

Kylie doesn't seem the slightest bit bothered, though, her cheery grin making her eyes sparkle. Meanwhile, Michael is still studiously avoiding looking at Tierney, scanning the menu with way too much interest. If only Riley would leave the pair of them alone, I honestly think they'd make a very cute couple. But there's no way shy, quiet Michael is going to piss off Riley, who is ten years older than him and basically his idol.

I catch Lincoln grinning at me, and I know he agrees, given he's watching them both with mischief in his eyes. I shake my head, giving him a silent warning not to stir up trouble, and he places a hand over his heart, giving me a mock innocent look.

It's impossible not to like Lincoln, but I do wonder how Adele manages to put up with him on a daily basis. He is a ball of energy, a massive flirt and way too happy. Probably why I take joy in making him whimper when I'm working on whatever his latest body complaint is.

One of our regular servers, Naomi, arrives to take our orders, and we order enough wings and ribs to feed an army. I always forget how much these guys can eat until we're together like this, and the table is soon laden with what feels like a hundred plates and glasses. We're eventually joined by the last of the group, Ollie and his wife Sarah, who is the marketing manager for the team. I know Sarah a little, seeing her around work often, and she's always trying to talk me into socializing with everyone more, with limited success. She's kind of the mother hen of the group, having worked with the team since before Ollie came to the Mounties eight years ago. Ollie's a fan favourite, being the only hometown player on the team, and the rest of the guys look up to him almost as much as Seth.

"So, Alanna, right?" Kylie says, and I look up quickly to find her smiling at me.

I nod and play with my pendant, slightly freaked out to have her attention on me. While I'm fine talking to people I know, or in a professional setting, new people make me nervous, and I tend to shut my mouth in big groups like this.

"The guys tell me you're a Kiwi? You have no idea how happy I am to see someone else from back home working for the team."

I clear my throat. "Yeah, I'm from Auckland. You're from Brisbane, right?"

She nods. "Sydney originally, but my family and friends are all in Brisbane now. I've been to NZ a few times but just the South Island. Do you get back home much?"

Hearing her refer to New Zealand as NZ sets off another wave of nostalgia. Everyone else around me calls it by it's full name when we've discussed my homeland, but Australian's love to shorten everything. Apparently it's much easier to say two letters than two words.

I shake my head. "No, I haven't been back since I moved here at the beginning of last season. I don't really miss it."

She cocks her head to the side, studying me for a moment, and I can feel myself start to sweat.

Fabulous, nervous sweating now, too? Get it together, Alanna.

I pull my jumper off and hope that'll do the trick, although now that means the top that Tierney insisted I wear is on full display, along with more of my cleavage than I'm entirely comfortable with. But it's better than overheating.

"You worked with a professional sports team there, too, right?" Sarah asks, joining the conversation.

The guys are all too busy shovelling food into their mouths to talk, but everyone is watching me with interest.

I am not enjoying this.

"Yeah, with the rugby team."

Kylie's eyes widen. "Union or league?"

I snort before I can stop myself. "Union, of course." And then I blush when she claps her hands together as she laughs.

"Ah, yes, spoken like a true Kiwi."

"What's the difference?" Adele asks, looking between the two of us.

"League is only played in Australia and our one team, and the players think they are top shit. Union is what you see on TV everywhere in the world, and the players actually are top shit," I reply with more conviction than I'm used to in a group setting.

Kylie hoots again as the guys all look at me in surprise. Given it's the most I've spoken about something outside of injury recovery with most of them, I guess I'm showing a side of myself none of them knew about.

"I never realized you were a rugby fan," Lincoln says with a smirk.

Deciding to play down just how involved I was with the sport growing up, I shrug. "I mean, I'm not a huge fan or anything, but the New Zealand team is one of the best in the world, so we kind of get a bit patriotic about it."

"Ah, so like Canadians and hockey?" Michael asks.

As the only American in this group, he is well aware of just how seriously Canadians take their national sport.

I nod. "Very similar."

"I bet the players aren't as tough as us, though," Ollie says, puffing his chest a little.

Kylie rolls her eyes. "Mate, these guys play a highly physical contact sport without an ounce of padding on their bodies."

I sit back and smile as the guys all give her incredulous looks.

"What's that supposed to mean? We get bashed into boards and stuff, of course we need padding," Lincoln says.

She shrugs, not the slightest bit concerned about the defensive tone from her husband's best friend. "These guys smash into each other. I guess we just breed them tougher Down Under." She winks at me as protests erupt around us.

I've decided I really like her now. She clearly doesn't worship the ground hockey players walk on like a lot of the other women I've encountered since I started working with the Mounties. Then again, hockey really isn't a thing in either of our home countries, so that is probably a large part of it.

As I smile, I find Dean watching me with that slightly intense, moody expression that does all sorts of stupid things to my insides.

He's been quiet throughout the entire conversation, almost as though he has lost the ability to socialize. Despite that night we had together, I really don't know him well enough to have any idea what might be up with him, but Kylie was right. He has been super grouchy for months. It all started last season, when he was getting crabby every time they lost. I've heard a few of the guys comment on it, but no one seems to know what's up with him.

I'd heard that he had a reputation as a bit of a player in prior seasons, which I'd tried not to think about, as it only reminded me how shitty my judgement had been. But from what I've seen, he hasn't been dating or anything. There were a couple of women that he talked to at dinner after games, but he didn't leave with any of them.

Not that I've been keeping an eye on him or anything...

But whatever is up with him, I'm finding the way he's looking at me now both unnerving and far too dangerous.

And very hard to ignore.

Chapter Eleven

DEOXYRIBONUCLEIC ACID

Dean

Everyone else at the table is happily defending the honour of hockey players against the two women who are adamant that rugby players would knock us flat on our asses. I wish I could get in on the fun, but my hip is sore as fuck, and I'm still pissed about Kylie's little 'Hop-Along' dig.

I also really want to hate the little redhead who put me through the ringer today, but instead, I just find myself watching her. She's always been pretty quiet when I'm around, other than to tell off the guys she was working on for being oversized babies, so this is the first time I've seen her relaxed enough to joke around since the night we met. Although I notice she's still clinging to that pendant like it's a lifeline. I wonder why she does that when she's anxious or thinking.

Since that night, I've only seen her wear her work uniform - workout tights and a Mounties polo - which is about three sizes too big for her petite frame. But tonight she's wearing a figure hugging top that shows more than a little skin, and from what I can tell, actual make-up. I don't think she really needs the make-up, because she looks great without it, but I'm not complaining about the top.

I might be a grumpy asshole, but I'm not blind. And this woman has had me in knots for over a year now, with no sign that it's going to end any time soon.

She looks up and meets my gaze, and it takes me a moment to realize I'm staring. I shift in my seat and look down at my plate. I've barely had any appetite since the accident, but I've managed to eat a decent portion of wings tonight. Probably because I was avoiding talking and needed something else to do with my mouth.

Wishing she hadn't caught me staring, I spend the next few minutes avoiding looking at her. I refuse to acknowledge how hot I still find her. There's absolutely no future for us and I really need to get a grip.

When Buck finally announces that trivia is about to start, I almost cry with relief. All this socializing is giving me a headache.

Riley, as the unofficial trivia team captain, gets up to grab pens from the table at the front of the room, returning with the answer sheet in his hand, along with a handful of scrap paper.

He spends the next few minutes informing us all about how it works, and gives Lincoln a stern look when he says not to go screaming the answers loud enough for the other teams to hear, but to write the answers on the pieces of blank paper he hands out instead.

At least O'Malley is self aware enough to just shrug good-naturedly. Adele rubs his back before leaning forward to grab a pen when Buck begins asking the first questions. She is incredibly competitive, and I'm sure she's going to be crabby when we ultimately lose.

"Okay, first question in our general knowledge round. The shooting of which person in 1914 started the First World War?" Buck is in his element, wielding the power over us all as he stands on the low stage with the microphone in his hand.

"Franz Ferdinand," I mutter, trying to keep my voice low so that none of the other teams hear me.

Riley stabs his finger at the pieces of paper in front of me before scribbling the name down on the answer sheet. Alanna shoots me a look I can't quite decipher.

"What is the largest organ in the human body?"

Lincoln clicks his fingers excitedly. "Oh, the small intestine!"

Riley shakes his head, most likely already realizing there's going to be no point to the scraps of paper, and goes to write it down, but I stop him. "No. It's the skin."

"As if. The skin isn't an organ," Lincoln retorts.

"Actually, Dean's right," Alanna says, and I realize the look she was giving me was surprise.

Which now seems to be morphing into *impressed*.

"Really?" Lincoln doesn't seem to believe her.

She rolls her eyes. "Who here has the sports medicine masters degree?"

"Well, Seth has a sports medicine degree." Lincoln looks over at his best friend for support.

Seth nods. "Alanna and Dean are right. Sorry, bud."

"Can't believe you were actually questioning the person who is responsible for making sure you aren't in pain every day," Adele says, rolling her eyes at her boyfriend.

"How many wives did King Henry VIII have?"

"Six," Alanna and I both say at the same time.

Several pairs of eyes turn to look at us in surprise. Well, at me. Guess they expected Alanna to be smart.

"What? I know stuff," I say, sitting back with my arms crossed.

"But... How?" Lincoln asks.

I scowl. "You guys weren't the only ones who went to college, asshole."

Too many people think that hockey players are just dumb jocks. I hadn't realized that I'd be copping this sort of ignorance from my own teammates, though.

Lincoln opens his mouth to reply, but Buck barks out the next question, shutting him up.

By the end of the first round, it's clear that Alanna and myself are fairly evenly matched when it comes to random knowledge.

"I never realized you were a closet nerd, Dean," Ollie says as Riley gets up to take the answer sheet to Buck.

I guess they've all forgotten that I spent my childhood in a series of snooty international private schools, and played on the Harvard NCAA team before starting my professional hockey career.

I shrug. "I have a weird memory where this stuff just sticks."

"Funny, so does Alanna," Tierney says, nodding towards her friend, who is still giving me a weird look.

It's unnerving, and I don't like it.

"Dean might give you a run for your money, Lahney," Riley says as he sits back down.

"I'm happy to have someone else help carry the load," Alanna says, grinning when Riley and Tierney protest loudly.

When the answers come back, we have a perfect ten out of ten, and the others share excited cheers. I don't think anyone had expected us to have a chance at winning. Spurred on by success, now they are all taking it seriously, grabbing the scraps of paper and pens to write the answers down for the next round.

"Right, so the next round is the music round. Which everyone sucks at, so good luck." Buck glances around the room, as if daring anyone to challenge him.

"I'm going to win this one, you just watch," Lincoln says,

grabbing the pen out of Riley's hand and dragging the answer sheet across the table.

Riley chuckles. "Sure, you can write the answers, O'Malley."

Buck starts playing a series of different songs that we need to give the titles of, and once again, it's Alanna and me with most of the answers, much to Lincoln's dismay. He does know quite a few, but isn't fast enough to get in before Alanna and I are already shoving bits of paper in front of him.

"You might as well just give the pen to them, babe," Adele says, patting his arm gently.

Lincoln flicks her a look of disgust, but pushes the paper across to Alanna.

The rest of the night continues like this, although Lincoln comes into his element when the specialty round is on random nineties TV shows that most of us haven't even heard of. Kylie also wows us with her sport knowledge, and Seth grins, wrapping an arm around her shoulders when she started rattling off random surfing facts. I guess trivia is helping her feel better after all the throwing up she was complaining about on the car ride over. Pregnancy seems awful. Not that I've really been around many pregnant women.

"Okay, now for the bonus questions. These are all worth five points each, so listen up." Buck is taking this far too seriously.

Anyone would think he's the new *Jeopardy!* host with how into it he's getting.

"What does DNA stand for?"

Everyone looks at Alanna, but the answer slips from of my lips first. "Deoxyribonucleic Acid."

Alanna nods, her eyes wide, and Michael gapes at me. "How the fuck did you know that?"

I shrug. "I told you, I know stuff."

"But that's not just stuff... that's like genius level stuff."

I sigh, rubbing the back of my neck. "I don't know what to tell you, man. I'm more than just the dumb goalie."

"What's the process called when plants release water vapour in the air?"

"Transpiration," Seth says.

No one bats an eyelid in his direction, which irks me. Clearly it's just me everyone thought was dumb.

"What is the national animal of Scotland?"

"Unicorn," I murmur.

"That can't be true, surely?" Kylie asks, looking at her husband.

Seth shrugs. "Dean's the one with a Scottish father, so I'm gonna go with him on this one."

I give her a smug smile.

"But unicorns aren't real." The confused look on her face is cute.

I chuckle. "Don't tell a Scotsman that, Kyles."

She scowls but doesn't say anything further while Alanna writes it on the sheet.

"And for the last question, which I wrote before I knew that half of the damn team was going to show up. How many times have the Mounties made it to the play-offs?" Buck glares at our table as half the room starts laughing, and the rest of them demand a new question.

"It's okay, Buck. I'm sure that there are plenty of Mounties fans in here who would have known the answer, even if we weren't here," Lincoln calls out.

"Shut it, O'Malley, or I'll let them all demand you sign their shit before you leave."

Lincoln grins back. "I'll happily sign whatever they want."

"No boobs!" Adele yells out, and everyone in the room starts laughing again.

Thankfully the people at our table, except Kylie and Alanna, know the answer to that question is forty-three. Would have been embarrassing if we got that one wrong.

When the scores are tallied, Buck begrudgingly announces that our team are the winners. Good thing we were already ahead even without that Mounties question, otherwise there may have been a riot occurring.

Riley shakes his head. "I can't believe we won. Who would have thought Dean knew so much stuff?"

I roll my eyes. "Seriously, it warms my heart that you all thought I was an idiot."

"We didn't think you were an idiot. But you kept your random knowledge to yourself. Guess there's more to our grumpy goalie than chasing tail and ninja reflexes," Lincoln says.

While his smile tells me he meant it as a compliment, having him mention chasing tail irks me. While I'm the first to admit I've slept with quite a few women, I never chased after anyone. I can't look at Alanna again after that comment. It's just proving her point from when she called me a player last year.

Keeping my head down, I don't bother replying, and he's distracted when a few people take him up on the whole 'I'll sign anything' statement from earlier. Adele watches with narrowed eyes - no doubt checking to make sure none of the women whip out their boobs - and the rest of us also agree to sign various napkins and other hastily gathered items.

"How's the hip?" an older man asks while I sign a mug that Buck is one hundred percent never going to see again.

"Getting there," I reply, not wanting to discuss my injury.

"Well, at least we have the young guys to keep us going while you're out. Be good to see you back between the pipes, though."

The reminder that I now have two younger players doing my job brings everything back that I'd managed to forget about over the past two hours, and I try not to scowl. My teammates are all distracted with their own fan interactions, but I look up to find Alanna watching me. She cocks her head to the side, looking thoughtful, and I wonder what she's thinking.

She probably just wants to tell this guy that I'm pushing myself too hard to get back out there and what a baby I am.

Chapter Twelve

THAT'S THE SPIRIT

Alanna

After watching Dean last night, I'd realized that he was really struggling mentally with his injury, and not just because he misses being on the ice. I'd seen the way he'd interacted with the fans last night, and his scowl had deepened each time one of them asked him how he was, or commented on how well Mark and Connor were doing in his absence.

I've seen this happen over the years I've been working with professional athletes. As they get older, while they are still deeply in love with the sport, their bodies begin to demand rest, and they have to work through those changes mentally. No one else seems to have picked up on the fact that Dean's moodiness started when Mark joined the team and started playing more games.

And Dean's clearly not talking about it.

Which means day two of being his primary trainer is going about as well as I thought it would.

"Did you ice your hip when you went home yesterday?" I ask him, watching the way he winces through the stretch I've given him to start with.

He's lying on one of the mats in the training room after

basically falling down to get there. I'll have to find a better way for him to do these stretches that doesn't require him getting on the floor until his hip stops giving him grief.

"Yes, Mom," he snips.

I raise an eyebrow, meeting his grumpy gaze with my own steely one. He might think he's intimidating, but I've dealt with men twice his size and I don't back down. He glares right back at me, determination etched all over his face.

It seems I've met a man as stubborn as I am.

Unlucky for him, I'm the one calling the shots here. "Are you this painful with Simon, or is this attitude something special you've been saving just for me?"

He sighs and rolls onto his back, staring up at the ceiling. "Honestly? I don't even know anymore."

I wait quietly while he sorts through whatever the hell is going through his mind. Finally, after a few minutes of silence, he rolls his head to look at me.

"Look, I don't mean to be an asshole. I just really want to get back out there and do my job."

Seeing the sincerity in his expression, I nod, softening slightly. "And I want to help you get back out there, too. But you can't rush this." I sigh, feeling a little more of the fight drain out of me. "This is my job, Dean. I know how hard it is to want something and not be able to get it straight away. If you keep pushing yourself, you risk making this injury worse and being out of commission even longer. Or worse, you'll end up needing surgery, and then you're out for the rest of the season."

His eyes widen, and I can tell he hadn't really considered surgery. I'm sure that Nicholas went over this with him when they were in the hospital after he was hurt, but it seems as though he didn't want to believe that there is a real risk of doing permanent damage if he keeps pushing himself too hard.

I can practically see the wheels turning in his mind as he

processes my words, and I remain quiet. It's only the two of us in the training room right now, which is rare, especially on a game day. But the rest of the team is in a strategy meeting right now ahead of tonight's game. Dean could have gone if he'd wanted, but instead, he'd asked if we could have his session now.

Finally, he nods stiffly. "Okay. So what do you recommend?"

I'm surprised that he's listening to me so easily. I was prepared to fight this out with him, but now he's looking at me expectantly, and I'm momentarily lost for words.

Straightening slightly, I cross my arms. "Well. I know you're not going to like this, but Nicholas was right. You really should have another week of resting it." His grimace tells me exactly how he feels about that. "The injection should help, but you jumped straight back into rehab before you gave it a chance to do anything. That's why you're in so much pain today."

He groans and rubs his hand over his face. "Fuck," he says, and then cringes. "Sorry, I didn't mean to swear at you. So what, more sitting around?"

I laugh. "I always forget how polite Canadians are when it comes to swearing. It's cute." He looks slightly horrified at being referred to as cute, causing me to laugh again. "You can swear around me, Dean. This whole situation sucks, and I'm a big girl. I only ask that you trust I know what I'm talking about when it comes to your recovery and stop fighting me on it."

The muscle in his jaw tightens for a moment, before he nods. "Okay. I'll do my best not to be a complete dick."

I grin. "That's the spirit."

He rolls his eyes, but I see a hint of a smile, which is a first. I mean, he'd kind of smiled last night, but that was a smug 'fuck you' smile when someone questioned his random trivia knowledge. That had certainly been a surprise. From what little I know about Dean, he hasn't really struck me as a trivia nerd.

But I'm realizing there is a lot more to this grumpy goalie than I originally thought. Then I'd reminded myself of the easy conversation we'd had that night, before we jumped into bed together. He'd shown incredible intelligence then, too. I'd just forgotten about it amongst my frustration when I realized I was just one of many women he's slept with.

He sits up, wincing again, and I move forward to help him get to his feet. He looks like he's about to insist he doesn't need help, but the pain in his hip clearly reminds him he's not running at full strength right now, and he begrudgingly takes my outstretched hand. I grip his elbow to give him the added support when he rises.

"Jeez, for a tiny person, you are remarkably strong," he says once he's back on his feet.

This is the closest I've stood to him in over a year, and the top of my head only comes to his chest, forcing me to crane my neck to look up at him. I've always thought I was average height, but hockey players are tall, and Dean is the tallest on the team.

I shrug, taking a subtle step back. "Kind of have to be when I'm working with men triple my size. Takes a lot of strength to get into those hard muscles you guys work to the bone."

Too late, I realize that I probably shouldn't have mentioned hard muscles and bones, feeling my cheeks heat up.

There's a flash of humour in Dean's eyes, and I shoot him a warning look.

"Look... If this is going to work with me training you... We need to put everything that happened last year behind us," I tell him.

He studies me for a moment with an unreadable expression on his face. "I didn't say anything, Alanna."

"No, but you were thinking it."

He crosses his arms. "So you're a mind reader now?"

I sigh. "Dean." I can't help the almost pleading tone in my voice.

He clenches his jaw, holding my gaze for a moment longer, before dropping his arms to his side with a nod. "So what am I supposed to do now? I swear, if you tell me to go home and rest it for another week, I will go crazy."

I let out a breath, hopeful that we really will be able to get to a point where the events of last year aren't hanging over every conversation.

"Some light walking will help. If you just sit around, that will most likely make it stiffen up more. Do you want to jump on the treadmill?"

He flicks his gaze towards the treadmills in the gym on the other side of the glass wall. "I kind of hate treadmills. While it's still not too icy, I usually prefer to run outside. Feels good to be out in nature, you know?"

I nod. "Yeah, I feel the same. Okay, how about this? Every morning for the next two weeks, we can go for a walk outside and I can assess you day by day to see when you're ready to start rehab? If we keep you moving slowly, given your overall fitness is high, this should get you on the right track. And I'll work on the area every few days."

He considers this for a moment. "So just walk around the arena every morning?" He doesn't seem particularly enthusiastic about that prospect.

I shrug. "Unless there's somewhere else you'd prefer to walk?"

He nods. "Yeah. You live with Tierney, right?"

"Yeah..." I reply slowly.

The question throws me, and I narrow my eyes as I try to follow why he's suddenly asking about my living situation.

His lips twitch, like he finds it amusing that I'm guarded about him knowing where I live. "So you're not that far from

Glenmore Reservoir. I usually try to go there for my runs. It's got nice views."

Relieved his weird question had a purpose, I nod. "Yeah, we go there on the weekends in the summer. Tierney runs a boot-camp there."

He grins. "I know. I went to one of them when she first started. Riley was trying to help her get clients and dragged us all along at the crack of dawn."

I laugh. "Well, I guess that plan worked, because she's in high demand now."

He nods. "So, do you want me to pick you up, or just meet you there?" He's still smiling, and I find myself wanting to see him do it more often.

It really is a beautiful smile, lighting up his entire face and erasing any sign of the grumpy goalie persona that he wields like a weapon.

I give myself a mental shake for obsessing over his smile and shrug. "It depends. I need to be in here by nine unless it's a game day. How early can you pick me up?"

He shrugs. "I'm an early riser, so I guess like six?"

I nod. "Okay. Well, if you're okay with picking me up, we can go for an hour each morning."

I try not to think about the fact that this is a rather unorthodox plan, and likely a very bad idea. Normally I would never agree to meet one of the players outside of the arena for something like this, but I can tell that Dean is trying his best to make this work in a way he's comfortable with.

He frowns after a moment. "What about when the team hits the road in two days?"

I shake my head. "I won't be travelling with them."

He raises an eyebrow. "Yeah, I noticed you rarely seem to travel with us. Why is that?"

I cock my head to the side, surprised he hasn't worked it out. "Um... well... Because that's just the way it is."

He's quiet for a moment, his expression clouding over once again. "Ah... Right... That sucks, Alanna."

I wave it off, not wanting to get drawn into making a comment about my boss I can't take back. "It's okay. One of us needs to stay around for anyone injured, anyway. I don't mind. I mean, I love travelling with the team as well, but that wasn't why I got into this line of work."

"Okay, well, I'm still sorry."

We make a plan for him to pick me up tomorrow morning and he heads towards the door. I'd thought he was going to go home, but he turns right, towards the small auditorium where the team is still going through tonight's game play, and I smile. Guess having a plan was enough for him to feel confident enough to sit in on that conversation.

Chapter Thirteen

YOU'RE NOT THAT OLD

Dean

At exactly six o'clock the next morning, I pull up in front of the small house that Alanna and Tierney are renting. I've been here once before, when Riley and I were carpooling to a Mounties family event and we picked up Tierney. Alanna didn't come along, and I hadn't gone inside, not feeling like I would be very welcome in her personal space.

Alanna appears at the door, pulling it closed behind her before jogging down the path. She's wearing her usual black workout tights, but instead of the oversized polo I'm accustomed to, she's wearing a fitted green tank top, with a dry-fit sweater zipped up half way that hugs every one of her curves.

I've spent the last year trying not to think about the toned body she keeps hidden away under the Mounties polos she wears. But it's incredibly hard when she looks so fucking good right now.

What I wouldn't give to have those powerful thighs wrapped around my waist again. She didn't even need me to hold her up.

I give myself a mental shake, disgusted by my lack of self-control.

Fuck, stop checking out your trainer, you pervert.

I fully intend on respecting her request yesterday about putting last year behind us, and I need to forget that night ever happened.

Thankfully, I manage to pull my thoughts out of the gutter before she climbs up into the passenger seat of my truck.

She gives me a brief nod. "Good morning." She yawns and covers her mouth with the back of her hand. "Sorry."

I grin. "Not a morning person?"

She buckles up her seatbelt and glances over at me. "I am, but I was up late going over my case files and lost track of time."

I pull away from the curb, keeping my eyes on the road so as not to stare at her any more than I already was. "Do you do that often?"

"Depends on how many of you are injured. I've got Timo off now too, after last night's game."

I cringe at the memory of watching the Swiss forward clutching his knee as he writhed around on the ice. One of the New York players had taken him out when they'd tripped and slid into him from behind while he was scrambling for the puck.

"Yeah, that looked brutal. I was going to check in on him later."

"I'm sure he'd appreciate that. He was pretty low last night. I guess you can relate," she says, and I glance over to see her giving me a sad smile.

"Yeah, although he's younger than me, so he'll probably bounce back quicker."

She's quiet for a moment, and I figure that's the end of the conversation, but then she finally responds. "You're not that old, Dean."

I huff a laugh. "I'm thirty-two. That's ancient, in hockey years."

She shakes her head. "It doesn't have to be. You're in great shape, and other than this injury, you've had a pretty good run."

I shrug. "Probably need to tell my old bones that, because things hurt a lot more these days."

It's the first time I've really admitted to anyone that I'm beginning to feel the wear and tear on my body after so long in the industry. Before my injury, Simon had been working with me on my right shoulder, lower back issues and sore knees, the usual shit goalies end up complaining about. I've been following his instructions on how best to take care of myself to the letter, and we've kept the pain from getting worse. But throw this injury in, and it's only a matter of time before my body just decides enough is enough.

"Good thing you've got Simon, and now me, in your corner, then."

"Yeah." I don't really know what else to say to that, so I just nod, and a semi-comfortable silence falls over us, broken only by the quiet music playing on the radio.

After a few minutes, she snorts and shakes her head. I glance over as she turns the radio up.

"Of course you're into country music. How very Calgary of you."

"Hey, country music has come a long way. This is like, new country, or whatever they call it," I reply, defending the music that I've come to enjoy since I moved here. "I'm not from Calgary, so I don't think we can blame it on that, anyway."

"That's right, I remember you said you grew up in Italy... But you're Canadian, right?" she asks, turning the sound back down slightly.

Normally, I'm protective over my sound system, but I don't seem to mind that Alanna is comfortable enough in my space to fiddle with the controls.

"I'm from Toronto, originally. But I grew up all over Europe because of my dad's job."

She cocks her head to the side. "What's he do?"

I hesitate for a moment, before deciding to give her more information than I usually do.

"He was an ambassador."

I see her straighten her posture out of the corner of my eye. "Like... *The* ambassador?"

I chuckle. "Yeah. He was the British Ambassador for Canada, then he was moved to Germany before being assigned to Italy. They stayed in Rome when he retired because they love it there. He's Scottish, but Mom's Canadian. So I'm a dual citizen."

"Ah, that's right, the unicorn thing. Wow, that's impressive. How'd you get into hockey then? Doesn't seem like the usual pastime for an ambassador's son."

"I played as a kid here until I was seven, and when we lived in Germany for the next few years. It was a bit harder when we moved to Rome, because it's not really that popular in Italy, but Mom managed to find me a team to play with. I moved to the States when I knew I wanted to play professionally. I promised my parents I'd get a college education first though, which is why I played on Harvard's NCAA team. They weren't big on the whole NHL career idea, although they've come onboard now."

She laughs. "You'd want to hope so, seeing as you've been doing it for so long now. I guess that explains why you're so smart. I'm guessing your parents are big on education?"

I raise an eyebrow as I shoot her a quick glance. "Yeah, about that. You seemed really surprised when I knew so many of the answers last night. Did you think I was just dumb jock?"

"No... It just reminded me of our conversation that night..."

Right. The night we promised never to discuss again..

I clear my throat. "What about you? Have you made it back home?"

I know she hasn't been back - I heard her tell Kylie as much last night. But I'm interested to see if she gives me a more detailed answer than she gave Kylie.

Alanna screws up her nose and shakes her head. "No. I haven't been back since I started working with the Mounties."

I want to ask so many questions, but we don't know each other well enough for me to pry, so I change the subject instead.

"Well it's good you've found Tierney and Riley, then. Like your own little family, I guess."

"Yeah. Tierney has become my closest friend since she moved in. She's a lot of fun, and Riley is cool. He can't seem to turn off 'big brother' mode, though."

I chuckle as I turn into the entrance of the reservoir. "Yeah, he's still got the majority of the younger guys terrified to even look in Tierney's direction. I guess it would be hard to switch from 'dad mode' back to big brother after raising her for like ten years, though."

With an eleven year age gap between the two of them, it's easy to see why he's so protective of his sister, even without everything else that happened.

Alanna sighs, her tone sad as she glances my way. "Yeah, I guess. It sucks that he had to do that. Tierney says she can only remember bits and pieces of her parents. I'm still amazed that Riley was able to take on caring for her while he was in college and just starting out in his career. This lifestyle doesn't make it easy for single parents."

The parking lot is almost completely empty, so I pull into a space close to the pathway. I'd managed to forget about my hip for most of the drive, but when I climb out of the truck, pain radiates through to my groin once again, and I stifle a groan, hoping she doesn't notice.

No such luck, though. "You should have turned in the seat and then stepped down," she says, coming around to my side.

I sigh. "It's too early for the telling off part of the morning."

She grins. "Not gonna happen, buddy." She pats my bicep. "Sorry."

I narrow my eyes as I try to glare at her, but it's hard to keep up the grumpy facade when she's smiling at me like that.

Ignoring my attempts to maintain my grouchy goalie reputation, she nods towards the entrance to the path. "So, I don't think we should go too far. I don't want to push your injury too much, but it's good to get some movement happening."

I can see she's switched from relaxed to professional now, and I have to squash down the disappointment that makes my stomach sink. I'd been enjoying the lightness between us, reminding me of when we first met. But I nod, reaching back through the open door and grabbing the walking stick that I have begrudgingly been using. She nods her approval, and I allow her to lead the way to the start of the path, trying not to think about how much I want the woman who is tasked with getting me back on the ice.

Once we've walked for a short amount of time, Alanna calls it, and we head back to my truck. I'm torn between relief at being off my feet again, and frustration that my body is refusing to make a miraculous recovery. Although we'd spoken a little on the walk, the drive back to Alanna's house is quiet while I stew over my thoughts.

When I pull up out the front of the house, Alanna turns to look at me, a thoughtful expression on her face.

"You did well, Dean. Remember what I said. It's just going to take time."

I sigh, staring ahead as I tap the steering wheel. "I know. If you haven't worked out yet, I'm not the most patient person on the planet, so unless I wake up tomorrow suddenly all better, I'm going to be annoyed."

She shakes her head with a sigh. "It's just a couple of weeks. It's not like you're permanently sidelined."

I grip the wheel as I grit my teeth. "A couple of weeks may as well be a lifetime in the NHL."

"No, it's not, and you know it. I won't sit back and let you feel sorry for yourself. That will get you nowhere and most likely lead to you hurting yourself further because you've pushed your hip too hard." There's a hint of annoyance in her tone, and I look over to see her glaring at me.

"Aren't I allowed to be pissed that I'm forced to sit around while my teammates need me? Because that's not fair." I cringe inwardly, knowing I sound like a child right now.

"You can be pissed, but wallowing is unacceptable. Now... Do you want to come in for breakfast, or are you going to go home and sulk?"

I blink a couple of times, thrown by the invitation as she twists her necklace around her finger. "Ah... what's for breakfast?"

Her glare gives way to a heart-stopping smile, and it takes all my concentration not to get lost in those beautiful green eyes.

"Eggs, fruit and coffee."

My stomach chooses this exact moment to growl, and I shoot her a sheepish grin. "Guess my stomach liked the sound of that. Are you sure it's okay?"

She shrugs. "I don't see why it wouldn't be. Riley is here all the time."

I resist the urge to point out that Riley is Tierney's brother and, therefore, it wouldn't be out of the ordinary for him to be here. Because although it feels like we're about to cross some imaginary line, I really want to spend more time with her when she isn't inflicting pain on me, cussing me out for being an impatient crybaby, or glaring at me for being an alleged playboy that just slept with her to add another notch on my bedpost.

Even though I know I should drive away right now, I cut the engine and follow her inside… Pretending this isn't a really bad idea.

Chapter Fourteen

EXTREMELY UNPROFESSIONAL

Alanna

The next week follows the same routine each day - early morning walks with Dean followed by breakfast, which he's taken to having with Tierney and me, before we head to the arena. He's been following my recommendations to the letter, and I'm pleased to see that his limp is improving. We'd started out with an easy two kilometre walk the first two days, before slowly increasing the distance as his pain decreased. By the seventh day, I was comfortable enough with his progress that I started adding in more stretches and some core work, and now here we are, with him lying on his back on the exercise mat once again while I have him doing glute bridges and resistance band work.

"Fuck!" he spits out when he raises his hips for the second set of bridges.

"What? Don't push through it if it hurts too much," I say, straightening from where I've been leaning against the wall while I assess his form.

I move to stand beside him, looking down at his face while he continues through the set.

"It's not too much, but it just fucking sucks that an exercise

I could do without any problem three weeks ago is now hurting."

I squat down beside him. "These things take time. Remember, this isn't a race."

This has become my mantra, and he gives me a dark look filled with frustration while continuing to complete the set, dropping his butt down to the ground with a groan. "Give me the band," he grinds out, nodding towards the resistance band behind me.

I shake my head. "Not yet, you need to rest between each exercise."

He glowers at me. "I know my limits, Lahney."

After a week spent having breakfast with Tierney and me, he's begun using my nickname, and I try not to focus on how much I like it.

I raise an eyebrow. "Clearly you don't, because you are pushing them too hard."

It's yet another stand off between us. Once the pain started to settle, he'd begun fighting me again. But he's learned that I'm just as stubborn as he is, and he just needs to suck it up.

Not that he has much of a choice. I'm the one Nicholas will be checking in with to see whether I think he's ready to strap his skates back on, so Dean has begrudgingly given in each time.

"You are such a pain in my ass," he grumbles.

I grin. "No, that's the glute bridges."

He snorts, rubbing his hands over his face. "Smart ass."

Despite the push back he's been giving me, we've developed a friendship of sorts over the last week. I hadn't expected him to follow through on my request to put last year behind us, but he seems to be comfortable enough around me to drop the grumpy persona now, and we've even joked around a little.

"Hey Big-D, how's the hip?" Mark calls out as he walks into the gym.

The team got back from a two game road trip last night, and he's the first one in for the day.

Dean's expression shutters a little, and he nods towards the younger goalie. "Getting better. I'll be back up and running in the next week or so."

Given that I am not even close to giving him the all clear, this is definitely pushing the timeline, but the look he shoots my way keeps me from opening my mouth to argue. His blue eyes plead with me not to say anything in front of Mark, which I find interesting.

Joel comes in a moment later and starts working with Mark, pulling the younger player's focus away from Dean.

"Wanna tell me why you just lied?" I murmur, still crouching at Dean's side.

"I didn't lie." He reaches out towards the resistance band, and I sigh, handing it to him.

"So you're just living in dreamland, thinking you'll be back on the ice in a week?" I know my words are harsh, but his determination to live in denial is driving me crazy.

"I didn't say I'd be back on the ice." He sits up to slip the band over his feet, dragging it up his legs and positioning it just above his knees. "I said back up and running in a week or so."

I shake my head. "How is that different?"

"Because you've already got me further than you thought you would by this point, so I have faith that you'll have me ready to start working with Oscar again by the end of next week." He rolls onto his right side and brings his knees forward to start doing the clam shell exercises we've worked into his regular workouts from now on.

"No pressure then," I mutter, rising back up.

As much as he's confident he'll be working with the team's goalie coach within the next week, I just don't understand why he's so insistent on pushing himself. It's not like his job is at risk. Dean is still the more experienced between him and Mark, and he's a fan favourite, so why on earth would he risk that by pushing his body too hard?

Once Dean has finished his session, I head into the office the trainers share to start doing inventory on the supplies again. I seemed to have drawn the short straw when it comes to this oh so riveting job, and I try not to sigh when I grab the clipboard with the stock levels outlined, moving to stand in front of the shelves to start counting.

"What are you doing?" Dean asks, startling me.

I hadn't realized he was still here.

"Just inventory. You'd be surprised how often we need to restock all this stuff with how much you guys need strapping up."

He eases himself into the chair at one of the desks. "Why are you the one doing it? Don't we have, like, assistants for that?"

I smirk. "As the newest trainer on staff, the job gets handed to me more often than not."

He scowls. "That's bullshit. You're more qualified than most of the rest of them, and they have you in here counting strapping tape?"

I turn back to the shelves as I shrug. "Someone's gotta do it."

"Yeah. An assistant," he shoots back, and I'm taken aback at the anger I can hear in his tone.

I start counting the rolls of strapping tape and note it down on the form before looking back over at him. "Did you miss the 'assistant' part of assistant trainer? Why are you so concerned about this, anyway?"

He shrugs. "Because I don't like seeing them treat you like shit when you're clearly the best trainer on staff. Bet they wouldn't be pulling this shit if you were a guy."

I choke on a laugh. "I didn't realize you were such a feminist."

He scowls. "Just because I'm a guy doesn't mean I think that it's acceptable that they treat you any differently just because you're one of a the few female trainers in the league."

I stare at him for a moment, stunned by the conviction in his expression. "It's nice to know you think that female trainers are just as competent as the men."

He shrugs. "We should be seeing more women working within the league. It would go a long way to deal with the rampant sexism I've seen over the years."

I put the clipboard down and lean my hip against the desk beside me. "I think that's the first time I've heard that from one of the players."

"It's true, though. You're what, one of seven female trainers in the whole league? And only one of them is the head trainer out of all thirty-two teams. I've worked with three female trainers over my career, and you have all been the most dedicated out of each group. You deserve better. Other sports have progressed but we're still years behind."

I have to admit, the determined expression on his face is incredibly attractive right now. "That's a lot of numbers for you to just rattle off the top of your head. I didn't even know how many of us there were. I mean, I knew about the head trainer, but are there really only seven of us overall?"

He nods, and I sigh. "Well, that sucks. No wonder Trevor doesn't like me." Too late, I realize I shouldn't have said that last part out loud. Dean's eyes widen as I groan. "Ignore that last part. That was extremely unprofessional."

He does not ignore it. "I've already noticed how he treats you, Lahney, and it's bullshit."

I pick the clipboard up once again. "I shouldn't have said

anything. Don't worry about it. Let's just focus on getting you all better."

He scowls, but I turn back to the shelves and start counting again, hoping he'll get the hint. Eventually, he sighs and stands again.

"See you in the morning?"

I turn back to look at him. "It's my weekend the next two days. Gotta rest us poor trainers every now and again," I say, making a lame attempt at a joke.

A look I can't quite decipher flits across his face before he nods. "Okay. I can just use the treadmill at home."

I hesitate for a moment before replying. "I mean... I guess we could still go for a walk. But can we make it later in the morning? I'm going out tonight and don't really want to get up super early on my day off."

"What are you doing tonight?" he asks.

"Um, just going out with Tierney and some of her friends from work?" His jaw tenses a little, and I find myself explaining further for some unknown reason. "She's been at me to check out that new club downtown, and I promised her I'd stop making excuses. I think she just wants to dress me up again."

"So like, a girls' night?" Yeah, there's definitely something off about how he's looking at me right now, his gaze growing more intense.

"Maybe. I don't know if it's only women from her work, actually. I didn't ask."

He doesn't reply straight away, and I shouldn't be as excited as I am that he's obviously jealous.

"Well, have fun. Send me a message or something in the morning, and I'll come pick you up." He turns and leaves the room without saying goodbye, leaving me standing there, trying to work out what the hell just happened.

Chapter Fifteen

ALIEN, OR JUST A BODY SNATCHER?

Dean

After leaving the training room, I head towards our locker room. I've kind of been avoiding it since my injury, but I figure it's time to come out of my self-imposed exile. And I want to talk to the guys.

Lincoln and Seth are the first ones I see when I walk in. They're both dressed in their team shirts and athletic shorts, ready for dryland training. They've got a few days off between games, but both of them prefer to work out at the arena when possible.

Seth nods at me as I take a seat on the bench in front of my cubby. "Hey stranger, looks like you're walking a bit better."

"Yeah, Alanna is a miracle worker. I'm hoping she can give me the all clear to work with Oscar in the next week or so."

"That's great. We've missed you out there the last few weeks. Just isn't the same without your grumpy ass yelling at us every five minutes," Lincoln says with a grin.

I scowl. "Well, if the guys didn't -" I stop myself and sigh. "You know what, no, I'm not going to mouth off about the shitty defence lately."

They both look at me with raised eyebrows. "Who are you

and what have you done with Dean?" Lincoln nudges Seth. "What d'you reckon? Alien, or just a body snatcher?"

Seth smiles but ignores Lincoln's ribbing, like usual. He's always been pretty reserved, and I find the friendship between them interesting. Lincoln forces Seth out of his comfort zone, while Seth keeps Lincoln grounded. They are two of my closest friends - along with Riley, Anders and Ollie - not just on the team, but in everyday life, and we often hang out when they aren't busy doing coupley stuff with Kylie and Adele.

"What's brought on the sudden change in personality?" Lincoln sits down to tie the laces on his trainers.

I shrug. "Nothing. Just don't feel like complaining. Besides, it's not my problem at the moment. Let Mark and Connor deal with it for a bit." I can tell that neither of them is sure how to take my relaxed attitude, so I continue talking. "What are you guys up to tonight?"

Lincoln shrugs. "Adele is on a tour until tomorrow. So, nothing, I guess. Why?"

Adele and Kylie work for their family tour company, although Adele is on the road far more often than Kylie, who went part time when she fell pregnant and started dealing with almost constant morning sickness.

I look at Seth. "How about you?"

"Kylie has finally stopped getting all day morning sickness, so we were thinking of going out for dinner."

"Don't suppose you guys feel like checking out that new club downtown?"

They both stare at me. "You-You want to go to a club?" Lincoln asks, stumbling over his words.

I shrug. "Why not? I'm starting to go stir crazy and we never do anything fun anymore."

They exchange a look, and then Lincoln shrugs. "I mean, I'd

be up for it. Just doesn't seem like your usual scene these days, though."

Seth shakes his head. "I don't think Kylie would be up for a club, but I can check. She hasn't been as tired this last week, so maybe. And once the baby arrives, I doubt either of us will be going out much."

I'm actually surprised he's even entertaining the idea. He is not a fan of being social, and I figured it would just be Lincoln and me. But Kylie is a social butterfly, so maybe he wants to try and get her out and about more before they are trapped at home with a screaming child.

"Great. Will be good to get out, there's only so many video games I can play without my brain dribbling out of my ears."

Riley walks in with giant headphones covering his ears. Seeing us all sitting there, he taps the screen on his phone and slides them off to rest around his neck.

"Hey. Didn't expect to see you guys in here this early." He heads towards his own cubby and tosses his backpack onto the shelf.

"Wanted to get some weights in," Lincoln replies, and Seth nods quietly in agreement.

"Cool, me too. And I need Alanna to work on my shoulder again. I think I tweaked it yesterday." He pulls his own trainers out of his bag and kicks off his slides.

"What are you doing tonight? Wanna come check out that new club with us?" Lincoln asks.

Riley looks up as he takes a seat on the bench. "The one downtown? Tierney is heading there tonight with Alanna and a bunch of her workmates."

Lincoln slowly turns to look at me with a smirk. "Are they now? Interesting. Did you know this, Dean?"

I shrug. "She mentioned it. That's how I knew about it."

Seth studies my face but doesn't say anything. I can tell he's got an opinion, though. I just don't want to hear it. There's nothing weird about going to a club, regardless of who else might be going, and I don't need to explain myself to him.

Lincoln chuckles but turns back to Riley instead of giving me a hard time. "So is that no for you, then?"

Riley shrugs. "Well, I wouldn't mind going, but I'm sure Tierney will think I'm checking up on her."

"Ah well, Tierney can just deal with it. It's not like we're going to be hovering over them or anything. Right, Dean?"

Guess I was wrong about Lincoln not giving me a hard time.

I scowl at him and cross my arms. "I don't hover over anyone."

He grins, taking far too much joy in the situation, and I'm beginning to regret asking them to come along. But it would have been weirder if I went on my own.

"Alright, I'm in. Want me to pick you up, Dean?" Riley asks, rising to his feet now that his shoes are tied.

"Yeah, if you're up for driving? Unless you want to drink?"

Riley shakes his head. "Nah man, you know I don't drink during the season."

I nod. "Yeah, right, I forgot. I'm not really drinking at the moment either." Not that I drank much before my injury, but I don't want to do anything that might even slightly slow my recovery.

"Okay cool. I'll swing by around nine." He nods and heads off towards the gym.

Lincoln and Seth follow, and I look around the empty room. I miss being here with everyone and can't wait to just get back to normal. Even though that will probably mean not getting to hang out with Alanna like I have been. But I refuse to think about why that prospect makes me feel a little sad.

• • •

Riley is five minutes early, but I'm already waiting on the curb for him when he arrives.

"Someone's eager," he comments when I slide into the passenger seat of his car.

"Just over my apartment," I reply, buckling my seatbelt.

"Yeah, that's how I was last season when I did my knee. I get it, man. Just glad you're finally taking it a bit easier."

We chat about the last road trip on the drive into town. I live close to the city and it's not long until Riley is pulling into the closest parkade to the club.

My phone pings, and I fish it out of the pocket of my jeans. "Lincoln says they just got here. Guess Seth and Kylie decided to join."

"Cool," Riley replies, pulling into the first empty space he sees.

We walk the block to the club and join the line out the front, but the security guard waves us over.

"You guys are in." He nods towards the door.

The guy at the front of the line speaks up. "Why'd they get to jump the line?" He sounds pissed.

His friend elbows him in the side. "They're Mounties, dickhead."

The guy is clearly not a hockey fan, judging by the scowl on his face. "So what?"

I shrug and follow Riley inside, happy to use my tiny bit of fame to avoid lining up in the cold night air. It still hasn't started snowing, but I know it's only a matter of time before it starts. Summer has well and truly disappeared for the year, and even after living here for eight years, I don't love when the temperature plummets to the minus twenties and lower. I might choose to spend most of my time inside cold arenas, but that doesn't mean I want to freeze my ass off in my downtime.

Once we're inside, the thumping music washes over me,

and for a brief moment I wonder what the hell I'm doing here. Even when I was younger, I never really went to the clubs, unless it was for some work event. I'd forgotten how loud they are, and I'm pretty sure my ears are going to be ringing by the end of the night.

I scan the crowd and see Lincoln, Seth and Kylie at the bar. I nudge Riley, and he follows me as I weave through the people on the dance floor to join them.

"Hey," I say, bending to give Kylie a quick kiss on the cheek.

She grins. "Hey you. I didn't believe the guys when they said you'd be here."

I shrug. "Needed to get out of my house. Glad you're feeling up for a night out."

She rubs her belly. "Yeah, baby decided to stop making me feel sick, so I'm going to take advantage of my free time while I still can."

Riley waves down one of the bartenders and orders a round of non-alcoholic ciders for us all before joining the conversation. "Have you guys found out what you're having yet?"

Kylie shakes her head. "I have my first scan in a few weeks. This guy wants to keep it a surprise," she says, jabbing her thumb towards where Seth is standing beside her. "But the pregnancy was enough of a surprise for me."

"That's cool. Will you be able to go to the scan?" I ask Seth, who nods with a grin.

"Yeah, we timed it for when I was in town. I don't want to miss any appointments, if I can help it." Despite the pregnancy being unplanned, I know he can't wait to be a dad.

Given he's basically the dad of all of us, he'll be a pro at the fatherhood thing. And while Kylie can be a little crazy at times, I know she's going to make a great mom. Or, mum, as she keeps reminding everyone.

While we wait for our drinks, I look around the crowd,

trying to make it seem like I'm just taking it all in while I scan the faces in search of a certain redheaded trainer.

I know I shouldn't be looking for her. That I'm meant to be her friend and nothing more. But the prospect of seeing her outside of work again was too good to pass up. I hadn't asked Riley if he'd mentioned our plans when he saw her about his shoulder, not wanting to seem too interested.

After a few minutes, I see a group women walk through the door, and I spy Tierney amongst them. She's laughing as she pulls someone along behind her, and it takes me a moment to recognize Alanna.

I'm pretty sure I've stopped breathing as I take in her appearance. She's wearing a short black dress so tight that it may as well be painted on, with her long hair falling down her back in waves. Her stilettos make her legs look impossibly long, and I stifle a groan as she turns our way and I see the plunging neckline that goes right to her belly button. There's no way she's wearing a bra under that.

Kylie looks over to see what has my attention. "Oh wow, Alanna looks amazing!" She abandons us to go say hi to the two women, pointing back over towards us after she gives them both a hug.

Tierney's eyes narrow when her gaze settles on her brother, and Riley chuckles. "Ah crap, spotted. She looks pissed."

But I'm too busy holding Alanna's gaze to take much notice of the look on Tierney's face. Alanna is eyeing me with a mixture of surprise and barely masked attraction, which shouldn't excite me the way it does. Her gaze drifts down my body, pausing on where my sleeves are rolled to my elbows. I'd heard that some women think arms are hot, and I guess she's one of them, because it's obvious that Alanna likes what she sees when a blush creeps up her throat and over her face.

I'm not an idiot. I know women think I'm hot. I've just

never wanted the attention of one this badly before. Even though, of all the women in my life, she's the one I definitely can't have.

But that doesn't stop me from smiling at her and imagining what it would be like if she didn't work for the team. And what I'd give to be the one peeling that dress off her later tonight.

Chapter Sixteen

JUST MOVE YOUR HIPS

Alanna

One would think that, after six months, I would have learned that if I let Tierney treat me like her very own life size barbie doll, I'm going to end up wearing clothes so tight I can't breathe. But clearly I have the memory of a goldfish, because here I am, wearing a dress so short that I'm scared to take even the smallest step, in case it reveals my underwear to the world. A see-through mesh panel gives the illusion that the front is open right down to my belly button, which means I wasn't able to wear a bra. Not that I needed one, because the damn thing is so tight that my boobs are squished flat.

"Holy crap lady, you look amazing!" Kylie says, appearing in front of us after Tierney drags me down the stairs towards the dance floor.

I look down at my outfit, then back at hers as a stab of jealousy hits me. I think this is the first time I've ever been jealous of someone's outfit before, but she's dressed comfortably in jeans and a low cut sweater, and I very much wish I was, too.

"Hey! What are you going here?" Tierney asks, leaning in to give Kylie a quick hug.

"The guys decided they needed a night out," Kylie replies, nodding back towards the bar.

Tierney and I follow her gaze, and my eyes widen when I see Dean, Riley, Seth and Lincoln. None of them had mentioned coming along when I saw them today at work. Although, now that I think about it, I did tell Dean I'd be here... Surely this can't be just a coincidence.

"Seriously? What is my brother doing here?" I can hear the frustration in my best friend's voice, but I'm too busy looking at Dean to pay attention.

I have seen all the guys in various outfits, and more often than not, without their shirts on, so I have no idea why seeing him dressed in dark jeans and a button up shirt with the sleeves rolled up has my stomach fluttering. His tanned arms are crossed, and my eyes lock on them for a moment. I don't even notice I'm staring until I look up and meet his gaze, seeing a small smirk on his face. I'd be embarrassed, except he's blatantly checking me out as well. But I can't really hold that against him, because this outfit kind of demands attention.

"Don't worry, I'll keep your brother in line," Kylie says, pulling my attention away from Dean and those arms.

"Did Michael come, too?" Tierney glances around the room, missing the amused look on Kylie's face.

"Sorry little Butler, no Jenson tonight. Besides, he'd probably freeze if he saw you dressed like that." She waves her hand over Tierney's equally revealing red dress. "And he would have a major loyalty crisis on his hands while he tried to respect Riley's 'no dating Tierney' law while having incredibly indecent thoughts." Kylie winks, but that doesn't stop Tierney from pouting.

"I really wish the guys would realize that I am not some kid that Riley gets to boss around."

Kylie pats her arm. “I know, it’s hard. But he’s just being protective. Give it time. He’ll come around.”

“Did your brother try to tell you who you can date?”

Kylie snorts. “Will wouldn’t dream of it. He was kind of protective of me in high school. But he had his own relationship stuff to deal with, and he’s only a year older than me. He also never had the lines blurred between sibling and parent.”

Tierney sighs. “Fine. Guess I better go say hello to the overprotective pain in the ass. Come on, Lahney.” She proceeds to pull me along behind her and Kylie as they weave through the dancers on the crowded dance floor, and I follow without saying a word.

We stop in front of the guys, and they all nod in greeting.

“Are you going to go all caveman on me and keep me from having fun?” Tierney demands, glaring at Riley.

“That’s a strange way to say hello,” I say, and Riley chuckles, holding his hands up in surrender while Tierney turns her glare towards me.

“Hello little sister, it’s good to see you, too.”

Tierney turns back to him. “Answer the question, Riley.”

He sighs, dropping his hands back to his side. “I promise, I’m only here to hang out with my friends, just like you. I won’t interfere with your fun. Besides, it’s not like any of these guys are going to hit on you. Seth’s married, Lincoln may as well be, and Dean’s... well, Dean’s Dean. He only goes out with the puck bunnies.”

I raise an eyebrow at that comment, noticing the way Dean frowns at that statement, flicking a quick glance my way before glaring back at Riley, who is completely oblivious.

“I’m surprised to see you here,” I say to Dean, trying to distract him from scowling at his friend.

His attention shifts from where Riley and Tierney are still bickering, and his gaze meets mine properly.

"Had enough of hanging out at home, and I've wanted to check this place out."

While he's doing a good job at acting casual, I don't buy it at all. Especially as he seems to be having trouble looking me directly in the eye.

Beside me, Tierney's snippy tone snags both our attention, and we look towards where Riley is running a hand through his hair while trying not to laugh. "Well, you just stay here with your friends and don't interfere with my fun, Riley. I mean it. I just want to dance and have fun with the girls without worrying about you being your usual overprotective self."

"I solemnly swear that I will not interfere with your fun. I won't even look at you," Riley says, looking at the ceiling, as though praying for patience.

Tierney growls, before looking at the rest of the group. "Good to see you all. Bye! Oh, except you Kylie. You can come play with us."

Kylie chuckles as Tierney drags us both out to the dance floor towards her friends from work. "Guess I'm coming to play with you guys."

I laugh. "Yeah, it's best to just go with it when it comes to Tierney and her relentless pursuit of fun. You sure you're up for dancing?"

She nods with a smile. "I'm feeling better this week. The nausea has finally gone away and I have a bit more energy. Seth and I aren't going to stay too long, though. This isn't really his scene. Even though I'm usually just as relentless in my pursuit of fun as Tierney is."

I laugh. "Yeah, I can tell Seth isn't loving it here."

We both look back over at the guys to see Seth rest his elbows on the bar, staring at the drink in his hand.

"Poor husband. He only asked if I wanted to come because

he knows I'm going to miss socializing once the baby arrives and I'm up to my eyeballs in dirty nappies."

"What the hell are nappies?" Tierney asks as she dances away beside me.

"Diapers," Kylie and I say at the same time, and then laugh at the disgusted look on Tierney's face.

"You Aussie-Kiwi's are weird."

Kylie grins. "Yep."

Tierney grabs my hand again. "Come on, Lahney. Loosen up a little and dance with me. You look absolutely smoking in that dress."

I groan. "I'm not much of a dancer, T. And I can barely walk in these shoes you made me wear, let alone dance."

"You don't need to do anything crazy. Just move your hips." She grabs my other hand and forces me to move in time with the fast beat.

Kylie dances along with us, and eventually I manage to find a rhythm, starting to enjoy myself despite still feeling self conscious in my outfit.

The next song starts, and I notice a group of guys nearby. It's obvious they are trying to get closer to us, seeing a group of women with no men to cockblock them.

I ignore the guy who's trying to catch my attention, continuing to focus on Kylie and Tierney. Over at the bar behind them, Seth straightens, keeping an eye on his wife while the strangers start to close in around us. Unfortunately, this isn't my first rodeo when it comes to unwanted male attention in clubs, so I continue to act as though they aren't even there. Kylie and Tierney do the same, although I notice the uneasy look on Kylie's face. After a moment, I catch Seth's eye behind her, and he nods, saying something to the guys.

Riley stays where he is, most likely not wanting to incur his sister's wrath, but Lincoln and Dean follow Seth as he heads our way. When they get close enough, Lincoln begins dancing casually, sliding in between Tierney and the guy who had pressed in behind her. Tierney tenses, but Lincoln bends to say something in her ear, and she relaxes a little when she realizes it's him behind her. Seth does the same with Kylie, and she turns in his arms to smile up at him while not so subtly waving her wedding ring in the face of the guy who'd been trying to touch her.

Dean's face is stoney as he glares over my head at the guy behind me, who stupidly chooses this moment to place his hands on my hips. The other two guys seem to have recognized the Mounties players, backing right off with wide-eyed looks. But I'm not sure the one behind me has realized that Dean is ready to take him out, instead tightening his grip on my hips. I frown and move out of his grasp, which brings me closer to Dean. He slides his arm around my back, continuing to stare down the guy while holding me close and swaying with me in time to the music.

"You okay?" he asks once the strangers finally take the hint and leave without a fuss.

I nod. "Yeah, I was more worried about Kylie."

He looks over to where Kylie has wrapped her arms around Seth's waist. She's still smiling, but I can tell the exchange had made her uncomfortable. No doubt her maternal instincts had kicked in and she wanted to protect her growing belly from unwanted attention.

After a moment, I realize I'm still pressed up against Dean's chest with my hands gripping his biceps. He hasn't loosened his hold on me, and I know I should put some distance between us, but I kind of like it.

Actually, there's no kind of about it.

I very much like it.

And I really, really shouldn't.

There's just something about the protective way he's got his arm slung around me, while casually taking a mouthful of his drink in his free hand. He just oozes alpha male confidence, and clearly my feminist ideals have fled the building, because instead of pushing away, I lean in closer.

His hand flexes as it rests on my back, sliding a little lower, and my heart rate picks up as it comes to a stop just above my butt. My back is entirely exposed in this dress, and the feel of his hand on my bare skin gives me goosebumps. Neither of us says anything as we continue dancing, even when I slide my hands up his biceps and loop my arms around his neck. Despite these ridiculous heels I have on, my face only just reaches his chin, and I keep my eyes down, scared to look up at him in case he see's the effect his body is having on mine. His muscular chest and abs are hard against me, a wall of pure muscle, and I feel safe here in his arms.

Riley eventually joins us when it becomes clear that the guys aren't coming back, and while Tierney looks a little annoyed, she relaxes when one of her friends starts dancing with her brother. He grins at Tierney before turning his back to her, no doubt happy that it's Lincoln she's dancing with and there's a healthy distance between their bodies as they laugh together.

I lose track of how many songs we dance to, focussed entirely on the way Dean's hand is splayed across my back. His cologne is something spicy and intoxicating, and the attraction is burning through me like a wildfire. My heart skips a beat when his nose skims down my neck, and I swear he's breathing me in as his hold tightens.

Fuck, I should stop this. I try to tell myself this is crossing into inappropriate, but my body just doesn't care as my mind conjures up all the what-ifs. What if I turned my head? What if I brushed my lips against his? What if I grind myself against his crotch?

Memories of his mouth on mine race through my mind,

and my nipples harden as a shiver runs through me. His hand flexes again, and a single finger strokes down my spine, stopping when it meets the fabric that's just covering my ass. Everything else around us ceases to exist as his finger ghosts along the edge of the fabric. My arms tighten around his neck, and I tilt my head slightly as his lips brush against my neck.

God, I want to kiss him so badly right now. All it would take is for me to turn my face and it would be game over.

But with three of his teammates present, and Tierney and Kylie right there, this is a dangerous game we're both playing.

Dean's body tenses as he raises his head, and I glance over to see Seth's gaze on us, the warning in his eyes more than obvious as he looks at Dean above Kylie's head.

Reality crashes back down around me, and I step back, breathing heavily.

"Um, I'm going to grab a drink." Reaching to grip my necklace with one hand, I grab Tierney's arm with the other and make a dash for the bar, avoiding looking Dean in the eye.

But I can feel his eyes on my back as I run away from whatever the fuck that just was.

Chapter Seventeen

BARELY EVEN HURTS

Dean

When I open my eyes the next morning, I stare at the ceiling for far too long as the memory of holding Alanna close runs through my mind.

I knew I was playing with fire when I put my arm around her, but seeing that creep grinding up against her ass had me seeing red. I knew the minute he recognized me. His eyes had widened, and he'd backed right off, so there was no need for me to keep holding her. But the second my hand hit the bare skin on her lower back, I'd lost all ability to think. I hadn't seen the back of her dress, and realizing her entire back was exposed had my heart racing. It had taken all my self control not to dip my fingers beneath the fabric of her dress, especially when she'd pressed herself closer. She'd been soft and pliant in my arms, and fuck, she'd smelt so good.

I shouldn't have breathed her in.

I definitely shouldn't have brushed my lips against her neck when she tilted her head.

And I most definitely should not have done either of those things in front of my captain. When I'd looked up to see him staring at us, shame had hit me like a bullet to the chest.

If Alanna and I cross that line again, it won't be my career at risk, but hers. There's a reason they don't allow the players to fraternize with female employees. It leaves the women in vulnerable positions with their jobs on the line.

The players earn millions of dollars, and unless they are forcing themselves on the women, there's no way the team is going to be firing them. Hell, I've heard plenty of horror stories of players getting off with nothing more than a slap on the wrist when they were harassing female staff, while the women were left with no one to protect them.

I scrub a hand over my face and groan, mentally kicking myself for my stupidity. This little crush needs to be squashed before things become any more complicated between us. I knew she was just as into it as me when she was pressing herself closer. I'd felt every shiver that coursed through her body as I ran my finger down her back. I also know she was just as freaked out by our actions as I was when she ran off with Tierney two seconds after Seth was glaring daggers at me.

We'd all left not long after. Kylie was uncomfortable with how crowded the place was becoming, and I needed to put myself in timeout, so had followed Riley out the door when he declared he was done, too. And as Seth and Kylie were his ride, Lincoln followed along without arguing.

Seth hadn't said anything while we were with the others on the walk back to the cars, but I know he'll have something to say once he gets me alone. There won't be any need, though, because I know I fucked up. And it can never happen again.

My phone vibrates on the bedside table, and I roll over to grab it. My hip only twinges slightly, which is a good sign, surely? Maybe I really will be back on the ice in the next two weeks, like I've been telling everyone.

Seeing the message symbol on my phone, I swipe up to unlock it and note the message from Alanna.

ALANNA

Hey, I'm not feeling so great this morning. Are you okay if I bail on our walk?

Despite the disappointment I'm feeling, I know it's for the best. I have no doubt she feels fine and is just avoiding being alone with me, and the last thing I want is to make her uncomfortable.

DEAN

Yeah, that's fine. I should probably just use the treadmills anyway, now that it's getting colder.

The thumbs up she sends me back confirms my suspicions, as she knows I prefer to walk outside and she would have definitely told me she'd still be coming if things between us hadn't turned weird.

Simon needs to come back from paternity leave now so that things can go back to normal and I can get back to focusing on my recovery instead of obsessing over my trainer.

Two days later, I head straight for the gym, bypassing the trainers office. Alanna can come find me if she still wants to assess how I'm walking, but I don't need her permission to use the treadmill, and the radio silence between us over the last few days tells me to keep my distance.

Turning the speed to a level that I'm able to walk comfortably without my hip playing up, I slide my headphones on and stare off into space as the history podcast I was listening to earlier starts back up.

I usually listen to music when I'm running on the treadmill, but that would just annoy me right now when all I can do is a medium paced walk. I just wish my recovery was happening faster. It feels wrong to be moving so slowly, and I have to fight the urge to turn the speed up and just run. But I promised Alanna I wouldn't push myself, and despite everything else, I really don't want to piss her off. It wouldn't be doing either of us any good for me to set my recovery back even further just because I was an impatient dick.

After half an hour, I sense someone standing behind me, and I glance over my shoulder to see Alanna standing at the back of the treadmill with her arms crossed as she stares at my ass. In a professional way, I'm sure.

"You look like you're moving better," she says as I pull my headphones down to rest on my collarbone.

I switch the treadmill off and turn to face her once the machine comes to a stop. "Yeah, it barely even hurts."

She nods. "We can start increasing your speed now that you're on the treadmill. That way, we can keep the pace controlled. And we'll throw in some more exercises. I do need to do a bit more soft tissue work though, if you're okay with that?" Her expression is all business, and I can tell the tentative steps we'd been making towards friendship have halted.

I shrug, ignoring the disappointment I'm feeling. "Yeah, whatever you think. You're the expert, after all."

She nods and turns on her heel. Stifling a sigh, I follow her back into the training room. Seth is in there with Joel, who is taking him through some exercises for his foot, and he gives me a nod when he sees me. Lincoln is stretching his calf, using a foam roller, and Anders is doing some stretches on the floor.

I'm both relieved and disappointed that Alanna and I aren't alone. I want to apologise to her for the other night, but I know that would probably just make things worse. Best to just forget it ever happened.

Or at least try.

She pats a treatment table as she stops next to it. "Lie on your right side, facing away from me, and I'll work through the muscle to see how it's healing up."

I do as she says, and she presses her fingers into my hip. The pain has lessened, and it only hurts a little as she pokes around.

I try not to think about the way she's gently working the muscle that stretches across my hip. Or about how close she's standing behind me.

She eventually gets me to roll onto my stomach so that she can work through the muscles in my lower back that have tensed up to compensate for my hip, and I grit my teeth as she applies more pressure there. The pain is a welcome distraction right now, and I allow myself to focus on that rather than the way her fingers feel on my bare skin.

We've not said a word to each other since she told me to roll over, and I hate the weirdness between us, but I don't know how to fix it. So when she's finished, I slide off the table and give her a brief nod before fucking off out of there and pretending my insides aren't all askew.

She puts a [illegible] table at the [illegible]. "Lie on your right side [illegible] and I'll [illegible] the [illegible] up."

I [illegible] and she presses her finger [illegible]. The pain [illegible] as she [illegible]. I try not to think about the way she's gently working the muscle [illegible] across my hip. Or about how close she's standing to me.

She eventually gets me to roll onto my stomach so that she can work through the muscles in my lower back that have locked up to compensate for my hip and I grit my teeth as she applies more pressure there. The pain is a welcome distraction right now and I allow myself to focus on that rather than the way her fingers feel on my bare skin.

We're not supposed to want each other, since [illegible] and I hate the way the [illegible] between us, [illegible] don't know how to fix it. So when she's finished, I slide off the table, [illegible] a brief nod before I [illegible] out of there and [illegible] my head [illegible].

Chapter Eighteen

WE MAKE A GOOD TEAM

Alanna

It's been a week since the inappropriate dancing, and things between Dean and I are still tense. But at least we've made further progress with his recovery.

"Ready to strap on your skates?" I ask, walking into the gym, where he's once again walking on the treadmill, dressed in sweats and his Mounties hoodie.

We've been working on adding in some more exercises to help him improve stability in his hip, and I'm confident he can handle hitting the ice finally.

He smashes his hand down on the emergency stop button and spins to face me. "Really?"

It's like all his Christmases have come at once, and I can't help but grin at the excitement on his face.

"Really. I want to see how you move while you're skating, and if there's no pain, I think we can get you back on the ice with Oscar."

He practically bounds out of the room, and I follow him with a chuckle. I'd let the equipment manager know we'd need Dean's skates, and he's left them in the locker room in front of Dean's cubby.

"Hello, my babies!" Dean practically kisses his skates, and I laugh before I can stop myself.

He has them on in record time, and I watch closely as he stands up in them. With the extra height, he towers over me, and I have to crane my neck to look up at his smiling face. He doesn't seem to feel any pain in his hip as he balances on the skates, and I follow him back out and down the player's tunnel. The team has morning skate ahead of the night's home game, and there's a few cheers as Dean makes his grand entrance, gliding out onto the smooth, white surface with ease.

I step out onto the ice carefully. My shoes are non-slip and designed for me to be able to walk on the ice, but I'm still not one hundred percent comfortable walking around on the slippery surface, despite how often I have to come out here with the players.

Dean skates around me, and I watch as he glides in circles. The players make skating look so easy, but I know it could still hurt his hip if he turns the wrong way, despite years of practice.

"Any pain?" I ask, and he glides to a stop in front of me.

"Nope." His excitement is contagious, and I grin up at him.

"Well, in that case, I'll let Nicholas know, and if he agrees with my assessment, you'll be back with Oscar from tomorrow."

He pumps his fist in the air before reaching down to wrap me in a hug, lifting me up and spinning us both around.

I yelp and cling to him. "Be careful of your hip! And don't you dare drop me!"

Lincoln skates over as Dean's putting me back down carefully. "I take it this means you're ready to get back on the ice?"

Dean nods, the wide smile looking almost painful.

"He's okay to train again, but no games just yet," I reply, and Dean sighs.

"And here I was thinking you were cool, Lahney."

It's the first time he's called me that since the night we danced, and I relax a little. Perhaps we can put that entire episode behind us now.

Maybe...

If I can stop flashing back to the memory of his fingers stroking my back and the way my body burned for him to move them further south. Because of the dangerous game we were playing, it's almost harder to forget than the memory of him making me come over and over last year.

"I am cool. You know what's not cool? Pushing yourself too hard and being right back at square one." I fix him with a knowing look and he sighs.

"You're a tough one, Jameson."

I pat his arm before turning to head back off the ice. I make it two steps before losing my balance, and my heart jumps into my throat as I fall backwards.

A pair of muscular arms wrap around me, keeping me from cracking my head onto the ice. I don't have a chance to gather my wits before Dean's sliding an arm under my knees, carrying me in a fireman's hold while skating me over to the open gate. Thankfully, it isn't far, but my face is bright red by the time my feet hit the rubber flooring on the other side. I try not to look at anyone else, embarrassed that I'd nearly fallen in front of the team.

Sure, that's the reason you're blushing, and it has nothing to do with the fact that Dean just carried me like I weighed nothing.

"Gotta work on getting used to the slippery ice, Lahney. Especially if you want to be behind the bench," Dean says quietly.

I shrug. "I doubt that'll ever happen. Trevor won't let me anywhere near the bench."

In the fourteen months I've been working here, I've been behind the bench a grand total of three times during games.

Trevor always finds some reason for me to remain hidden away out the back.

Dean scowls and leans his forearms against the top of the boards, bringing his face to my level to meet my gaze. "Trevor's a dick and you deserve to be out there just as much as any of the guys. Look what you did for me."

I search his handsome face, the wall I've built around my heart crumbling at the sincerity I see there.

"Thank you, but a lot of that was you. Once you stopped fighting the process, you really stepped up. I'm glad I was able to help you, though. The team needs you."

He glances over towards the net, where Oscar, the goalie coach, is talking to Mark and Connor. I see a hint of sadness on his face, and wonder what he's thinking. But the moment passes, and he pushes off the boards, gliding backwards while he grins at me.

"We make a good team, Lahney. I'm glad Simon's wife had a baby, and you got stuck with my grumpy ass."

I laugh and shake my head. "Go play with your friends."

He shoots me another grin and skates off towards the net. I watch him for a little longer before heading back into the safety of the training room.

For the last three weeks, my focus has been on Dean's recovery. Now that he's almost better, I need to get back to my usual work. Timo's recovery had been less demanding than Dean's, and I had him back on the ice within a week. The rest of my players are all just dealing with superficial muscle tightness and the occasional dodgy knee.

I look around the room and fight back a sigh.

I'd become so used to having Dean to focus on that I'd been ignoring the work frustrations I've been dealing with. Trevor had handed me more busy work this morning, and I'm beginning to wonder how much longer I can put up with his sexist attitude. I might have waved Dean off when he mentioned me being behind the bench for games, but the truth is, I'm dying to be out there. And I've more than paid my dues.

Now to just get my misogynistic boss to see that.

Five days later, Nicholas gives Dean the all clear to be put back into the line-up. With Simon now back from paternity leave, I have to hand his guys back over, which sucks. But Simon has negotiated to stick close to home for the first few months of new parenthood, so he'll be sticking around for any players who are injured, and I'll get the chance to do more than count strapping tapes for a while, hitting the road with the team for their away games finally.

Chapter Nineteen

WHAT'S HURTING?

Dean

My first game in a month is going well.

You know, besides the aching hip, screaming knee and unhappy lower back.

We're fifteen minutes through the third period and currently leading against Boston two to one on their home ice. And while we might be ahead, Boston has been doing their level best, with thirty shots on goal, spurred on by their dedicated fan base who have been very vocal every time I've blocked their attempts. I've only missed one shot, and while I'm happy with that, my body is not.

I don't think I've ever been more ready for a game to end. I've been working my ass off with Oscar for the last week ahead of this game, but even with Alanna and Simon's help, I think the month off has set me back further than I realized. A part of me has wondered how I'd be feeling if Alanna was still my primary trainer.

Lincoln and Seth are working hard on their latest shift with Riley, keeping the puck down the other end. I'm relieved for the break, but when Boston's first line centre intercepts a pass between the guys just as they pull their goalie, I push through the pain and crouch down, readying myself to defend my net. Keeping my eyes trained on the puck, I let everything else in the arena fade away. It's the adrenaline that fuels me. That need to keep the little black disk from making it past me and into the net is all-consuming, and keeps me from focusing on the pain in my body instead.

Pieter reaches out with his stick to attempt to block the puck as Boston's captain takes the shot, but it just makes it past him. It doesn't matter though, because that puck isn't making it past me. My left leg shoots out and I direct the puck into the corner. The few Mounties fans in the arena cheer, and I smirk while I straighten, ignoring the pain in my lower back. Thankfully we chip the puck out of the zone and I can catch my breath as Boston goes offside trying to re-enter. Glancing up at the clock, I see that there's less than a minute left in the game. I have zero interest in this game going to overtime - or worse, a fucking shoot out.

Boston's goalie heads back to his net for the face-off, but as soon as his team wins the possession battle he's streaking towards the bench with another forward jumping over the boards. When Anders intercepts their centre's attempt to dump it in from the blue line, Mitchell and Maxim fly past him, and he smacks the puck towards them. Mitchell catches it with his stick and sends it flying towards the empty net. Our bench erupts, and I let out a relieved sigh. With only twenty-five seconds left in the game, there's no way Boston is getting two goals.

We run down the clock and as soon as the buzzer goes off, the rest of the guys on the bench hit the ice to come and tap their helmets to mine. A loss on home ice is never fun, so I feel for Boston.

But only a little.

Seth's the last one to get to me, and he grins as he taps his helmet against mine. "Great way to celebrate being back, man."

I smile back, hoping the pain I'm feeling doesn't show on my face. We skate back to the visitors' tunnel together, and even after being told I was named the first star, all I can think about is getting back to the dressing room.

Coach Stephens pats my shoulder as I walk past. "Stellar game, Thomas. Good to have you back."

I nod and continue on towards the bench in front of the locker the equipment manager had set up for me. As I pull my gear off, I finally allow myself to feel the pain that I've been ignoring since the first period, dropping my head down and taking a deep breath.

"You good, Dean?" Joel calls out from the other side of the room.

I look up to see him working on Maxim's shoulder. The big Russian forward winces as Joel lifts his arm to the side, assessing his mobility.

"Yeah, I'm fine," I reply, not wanting to draw any unnecessary attention.

Joel nods and returns his focus to Maxim, and I use the distraction to force myself to get moving. I strip down and head for the showers, doing my best not to wince as my hip protests the movement. I let the hot water wash over me and wish I could stay here for a few hours. Maybe then the heat will erase the pain in my body.

Sadly, we need to get back to the hotel ahead of our early morning flight to Chicago tomorrow, so instead of lingering in the shower, I shut off the water and grab my towel. Once I've dried myself off, I wrap the towel around my hips and shuffle back into the locker room. As I walk through the door and turn towards my locker, Alanna crashes into me, bouncing off my chest, an array of strapping tapes and stretch bands falling from her hands.

"Jeez, sorry!" I reach out to steady her and keep her from falling backwards.

"No, no. I should have been watching where I was going." She drops to her knees to pick up the stuff she dropped, and I crouch down to help her, inhaling sharply as my hips screams at me.

She looks up quickly, studying my face, and I school my expression to hide the pain. She frowns and glances over towards where Coach is talking to Trevor, before looking back at me again.

"What's hurting?" she asks quietly.

I shake my head and rise to my feet, holding my towel at my hip to keep it from falling. "Nothing. I'm good."

She narrows her eyes, but doesn't reply when she stands up. Her face is directly in line with my chest, and she flicks her gaze over my naked torso before her eyes snap up to my face. A slight blush appears on her cheeks as I study her face. I have no doubt that my own attraction is showing on my face as I run my gaze over her features, marvelling at her beauty. Am I ever going to be able to push past this ridiculous crush?

She swallows before nodding slowly, dropping her gaze to her feet and stepping around me to continue on towards the temporary training room next door. I let out a long breath and shake my head, before continuing on to my locker and getting back into my suit, before joining everyone on the bus.

Once we arrive at the hotel, everyone heads into the event space that's been set up for our dinner service while the hotel staff sort out getting our luggage up to our rooms. I fall into the empty seat between Lincoln and Anders with my plate piled high with food.

I eat silently, too shattered to contribute to any of the

conversations happening around me. On the other side of the room, the support staff sit together as they eat their own dinners, and I find myself watching Alanna as she talks to Joel. I know I shouldn't be staring, but it's hard to look away when she's so effortlessly beautiful. Still dressed in her work clothes, her long hair hangs in a braid down her back, and I imagine myself pulling it free and running my fingers through those silky strands.

Anders clears his throat, and I look over to see him grinning at me. I scowl and look back down at my dinner, annoyed that I've been caught staring at the pretty redhead yet again.

What the fuck is wrong with me?

I don't moon over women. Hell, I don't even really get crushes. My last relationship was five years ago, and I don't remember ever letting a woman get under my skin like this. But ever since I met Alanna, she has consumed me, and I have got to get a grip before I go crazy.

I need to find someone else to distract me from the woman I definitely can't have. Now that I'm back on the ice, perhaps it's time to hit up one of the women I have on speed dial and break the drought.

But the idea doesn't appeal to me... And I really don't want to think about why.

Once we've finished eating, everyone heads up to their rooms. When I arrive on my floor along with Anders, Lincoln and Seth, we peel off towards our own rooms. When I reach my door, I wave my card over the security panel, and nothing happens. I try a few more times before groaning and resting my head against the door.

"What's up?" Seth asks from across the hall, and I turn to

see him holding his door open with a raised eyebrow, his phone already in his hand.

"Fucking key card doesn't work," I mumble.

"Want me to come with you to sort it out?"

I shake my head. "Nah, man, go call your wife. I'll get it sorted. Just really ready for some sleep."

He nods and shuts the door, and I walk back to the elevator, cursing under my breath.

Back downstairs, I explain the issue to the lady behind the desk, and she activates the card, apologising profusely that her colleague hadn't done it properly. I wave her off with a "don't worry about it" and turn back towards the elevators. Alanna is standing by herself, an overstuffed duffle bag slung over her shoulder as she waits for one of the elevators to come back down.

Fucking perfect.

As if this night could be more of a clusterfuck. Now I have to try to make small talk with the woman who has been the source of endless sleepless nights lately, and who seems to be able to sense the second I have the slightest twinge in my body.

Chapter Twenty

THAT FEAR IS GOING TO BECOME YOUR REALITY

Dean

"Hey," I say, stopping beside Alanna. She startles and looks up from where she was staring down at her nails, her eyes wide. "Shit, sorry. I didn't mean to scare you."

She lets out a breath, rubbing her chest. "It's fine. I was off in my own little world."

I nod. "Headed to bed?"

"Yeah. It's been a long day."

An elevator arrives, and I wave for her to go first before following her inside. I lean against the handrail, forgetting about my hip for a split second. Pain shoots into my lower back and I suck in a breath.

She glares at me. "I knew you were lying about nothing hurting before."

I shoot her a sheepish look and shrug. "Nothing unusual about being in pain after a hard game. I'll be fine."

"Dean, no offence, but you are full of shit."

I choke on a laugh. "Why don't you say what you really think, Lahney?"

We reach her floor, but she stays where she is, staring me

down. "I need to work on that hip tonight, otherwise you're not going to be able to walk tomorrow."

I study her for a moment as the elevator doors close again. "Don't you want to go to bed?"

She crosses her arms. "Yes. So you're going to behave and let me look at your hip so that we can both get to bed."

I know I shouldn't read anything into her words, and I do my best not to grin at the double meaning behind her words, but she groans and stares up at the ceiling. "In our own beds. In separate rooms. On different floors."

I hold my hands up. "I didn't say a word."

"No, but you were thinking it."

I grin. "Well yeah, when you just make statements like that, of course my brain is going to go there. I'm a red-blooded male, after all."

She sighs and shakes her head as the doors open again, and I follow her out into the hall. Thankfully, the key card works this time, and I open the door, standing aside to let her in first.

She brushes past me, her arm grazing my chest and I ignore the zap of electricity that zooms through me, watching as she lets her bag drop to the floor beside the desk before sitting in the chair by the window.

"Get changed into your sweatpants or something, and I'll check you out." My lips twitch and she groans again. "Stop it! You know what I mean."

"Whatever you say, Lahney." I grab my duffle bag from where the concierge left it at the foot of the bed and grab my sweats, heading for the bathroom to change.

Once I come back out, she is very studiously not looking at my bare chest, and I smirk as I hang my suit on the back of the door before sitting on the bed.

"Where do you want me?"

She licks her lips, looking nervous, and I realize that we

shouldn't be doing this in my room. If someone sees her walk out of here, it's going to lead to problems for her.

"Want me to grab Seth or someone so we're not alone?" I ask, not wanting her to be uncomfortable.

She hesitates, then shakes her head. "No, it's fine." She gets up and comes to stand beside the bed. "Lie on your right side, facing that way." She points to the window, and I nod before following her instructions.

We don't speak as she pokes and prods my hip, working to release the muscles that have tensed up around the joint that is giving me grief.

There's absolutely nothing sexual about the way she's touching me, but I really wish I could see her face right now.

Wish I could run my hands up those toned thighs and cup that gorgeous ass in both hands. Wish I could bury my face between -

"Dean, you really need to keep doing those stretches I gave you. I know you think you're all better, but if you don't take care of yourself, this is going to get so much worse." Her words rip me from the very indecent daydream I'd drifted into, and I can hear the concern in her tone.

I turn to look at her over my shoulder. "I've been doing the stretches."

"How often?" she demands, pushing down on a trigger point, and I groan, burying my face into the pillow.

"When I remember," I mumble into the pillow.

"Well, remember more often. Because I don't want to tell them to bench you, but I will if you don't start taking better care of yourself."

I sigh and look at her again. "At least I have you to put me back together again when I'm broken." She scowls and finds another knot. "Fucking hell, Alanna," I spit out, burying my face into the pillow again.

"Oh, I'm sorry, did that hurt?"

I lift my head to glare at her. "Lincoln was right. You're a big bully."

She chuckles, beginning to massage my hip now that she's released the muscles. "You're at risk of sounding like him when you say that."

I close my eyes, relieved that the painful part is over. "Whatever. I'm not a wimp like O'Malley."

"No, but at least Lincoln knows to talk to me about his pain instead of trying to hide it."

"I wasn't hiding it." She stops massaging and pushes down again, finding another knot. "Ah! Okay, okay! Fine, yes, I was hiding it."

She goes back to massaging. "This would go so much easier if you just talked to me instead of trying to be all strong and silent."

I crack an eye open and look at her again. "Fine."

"Good. Now roll over, because I'm going to have to work through your lower back and glutes."

Great, more pain.

I spend the next twenty minutes trying not to cry as she treats me like human bubble-wrap, determined to get every single knot. But once she's done, it feels so much better.

She hands me a heat pack from her bag. "Stick that in the microwave and put it on your hip and back. I'll get them to send up an ice pack. I want you alternating between cold and hot for the next half an hour, okay?"

I sigh, nodding. "Yes boss."

Her lips twitch, and I can see the laughter in her eyes. "I know you don't like to hear it, but you really need to take better care of yourself."

"I know, I know. You said that already."

She narrows her eyes. "I mean it, Dean. If you're in pain,

you need to tell me. I'm here to help you, but I can't do that if you aren't honest with me."

I sigh and roll onto my back, looking up at her. "I've always found it difficult to admit when something hurts."

She nods. "I know. But please try. I'd hate to see this get any worse and you end up being out for the rest of the season."

I swallow, not wanting to even contemplate that.

Her expression softens again, and she takes a seat beside me on the bed. "I know you're worried about what happens if Mark and Connor are both covering for you."

My gaze snaps to hers. "What's that supposed to mean?"

She scoffs. "Come on, Dean. I'm not an idiot. It's obvious you're worried that the younger guys are going to take your position."

I clench my jaw, grinding my teeth. "I don't know what you're talking about."

"You just keep telling yourself that. But I've seen this before. And if you keep pushing yourself into the ground like this, that fear is going to become your reality."

I stay silent, and she eventually gets up, shaking her head. "I'll call them once I get to my room and get them to send up an ice pack. I'll see you in the morning."

I sit up as she moves to collect her bag, reaching out to grab her hand in mine as she moves past me.

"Wait."

She stops and turns back slowly to look at our hands. Mine dwarfs her tiny one, her skin soft against my callused palm.

When she doesn't immediately drop it, I swallow. "I just... Thanks..."

I can't believe that's all I can think to say after what she just did for me, but with the tension hanging over us like an unspoken storm cloud, it's the best I can come up with.

She brings her eyes to mine, and I can see the emotions

swirling behind them as she nods. We look at each other for what is probably far too long before she slides her hand from my grasp, turns back around and walks out the door without a backward glance.

I release a breath and flop backwards, groaning once the door closes behind her.

What the fuck am I doing?

Chapter Twenty-One

DON'T PLAY DUMB

Alanna

When we arrive at the Chicago arena fresh off the plane, the guys immediately hit the ice for morning skate. Usually they have at least two days between games on the road, but this was a tight turn around, and the players are all feeling it already.

Joel and I are sitting on the bench while the guys are practicing, going through our notes to check over any injuries we need to be concerned about while watching for any players that appear injured on the ice. Trevor is inside getting the temporary training room set up, and I'm relieved to be out from under his watchful eye. He's been watching me like a hawk since we left Calgary - like he's just waiting for a reason to make my life hell. I really wish I knew what it was about me that he can't stand - other than the fact that I have breasts and my reproductive organs are on the inside.

"Okay, so Riley's shoulder is still giving him some trouble. And Seth's foot was a problem after the game last night," I say to Joel, reading through the files in front of me.

"Yep, and Timo's knee was a bit tender, too."

"Great, hopefully he doesn't push it too hard. We had to do

a lot of rehab to get that sorted after the last time," I mutter, leaning over to grab the next file.

"Who's next?" Joel asks as I flip it open.

I grimace. "Dean."

"Well, he shouldn't need too much work, right? Simon said he's basically back to normal after his hip injury."

I don't reply as I frown down at Dean's file, reading over Simon's notes. One look at this and it's obvious that either Simon has become very rusty, or Dean lied to him about how much pain he's experiencing.

My money is on the latter. His stubborn determination is going to end in disaster. It's like he has no regard for how much he's fucking his body up by pushing through all these injuries instead of allowing himself the time to rehab them properly.

"Alanna?" Joel's voice pulls me back to the present and I turn towards him. "Is his file okay?"

I pause. I want to be honest with the other trainers about my suspicions that Dean is pushing himself to perform when he should still be benched. But I'd seen the look on Dean's face when I'd mentioned his obvious insecurities around the younger goalies getting more ice time.

So I do the one thing I thought I'd never do.

I pretend everything's fine.

"Yep, Simon says he's recovered well." I hand Joel the file and grab the next one, ignoring the stab of guilt at the truths I'm keeping inside.

Telling myself that it's on Dean - not me - if he ends up needing surgery. Or worse... with a career-ending injury...

A puck sails over the boards, smacking into the protective glass at the back of the bench, less than a metre from where I'm sitting. I jump, and a yelp slips from my lips while I stare at the projectile that lands next to me. Shaken, I look up to see who the culprit was.

"Sorry Alanna!" Michael yells from centre ice, looking horrified.

I think he was trying to pass the puck to Lincoln, but if he was, his aim was way off, because Lincoln is a good few metres away, and is currently gaping at the younger player.

"Are you trying to kill me, Jenson?" I yell back.

"No, total accident, I swear! I'd never try to kill the best looking out of all the trainers." He winks as he turns back to the pile of pucks next to him.

"I'd be offended if that wasn't true," Joel murmurs, turning back to his notebook where he's scribbling down observations while watching the players in front of us.

"Still, he probably shouldn't say that too loudly. Last thing I need is to be accused of fraternizing with the players," I reply, shaking my head.

"I doubt that anyone has concerns in that regard. You're incredibly professional with all the guys."

I nod absently, trying not to think about a certain player that I have been less than professional with. I still don't know what came over me last night when I basically invited myself back to Dean's hotel room to work on his hip.

Actually, that's a lie.

I *wasn't* thinking when I let the elevator doors close on my floor and allowed myself to continue on for the next four floors to where the players were staying. It had been incredibly stupid, and I had put my career at risk by being alone with him like that. And while nothing untoward had happened between us, if anyone saw me leaving his room, I could pretty much kiss my career in men's professional sports goodbye.

But a small part of me had imagined what I'd do if something had happened between us...

Another lie.

It wasn't a small part of me that imagined it... It was at least ninety percent of my thought process while he lay on the bed, shirtless and wearing only a thin pair of grey sweatpants. How is it that I see these men basically naked on a daily basis, but seeing this one in grey sweatpants has me all hot and bothered?

God, I know the answer to that, too. It's because I know just how good he is at making my body come apart with earth shattering orgasms.

Am I ever going to be able to forget about that night?

Without realizing what I'm doing, I watch Dean while he works with Oscar and Mark down at the net. My eyes track his every move as his lightning fast reflexes catch multiple pucks that Oscar shoots at him. There's absolutely no denying the way my stomach flutters at the determined expression on his face.

The Mounties often switch goalies between games so that Dean doesn't have to play every single game. But because he was off for so long, Coach Stephens has him rostered to play the two games on this road trip, leaving him only a day between games.

He's now listening intently to something that Oscar is saying, nodding alongside Mark as they watch Oscar demonstrate a series of moves. His face is a mask of concentration, and I marvel at how attractive he is. I never thought I'd be drawn to someone like him. He's grumpy, and frustrating as all hell. But when he allows himself to smile, it lights his entire face up. And he's been smiling a lot around me lately.

Dean glances my way, catching me staring, and I quickly look back down at Lincoln's file, even though I know all the details in there like the back of my hand. I feel my face heat up, and know it's bright red. One of the joys of being a redhead is that when I'm embarrassed, my face turns redder than a tomato and I can't hide how I'm feeling.

There's no denying that there's something between us. So I'd put distance between us after that night at the club, scared of the way my body had reacted to his. But the memory of his hard body pressed against mine while his lips ghosted along my skin is seared into my mind, and I'm having a lot of trouble blocking it out. It's been over two weeks and I've touched myself more than a few times to the memory, imagining what could have been if we'd been alone. I have no doubt it would be just as hot as our one night together. Maybe even more so, because we've been dancing around each other for weeks now, and the sexual frustration is close to boiling point.

"You going to be behind the bench tonight, Lahney?" Riley asks as he grabs his drink bottle, his voice ripping me from my very inappropriate-for-work thoughts.

The equipment manager and his assistant had lined the players water bottles up along the boards at the front of the bench, distinguished only by their jersey numbers printed on the side.

I shake my head, grateful to have someone else to focus on, even though I can still feel Dean's eyes on me. "Sadly no. Still paying my dues."

Riley frowns before squirting some water into his mouth. Once he's finished, he sets his bottle back down, continuing to study me.

"Why have you barely been out here with us?" he asks, his gaze shifting between myself and Joel.

I glance at Joel before shrugging. "Just how it is, I guess."

Joel can't seem to bring himself to look at me properly, and it's hard not to feel a little disheartened that he doesn't speak up about the way Trevor treats me.

Riley clearly doesn't like this answer, glaring at Joel when he continues to say nothing. "Well, maybe you should say something about that, Joel. Given that you've been behind the bench almost every game."

Joel opens and closes his mouth a few times, his eyes wide. It's almost comical.

Emphasis on the *almost* part.

"Yeah Joel. What's up with that?" Lincoln asks as he slides in beside Riley.

I hadn't realized he was close enough to hear this conversation. It would be embarrassing if I wasn't interested in knowing the answer myself. All three of us stare at Joel expectantly, and the guy looks like he wishes the ground would open up and swallow him.

"Uh, well... I mean... Trevor..."

I snort and pat his shoulder. "Don't strain yourself, bud." I look back over at Riley and Lincoln, who are wearing identical, unimpressed expressions. "Not everyone is as confident as hockey players. I'm sure Joel is just worried about his own job."

Lincoln's eyes narrow as he continues to stare at Joel. "I sure hope that isn't true, Joel. Because we all know how invaluable Alanna is, don't we?" he asks in a sing-song tone, but there's a measure of annoyance beneath it.

Joel nods quickly, and when Coach Stephens blows the whistle to get everyone to join him at centre ice, Joel lets out a long, relieved sigh when Riley and Lincoln skate off.

"Bloody hell, what the hell was that about?" he asks, his English accent more pronounced than normal.

I shrug. "Guess Trevor's obvious dislike of me is more noticeable than I realized."

"You know I'd say something if I thought it would make a difference, right?" His expression is pleading, and I want to cut him some slack, but I'm feeling a little annoyed now.

"I don't know, Joel. Would you? Seems like everyone is just out to protect their own interests. But it's fine. I don't need a big, strong man to fight my battles for me." I turn back and grab the next file, ignoring the way Joel stares at me.

Neither of us says anything further, and once morning skate

is finished, I head back down the players' tunnel to start working with the guys I've been assigned for the morning.

"Alanna? A word?" Trevor says, frowning in my direction when I walk into the locker room.

Stifling a sigh, I walk over, preparing myself for whatever perceived problem he has now.

He doesn't beat around the bush, frowning as he studies me. "Dean has requested to be switched to your care from now on."

I raise an eyebrow. "What? You mean, just for today? I thought Joel was working with him on the road trip?"

He shakes his head. "No. He wants you to be his primary trainer moving forward."

I frown. "Why?"

He crosses his arms, glaring at me. "I was hoping you could tell me. Because Simon has been working with him for years, and now after five weeks with you, suddenly Dean wants a new trainer?"

I shake my head. "I have no idea. I didn't tell him to do that."

He studies me for another moment before sighing. "Well, we have to take the players' preferences into account with requests like this. If there are no ulterior motives, I guess I'll have to honour Dean's wishes."

I cross my own arms, mirroring his stance. "What do you mean 'no ulterior motives'? What possible motives could there be?"

He scoffs. "I'm sure he just enjoys having someone pretty to look at."

I stare at him. "Did you seriously just say that?" Anger coils tight in my belly, and I have to fight the urge to raise my voice.

Can't have him telling me I'm hysterical, after all.

"We both know that you are only popular with the players because you're a woman, Alanna. Don't play dumb."

I am lost for words as I process what he's saying. No one is within earshot, so if I were to complain to HR, it would be a case of his word against mine, and he's been with the team for over a decade. They'd never believe me, and I'd just be giving them one more reason to never hire another female trainer again.

But the look I give him is filled with pure rage, daring him to say another word.

Just as he opens his mouth to do just that, Dean appears at his side. "Hey. Did Coach mention I'd asked for Alanna to be on my care team from now on?"

It's obvious he can see the tension between Trevor and me as his gaze darts back and forth between us, his jaw tense even as he plasters on a smile.

Trevor schools his expression, attempting to appear as though we weren't just arguing about this very thing. "Yes he did. It's a rather unorthodox request, but I'll allow it. Although I'm sure Simon will ask why you're replacing him."

Dean shrugs. "Nothing Simon did. Alanna was just so professional when it came to getting me back on the ice, and I preferred her way of doing things. It worked better for me. And besides, with Simon not coming along on the road trips for awhile, it makes more sense for Alanna to be the one in charge of my training."

Trevor looks like he's fighting an internal battle, and I hold my breath, praying he'll say something in front of Dean so that I have a witness to his bullshit. But he doesn't say anything further, simply nodding and stalking off to bark instructions at Joel.

"That guy is the biggest asshole," Dean mutters, watching my boss with a scowl.

"Yeah, well, you just gave him a reason to hate me even more," I reply, torn between anger at Dean for causing me more issues and happiness that I get to work with him again.

"I didn't realize that asking for you to be my trainer would cause problems. It should be a non-issue. You were the one who worked so hard to get me back between the pipes. Nothing against Simon, but your methods are obviously better suited to me than what his are."

I study his face for a moment. "And that's the only reason you asked for me?"

He rubs the back of his neck, not quite meeting my eye. "What other reason would there be?"

I'm not entirely sure how to feel about the way he's obviously leaving something out.

I should decline and tell him to stick with Simon. Because nothing good can come of us working so closely together on a permanent basis.

But I can't bring myself to say it.

Because I'm in way over my head with this guy... And I don't think I have it in me to tell him no.

Chapter Twenty-Two

PHONE SEX WITH YOUR GIRLFRIEND

Dean

After the second game of the road trip, I'm in even more pain than I was the previous night, but we'd won both games, and I refuse to let a little pain stop me from celebrating with the team.

"Seeing as we have no games for the next three days, who's up for a night out in Chicago?" Riley says as we walk towards the team bus with everyone else.

Michael's hand shoots up, as do a few others. Riley cocks his head towards me, and I shrug.

"Sure, why not?"

"That's the enthusiastic spirit I was hoping for." He claps me on the shoulder and turns to say something to Michael.

"You guys not coming?" I ask Seth and Lincoln, following them on to the bus.

"Nah, I'm beat. I just wanna talk to Adele and crash, man," Lincoln says, throwing himself into a seat.

"So, you want to have phone sex with your girlfriend? Got it." I slide into the seat across from him and turn side on to look at him, propping my leg up on the seat beside me and pushing my knee down slightly to stretch out my groin with no one noticing.

Lincoln tries to look as though whispering dirty words into Adele's ear isn't exactly what he was planning to do, but then just shrugs. "Whatever, she's been on this tour for like a week. You'd be doing the same thing if you had a girlfriend. Not that you want one."

I try not to let that comment hit me, knowing he didn't mean to insult me. I've done a pretty good job of leaning into the whole playboy thing for the last few years, and clearly it's worked, because everyone thinks I'm a man-whore now, apparently.

"And I want a decent sleep tonight, because Kylie has her scan tomorrow afternoon, and I don't want to be hungover for it," Seth says, taking the seat behind Lincoln.

Riley sits down behind me, and the four of us continue talking over the backs of the chairs and across the aisle.

"Oh yeah, that's right. I get to find out if we're having a boy or girl," Lincoln replies.

Seth raises an eyebrow. "We? I don't recall seeing you in the room when I impregnated my wife."

I splutter a laugh. "Jesus, it's official. You have now spent far too much time with Lincoln, because that is the most O'Malley thing you've ever said."

Seth shakes his head as Lincoln shrugs, not even slightly chastened. "Whatever. I may not have contributed to the baby making - which I also never plan to do with either your wife or my girlfriend, for the record - but we all know I'll be the kid's favourite."

Seth rolls his eyes but doesn't bother replying. Given that Lincoln is really just an oversized child, it probably isn't far from the truth that he'll be the kid's favourite.

The support staff follow us onto the bus, and Riley flags down Alanna as she walks past him. "Hey, Lahney. You guys coming out with us tonight?"

Alanna pauses, glancing behind her. I assume she's looking to see if Trevor heard the question, and I can't keep from scowling. That guy is such a douche. Alanna and Riley are just friends, and she's well within her rights to socialize with him, but her asshole boss is making her feel bad about it.

Trevor is still outside, overseeing the loading of the training equipment into the luggage compartment beneath us.

Alanna's gaze meets mine, her eyes lingering for a heartbeat before sliding back to my teammate. "Yeah, sure. But I didn't really bring anything to wear, so I guess it depends on where you're planning on going?"

Sarah, who had been a few steps ahead of her, turns back with a smile. "I brought a couple of dresses because I didn't know if we might end up going out. I can loan you one? We're about the same size."

Alanna hesitates, before eventually nodding. "Okay, cool. Thanks."

Plans made, the women continue on down towards the back of the bus. Riley goes back to talking to the guys, but I can't tear my eyes away from the redhead as she slides into the seat beside Sarah. She's smiling at something Sarah says, and I wish she was smiling at me like that.

Like she can feel my eyes on her, she meets my gaze again, and a weird fluttering sensation stirs in my stomach.

Great, now I'm getting fucking butterflies when I look at her. What the hell is happening to me?

I'd struggled to fall asleep last night, even though I'd been so exhausted before Alanna stepped into the elevator with me. The look she'd given me as she walked out of my hotel room has been playing over and over in my head. One that told me that maybe it's not just me with confusing feelings right now. By the time I'd finally drifted off, I'd decided I needed her back as my trainer, although I knew it was for all the wrong reasons. And despite the flash of anger on her face when I'd sidled up to her and Trevor when I could see he was giving her a hard time about it, I'd caught the glimmer of excitement in her eyes.

We stare at each other for a moment before she looks away, her cheeks turning pink.

I turn back to find Seth watching me, and I resist grinding my teeth. Why is that every time I slip up with Alanna, Seth catches me? It's like he's got a 'Dean's checking out his trainer' radar, or something.

Or maybe, it's just really fucking obvious that I'm crushing hard for her...

I don't say anything, looking away from my captain towards the front of the bus, trying to work through the mess of thoughts in my head.

Stripping my suit pants and jacket off, I throw on jeans and sneakers, keeping my button down shirt on, before heading back down to wait for the others in the lobby. Anders and Ollie are already there, and I raise an eyebrow when I notice the absence of a certain marketing manager.

"Where's Sarah?"

Ollie shrugs. "She kicked me out of the room so she and Alanna could get ready together. You know what Sarah's like. She's always adopting the ones from out of town. She's been trying to get Alanna to hang out since she started working here."

I nod, resisting the urge to smile at the thought of seeing Alanna more if she starts hanging out with the WAGs.

We sit and discuss the game for twenty minutes, slowly joined by our teammates every few minutes or so. By the time all the guys are with us, Ollie is sighing and shaking his head, looking at his watch.

"Why do women always take so damn long to get ready?"

I grin. "Shouldn't you know the answer to that by now? You guys have been married forever, after all."

He sighs again, slumping down in his chair. "You're right. It's going to be at least another hour."

Anders snorts. "An hour? If it was Bethany, she would have started getting ready before the game finished and we'd still be fucking sitting here."

Anders' wife is the cliche puck bunny, and they couldn't be more different. She's some sort of influencer, although I still haven't figured out who she is meant to be influencing. None of us can work out how Anders ended up with her. He's so laid back, and just a genuinely nice person, but Bethany is one of the most vapid women I've ever met. She'd been hanging around the team for a few years and somehow dug her claws into Anders when he was traded to us five years ago, marrying him within six months and trying to worm her way in with the tight-knit group of WAGs. Most of them avoid her like the plague, though. Especially after she and her little group of professional husband chasers tried to cause problems between Seth and Kylie in the beginning of their relationship.

Riley and I laugh as the two men grumble about waiting for their women, but thankfully it's only a few more minutes until we're joined by one of Sarah's two assistants. Tamara, I think her name is. She's only young and still gets tongue tied around most of us, so I've never actually spoken to her. She is doing her best not to look at one of the rookies, Declan, and I'm trying to work out if something is going on there... Or if something is about to start going on there. Given the way Declan keeps darting his eyes towards her, my money's on the former.

Wonder if anyone is going to warn him to keep his dick to himself, or if that warning is just for me?

"Looking good, ladies," Michael says, looking behind me with a grin.

Ollie's head pops up from the back of the couch, a slow smile spreading across his face, and I turn to see what's got him looking like all his wet dreams are about to come true.

Sarah's got a tight red dress on that hugs her curves while showing off almost every inch of her long, smooth legs. It barely covers her ass, and I can tell Ollie is into it. He's basically eye fucking his wife as she struts towards us in sky high matching red stilettos. Her long blonde hair is pulled back into a high ponytail, and she looks amazing as she gives her husband the same look. There's no way these two are staying out long - they look like they're about to tear each other's clothes off right here in the lobby.

But it's the woman behind her that has my full attention. Alanna's hair cascades over her right shoulder in a mess of curls, and she's wearing an equally tight, equally short, strapless black dress. My mouth goes dry as I watch her walk towards the group. My eyes slowly rake over her body, taking in every single curve. Every inch of exposed skin. And when my eyes meet hers finally, I swallow when I see the heat in her gaze.

Thank god Seth isn't here, because his 'Dean and Alanna' radar would be pinging left, right and centre right now. I'm surprised he hasn't leapt from the elevator to smack me up the back of my head.

I get to my feet as the women come to a stop in front of Ollie. He bends to whisper something in his wife's ear, and she giggles.

I move a little closer behind Alanna while everyone else is distracted, my chest brushing against her back as I dip my lips to her ear. "You look amazing, Lahney," I whisper.

A tiny shiver runs through her, and I have to fight the urge to shift her hair aside and brush my lips to her neck.

"Thank you. So do you," she murmurs back.

Emboldened, I raise my hand and stroke a finger down the back of her neck to the top of her dress, watching goosebumps follow in its wake. She shivers again, and I hear her breath hitch. It takes all my resolve not to turn her towards me and kiss the fuck out of those beautiful, plump lips.

Riley claps his hands to get everyone's attention. "Are we all here now?"

I step back slightly to put some distance between me and the achingly beautiful woman in front of me as everyone else nods. Riley leads the way out onto the street, and we flag down a few cabs. Some of the guys have found some female admirers that must have been lying in wait outside the hotel, and they all pile into the first three cabs, along with Tamara and Anders. I hang back with Riley, Michael, Ollie, Sarah and Alanna. When the next cab arrives, Sarah grabs Alanna's hand and drags her into the car with her and Ollie, and I fight down a wave of disappointment. I'd hoped to shove Michael and Riley in with them so that I could have Alanna to myself in the back of a cab to continue with what we'd just been doing. And from the look that Alanna flashes me as they drive off, I get the feeling she'd been wanting the same thing.

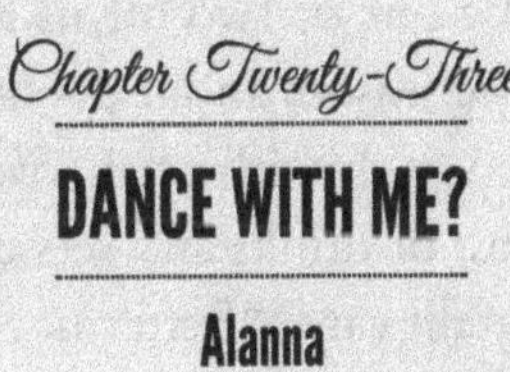

DANCE WITH ME?

Alanna

"What do you want to drink?" Sarah asks as we make a beeline for the bar.

Riley had called ahead and sweet-talked them into getting a VIP section set up for the team, and I can feel Dean's eyes on me from where he's sitting at the end of one of the booths behind the roped off area. I'd taken one look at him when he'd sauntered up beside us in the line and immediately looked away, unable to meet his gaze in case I spontaneously combusted. My mouth has been dry ever since I saw him in the lobby, sitting casually on one of the leather couches, his arm slung along the back while he talked to Anders. The addition of a backwards Mounties cap just added to the confidence oozing off him when he turned to look at me. And apparently, my inner cave woman really fucking loves that, because she really, really wanted to straddle his lap and suck on his face.

So that's why I agreed to go with Sarah to the bar. Because I need to put as much distance as possible between myself and the man who dragged his finger down my neck and sent my libido into overdrive.

Realizing Sarah is still waiting for an answer, I shake off the memory of Dean's breath on my neck and shrug. "Um... Vodka, lime and soda, I guess. I'm actually not a huge drinker, so I'll just have the one."

"Yeah, it'll only be one or two for us as well. Ollie doesn't drink much during the season, and it doesn't take much for me to feel tipsy. I'd rather not fly with a hangover tomorrow."

She orders a round of drinks and sets up a tab for the guys on Ollie's personal credit card. "Better not put that one on the company credit card," she says with a grin.

I huff a laugh. "Yeah, I don't think Tristan would be a fan of the team paying for the players to drink."

The new general manager, while not as uptight as the one that they fired last season, still runs a tight ship, and I'm sure he'd laid down the law with the younger players about being on their best behaviour tonight. Hopefully, the older ones have worked that out by now, used to protecting the team's image even when not in their jerseys.

"I'm so glad you agreed to come out with us," Sarah says, giving me a quick side hug while we lean against the bar, waiting for our drinks.

I smile. "Me too. I figured I need to start being more social. I mean, the other trainers hang out with the players, so why can't I?"

"Right? I keep telling the girls on my team that. If the guys can do it, then why should it be any different with the women on staff? These are adults we're talking about, not horny high school kids. Everyone knows how to keep their hands to themselves." She looks out towards the dance floor, thankfully missing my guilty expression.

While I've definitely kept my hands to myself, I'm not sure my hormones have remembered that I'm an adult and should, therefore, *not* be lusting after the ridiculously hot goalie.

The ridiculously hot goalie who is currently watching me

with a hungry glint in his eye from the other side of the packed room.

Heat coils in my belly as I hold his gaze. I've read the term 'undressing her with his eyes' plenty of times in romance novels, but until today, I'd never been on the receiving end of that look... And let me just say, it's no wonder the women in those books end up falling at the guy's feet, because the things that look is doing to my libido should be illegal.

Our drinks arrive, and I pick up my glass with a slightly shaky hand as I break myself away from his downright sinful gaze.

I honestly can't remember the last time I felt like this with any guy. Hell, I'm not sure I've ever had such a physical reaction to a guy.

This whole situation is so very dangerous. Now that I'm Dean's permanent trainer, we're going to be spending a lot of time together. Especially as he still seems to be nursing a few secret injuries. Having to touch his body and remain professional is becoming difficult, and if we're looking at each other like this, I know it's going to be almost impossible to keep him at arm's length.

Oh god, do not think about length right now, you idiot!

Too late. My brain goes right to the gutter, and I remember just how big his length is. The guy is tall and broad, and he's definitely in proportion. Men might think women want a ten-inch cock, but sometimes, too big is too much. But he knew how to take things slow...

We rejoin the guys, and I have to keep from looking at Dean again.

This might actually be torture. I'm basically having an internal war with myself as my common sense and inner horny teenager fight over who's going to be making decisions tonight.

Maybe I shouldn't drink at all...

Unable to control my thoughts any longer, my eyes meet his again over the rim of my glass, and I take a mouthful of my drink. The burn in my throat helps keep me from getting too lost in that look. It truly is a wonder that no one has picked up that something is going on between us. But the guys are oblivious, and Sarah's too busy flirting with her husband to pay attention to the way Dean and I are devouring each other with our eyes.

The women who'd joined us at the hotel drag a few of the guys out onto the dance floor, while the rest of us stand around, talking and laughing amongst ourselves. I've finally convinced myself to turn away from Dean and join in on a conversation with a few of the other players, and he's now in a deep conversation with Mark, most likely talking shop with the young goalie.

But it's not long before he abandons Mark. While I'm listening to Anders tell the group about Bethany's latest business collaboration with some protein shake company, a hand presses against my lower back, and a deep, commanding voice murmurs in my ear, "Dance with me?"

No one is looking our way, and I know Dean's picked this exact moment to steal me away without notice. I allow his fingers to twine with mine after he slides his hand down my arm, and he gently pulls me back so that my back is pressed against his chest.

"Please," he whispers, and I shiver as his breath brushes my neck.

I swallow before giving a small nod. He steps back from me, letting my fingers go as I feel him turn away. I put my drink down and excuse myself from the conversation when Riley finally looks my way again to say something. He nods and turns back to the conversation with Michael, Anders, Ollie and Sarah. Turning, I search the dance floor and spy Dean waiting for me off to the side. After checking to make sure no eyes are on me, I move towards him, and he guides me through the crowd with his hands on my hips, keeping me close. Once we find a space that's to his liking, he tugs me backwards into his chest. His arm circles my waist, holding me against his hard muscles with my back pressed firmly to his chest.

Goalie's need to be flexible, and that often means that they are fairly decent dancers if they can follow a beat, able to roll their hips while maintaining control.

And Dean can definitely dance. With his arm holding me in place, he moves us both together in time with the R&B song pumping through the speakers. I surrender completely and let him control the movements, and his arm tightens around me.

I feel his breath on my neck and tilt my head, silently consenting to the lips that ghost over my skin. He presses a kiss just below my ear, and I shiver again, clearly unable to control my body anymore. He chuckles and kisses his way down my neck while still guiding our bodies in time with the music. Drunk on lust, I bring my arm up and cup the back of his neck with my hand, sliding my fingers into his hair.

He brings his free hand up to tilt my face back, his eyes on mine as he slides his thumb over my bottom lip.

"I need to taste these, Alanna," he pleads, making no move to close the distance between our faces.

I nod, and he brings his lips to mine.

There's nothing soft or tender in the way he claims my mouth as his own. It's confident. Demanding. And any logical thoughts about how very wrong this all is fly right out of my head. Because I want this man to own every part of my body.

I have no idea if we're still moving, so lost in the way his tongue is stroking mine while he pulls my body even further into his. I grip the back of his neck, a silent request for more. He groans against my lips and kisses me harder before pulling away.

"If we keep doing that, this is going to go straight past PG-

13 and into an R rating." His eyes search my face. "What are we doing, Lahney?"

I swallow, not wanting to think about that yet. "I don't know... But I don't want to stop."

His jaw clenches, and he raises his head to scan the room. Nodding, he turns us towards the door and guides me through the crowd. Once outside, he tugs me around to face him.

"How far are we taking this? Because I will more than happily order us a car right now and take you back to the hotel to explore this further, but I don't want you regretting this tomorrow."

I study his face as he squeezes my fingers. "I've been fighting this for weeks, Dean. All I can think about is how it would feel to have your hands on me. How I need to kiss you again."

His gaze becomes downright feral, and he yanks me forward, crushing his mouth to mine and stealing my breath away.

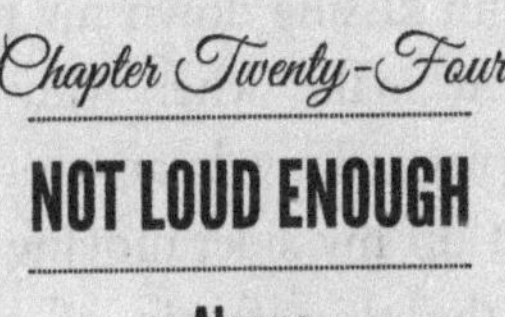

Chapter Twenty-Four

NOT LOUD ENOUGH

Alanna

I wrap my arms around Dean's neck, raising onto the very tips of my toes as he holds me tight against his chest. Even so, he still has to bend to kiss me, and I just barely keep myself from climbing him to wrap my legs around his waist.

Finally breaking the kiss, he pulls his phone out of his pocket while continuing to hold me against him. He orders us a car and then sends Ollie a text saying that I wasn't feeling well, and he'd decided to get a cab back with me because he was beat. Once that's done, he claims my mouth again, sliding his phone back into his pocket while his tongue urges my mouth open. The hand that isn't currently holding me motionless against him works its way into my hair, wrapping it around his fist so that he can tip my face upwards and take complete control. A moan slips out of me, and he chuckles darkly.

A black town car pulls up a few moments later, and I allow Dean to guide me towards it. He opens the back door and holds it wide for me to slide in before following behind me.

After confirming the hotel address with the driver, the privacy screen goes up between the front and back seats. Dean tugs me into the middle seat and buckles my seat belt as his mouth finds mine again. His hands bracket my waist as his upper body twists towards mine, and I slide my fingers into the hair at the back of his head.

He moves to begin kissing down my neck. "I can't wait to hear the sounds you make when you come undone," he murmurs. "They've plagued my dreams for the last year."

He slides a hand up my side, moving around to palm my breast gently over the thin fabric of the dress Sarah had convinced me to wear. As I'd had no strapless bra to wear under it, I'd gone without, and my nipple pebbles when his fingers slide over it.

"Can't wait to run my tongue over these perfect breasts again." My breath hitches as he runs his tongue over the sensitive skin where my neck meets my shoulder while he pinches my nipple gently. "Going to see if I can make you come if I play with them long enough."

His hand slides back down, ghosting over my hip and skimming along the bare skin on my thigh. He gently urges me to open my legs, and I slide them apart. He circles his finger around my inner thigh, and I inhale sharply as his hand slides upwards. When he finally reaches the apex of my thighs, I'm breathing heavily, needing more.

"Can't wait until it's my mouth that's doing this." He hooks a finger to pull my underwear aside before sliding his fingers over my clit. "But right now..." He kisses his way back to my ear. "I really need to hear you come."

With those words, he brings his mouth back to mine in a demanding, hungry kiss while increasing the pressure on my clit, circling firmly while I moan, before turning his hand to slide a finger inside me. His thumb moves to my clit as he curls his finger upwards, finding a spot that only he has ever found before.

My moans grow louder as he picks up the pace, and pleasure spreads throughout my body. My back arches, and he keeps his lips firmly on mine when I cry out, muffling the sound while I break apart. He keeps moving his hand between my legs while the other slides around my back to hold me still when my body tries to move away. "One was never going to be enough, Lahney. You've got at least two more in you before we get back to the hotel. And next time, you'll be screaming my name." He buries his face in my neck, sucking on the skin just beneath my ear while he continues thrusting his fingers in and out, hitting my g-spot every time while his thumb keeps moving in firm circles. Within minutes, I cry out again, his name slipping from my lips as my body shudders and a second orgasm crashes over me.

"Not loud enough, Lahney. I want them to hear you back in Calgary." He tugs the front of my dress down, exposing my right breast, and bends to suck my nipple into his mouth, hard.

My back arches again when his teeth graze over my skin.

"God, Dean," I whimper, gripping the back of his neck.

"You like a little bit of pain, don't you?" His teeth close gently over my nipple and I moan again. He chuckles. "Oh, baby... we're going to have a very good night."

He continues sucking and nipping my breast while his hand maintains the same pace between my legs. It takes a little longer this time, but with the combination of his mouth on my breast and his thumb on my clit, the third orgasm he'd promised bears down on me. My toes curl in my borrowed stilettos as my back arches clean off the back of the seat, and he covers my mouth with his as I scream his name, muffling the sound from our - hopefully oblivious - driver.

He finally moves his hand away, sliding it up my torso to pull my dress back up over my breast. I slump into his arms, still reeling from the final, explosive orgasm.

The car finally arrives at the hotel, and Dean climbs out

first, looking towards the lobby before reaching in to help me out.

Neither of us says anything when he leads me towards the elevators. One arrives within a minute, and once inside, he places a hand firmly on my lower back, tugging my body into his. I go easily, loving the dominance he's exerting over me. His lips return to my neck, sucking gently on the spot that he's worked out makes me shiver. When we arrive on the floor that we're all staying on, his hand drops away, and he waves for me to walk out first, putting distance between our bodies. The hall is blissfully empty, and he nods towards his room. I head that way, my muscles tensing as I peer around to make sure no one comes out of their rooms. He pulls his wallet from his pocket as my heartbeat thunders in my ears, and he waves the room key over the sensor.

He steps inside, holding the door open with an expectant look on his face. I hesitate for a moment too long, then freeze at the sound of a door opening down the hall. Dean reaches to grab my hand as I turn my head to see who is coming out. But for a goalie with fast reflexes, he appears to be losing his touch, because I'm still standing there when Coach Stephens walks out of his room.

"Alanna?"

Cursing internally, I turn to face the coach properly as he walks towards the elevator and plaster on a smile. "Coach. Hi." I try not to squeak the words.

He nods. "Having a bit of trouble sleeping, so I was going to head downstairs for some hot chocolate. You're back early. Did you have a good evening?"

I nod, forcing myself to keep my eyes on him. "Yeah. Just a bit tired. It's been a long day," I say, praying that my facial expression gives nothing away as Dean's door closes slowly. At this angle, I'm hoping the older man isn't able to see it.

"Well, I just wanted to thank you for all the help you've been giving us lately. You've really been going above and beyond, and it shows just how dedicated you are. You're a real asset to the training team. The whole team, really."

I swallow as a knot of guilt starts to form in the pit of my stomach. "Thank you, sir. That means a lot."

He nods, then wishes me goodnight as the elevator arrives.

Before Dean can reappear, I hurry down the hall and let myself into my room. Leaning against the closed door, I stare at the ceiling while I wait for my heart to stop racing. My phone dings, and I fish it out of my handbag.

DEAN

Is the coast clear?

ALANNA

That was too close. We should never have started that. I got swept up in the moment.

A bubble with three dots appears and disappears several times, and I grip the phone, terrified of what he is going to say. And when the message finally comes through, I know I've hurt him.

DEAN

Okay.

Chapter Twenty-Five

DO YOU EVEN KNOW ANYTHING ABOUT ME?

Dean

I didn't sleep a wink all night after Alanna blew me off via text. Between the raging hard on at the memory of her coming over and over in the back of the car, and the way my stomach had plummeted to my feet when she'd messaged to say it can never happen again, I'd tossed and turned all night.

When my alarm goes off ahead of the flight home, I've been staring at the ceiling for hours while cursing myself for my stupidity.

Of course Alanna has to put her job first - last night was a sure sign of just how dangerous this little crush is. Even though the way her body responded to mine last night was evidence enough that the feelings are most definitely not one sided.

And now that I've had the pleasure of watching her come once more - multiple times - all I want is to have the chance to do it again. And again. And again. Those whimpers she'd made are permanently etched into my mind after a year of trying to forget them. And the way she'd screamed my name? Yeah... it's no wonder I haven't slept and needed to beat one out in the shower.

Fuck my life.

As I enter the lobby with my duffle bag over my shoulder, I see her immediately. Like I'm drawn to her without even trying.

She's speaking to Joel near the front door, but her eyes lock on mine across the lobby. I can see the regret in her expression in the split second before she turns away, and my stomach turns to lead.

God, I've fucked this all up royally.

On the bus, she sits as far away from me as possible, and when we get on the plane, she races down the back to join the rest of the support staff without so much as a backward glance in my direction.

Message received, I guess.

Scowling, I flop into my seat, and Mark wisely decides to find somewhere else to sit when he takes one look at my face.

I spend the entire flight with my noise cancelling headphones on and my head resting against the window, trying to catch some desperately needed shut-eye. But the memory of her lips on mine plagues me, and I wonder if I'll ever be able to sleep again.

I've been with a lot of women, but I honestly can't remember being twisted in knots like this over any of them. Sure, they were all beautiful, and absolutely none of them left my company without being thoroughly satisfied. But none of them gave me the tingles like this. And now, because I'm an idiot, I have to see her every single day while we work together. I have to feel her hands on my body and will myself not to react.

By the time we land in Calgary, I'm exhausted and on edge. All I want is to get in my car and go home, putting as much distance as possible between myself and a certain redheaded trainer.

I follow the rest of the team towards the valet desk, where they'll bring the players cars around. I'm relieved to finally be out of Alanna's orbit, as the support staff park their cars in long term parking. But when I look up from my phone while I wait, I groan inwardly when I spy the redhead in question walking towards me, her arm linked through Sarah's.

Of-fucking-course.

"What are you doing here?" I ask, my tone harsher than I'd intended.

Sarah raises an eyebrow at me as Alanna's cheeks grow red while she avoids meeting my gaze properly.

"Apparently they were having trouble getting my car started in the long-term parking area, so Sarah and Ollie are going to give me a ride home. I'll have to arrange for a mechanic to come out and look at it."

I sigh, rubbing the back of my neck. "I can look at it for you."

She startles, her eyes widening. "Oh, no, it's fine."

"Actually, that's a great idea. I forgot you used to be into cars," Sarah says, nodding.

"I'm still into cars," I reply, then turn back to Alanna. "It's fine. I can get these guys to hold off on bringing my car around and go look at yours. Just let the parking guys know I'm coming."

She bites her lip, flicking a glance between me and Sarah, who is watching us with her head cocked to the side. "No, it's okay. I'll come with you."

I force my expression to remain neutral while I nod, surprised by her willingness to be alone with me after last night. With the way she's been acting this morning, I figured we'd need chaperones for even the simplest conversations from now on.

"Want us to wait around in case Dean can't get it started?" Sarah asks as Ollie slides an arm around her shoulders.

"I can drop her home," I reply, before Alanna can answer.

She frowns slightly, but nods, and I head over to the desk to ask them to hold off on bringing my car around. When I return, she hesitates briefly before moving stiffly towards the exit when I wave for her to lead the way.

Once we're out of earshot, I murmur. "Don't worry, I'm not going to be weird. I respect your decision, Alanna."

She looks up at me with wide eyes filled with regret. "I'm sorry. I didn't mean to lead you on. Just... after Stephens nearly caught us, I realized I'd be throwing so much away if..."

"I get it. I shouldn't have pushed," I say, my tone gruff as I turn to look ahead, unable to continue to look at her.

I didn't really want to get into a conversation about it, I just wanted her to know I wasn't going to be an asshole.

She sighs. "You didn't push, Dean. I wanted it just as much as you... But we can't. Even if I wasn't your permanent trainer now, I'd still be risking my entire career for a fling that would probably mean nothing to you... and everything to me." I just barely hear her last words as she lowers her voice to an almost whisper.

Almost like she's afraid to admit her feelings.

I stop walking abruptly, turning back to face her, stunned. "You think that all I want is a fling with you?"

She halts too, her eyebrows raised. "Isn't that kind of what you do?"

I gape at her for a moment, struggling to find the words for how her assumption has hit me like a punch to the gut.

"I'm not sure what you've heard, but no. That isn't 'what I do'," I reply, using air quotes while I glower at her. "Yes, I've been with a few women, and I make no apologies for that. But I never promised those women anything. They all knew what the situation was before we slept together, and I was always upfront with them if I wasn't interested in pursuing anything further with them. I've had girlfriends, and relationships that I thought would lead to something more. So I am not just some playboy who has left a trail of brokenhearted women in my wake."

She crosses her arms and glares right back at me. "Well, you never promised me anything either, Dean. We've never even discussed whatever this is between us. So forgive me if I was just protecting myself and my job!"

We're having this rather fiery conversation in the middle of the airport, and a few passersby give us uneasy looks while we face off. It takes me a moment to register that this probably isn't the best place to be discussing this. I jerk my head towards an alcove, taking her by the arm gently and leading her over to it.

She continues to glare at me as she recrosses her arms, and I half expect her to tap her foot like in cartoons. If I wasn't so annoyed, I'd be laughing at how cute she looks, all short and fierce.

I lean back against the wall, crossing my own arms to mirror her stance. "There was a reason we hadn't had that conversation. Maybe we would have talked more if you hadn't bailed, but given I had no intention of hitting and quitting it with you, I didn't think I needed to say anything."

She narrows her eyes as she studies my face.

After a moment, she sighs and runs her hand through her hair. "Do you even know anything about me, Dean?"

"What kind of question is that? We've spent hours together over the past two months. Of course I know things about you," I reply with a frown.

"Like what?" She smirks, like she thinks she's caught me in a lie.

I step forward and grip her chin, looking her in the eye as I tilt her face upwards. "I know you prefer tea over coffee, but still need at least two cups of coffee in order to make it through the morning. I know you spent your childhood dreaming about living in a different country and when you got this job, it was the best day of your life. I know you would do anything for Tierney, including letting her dress you up in clothes you hate, just to make her happy. I know that when you're frustrated with me, which is all the time, the cutest little frown line appears right here." I use my finger to smooth the line between her eyebrows gently as her eyes scan my face. "I know you've fought like hell for your position on the training staff and are terrified that if something happens between us, you'll be throwing all that away. I know that I've laughed more around you than I have around anyone else in a long time. I know I want you, and you want me, too, because I've seen how you look at me. And I know the ball is in your court, because you're the one with the most to lose if something happens between us."

With each point I make, her expression softens, and she stares up at me with wide eyes filled with emotion. "I just assumed that you were into me because I'm the one woman you couldn't have," she murmurs.

I scoff. "I'm not some alpha male who's just chasing you to prove I can get anyone I want, Alanna. But I guess you don't know me as well as I know you, if that's what you really think about me." I rake my hand through my hair, swallowing down my annoyance. "Look, there's no point in us having this conversation, anyway. You made it pretty clear where you stand on all of this, and I respect that. So let's just check out your car, and you'll be rid of me. If I didn't think it would make things worse for you at work, I'd organize to switch back to Simon. But we'll just have to make the best of a bad situation, and I'll keep things strictly professional." I step out of the alcove and move towards the exit again, done with this conversation.

She eventually follows, her expression troubled when I look back to make sure she's there. Maybe I was a little harsh, but I resent the fact that she clearly thought I was nothing more than a stereotypical jock who sleeps with any woman that throws themselves at me. While I thought we'd been building a friendship, or maybe something more, she'd decided that I was just going to use her to scratch an itch and move on. I can't control what others say about me, but I'd thought my intentions had been clear.

Guess I was wrong.

Once I determine her car simply has a flat battery, I get the long term parking guy to bring his car around - after I sign the Mounties jersey in his office - and jump start it. We haven't said a word to each other since I'd walked away from her. Once she's sitting in the driver's seat, I nod and turn to leave.

"Dean," she calls out the window.

I turn back with a sigh. "What?"

She swallows, hesitating for a moment before responding. "I'm sorry."

I shrug. "It's fine. I'll see you at work."

And then I turn and walk away without looking back. Because I'm not sure I can handle anymore rejection from this woman.

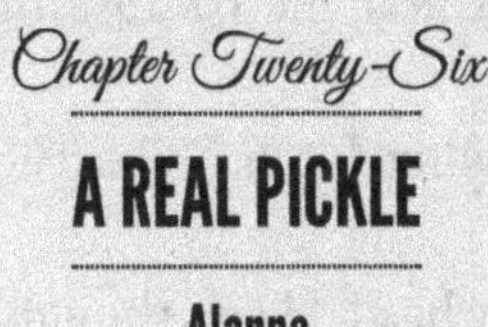

Chapter Twenty-Six

A REAL PICKLE

Alanna

For as long as I can remember, I've been known to jump to the worst-case scenario when it comes to relationships. When the man you're supposed to be able to trust above all others constantly disappoints you, it's hard to believe the best in people. More often than not, my assumptions about people have been right, and I've prided myself on my excellent people reading skills.

But this time my assumptions appear to be completely off. I knew I'd made a grave error in judgement when I saw the shocked look on Dean's face as I admitted that I thought he was only interested in me because he couldn't have me. But the damage was done, and now I'm pretty sure he's never going to forgive me.

When I get home, Tierney is sitting on the couch, scrolling idly through her phone.

"Oh, hey! How was your trip?" she asks with a smile.

The emotions I've been holding in for the last hour bubble up inside me, and I drop my bag beside my feet before burying my face in my hands.

"Oh, shit!" I hear Tierney jump to her feet, and a second

later, arms wrap around me as I choke back a sob. "What's going on?"

"I'm a raging bitch, that's what's going on!" I wail, although I'm not sure she can hear me because the words are muffled against my hands.

"You're not a raging bitch." She rubs her hand up and down my back.

I sniffle as I lift my head. "I am, though."

She moves back to hold me at arm's length. "You're going to need to walk me through this, babe. What's going on?"

Sighing, I let her lead me to the couch, sitting with a thump when she guides me down.

"So... what I'm about to tell you can never leave this room," I say as I turn to face her.

She studies me for a moment. "Oh-kay..." she drags the word out warily.

"I kissed Dean." She gapes at me, seemingly struck dumb, so I start babbling. "Actually, it was way more than kissing. He made me come three times in the back of a private town car last night. And then..." I swallow hard. "We were seconds away from sleeping together, but Coach Stephens caught me when I was about to go into his room." I bury my face back in my hands, just to avoid the stunned look on Tierney's face.

A few heartbeats later, Tierney lets out a long breath. "Okay... so... that was a lot."

I let out a bitter laugh and look up to find her smiling. "Why are you looking at me like that?"

"You just said that one of the hottest guys on the team gave you three orgasms last night, and you're acting like it's the worst thing in the world."

I glare at her. "It is! I can't just be letting Mounties players give me orgasms, Tierney! And..." I take a deep breath, preparing myself. "We actually slept together back when I started working for the team..."

She gapes at me. "You... You did what?!" she screeches.

I bury my face back into my hands. "We didn't know each other yet. I was at the practice arena, doing all the stupid shit that Trevor had me doing to keep me away from the team. Dean and I ran into each other at the coffee shop in my hotel and hit it off. He asked me to go to dinner with him, and I invited him back to my room afterwards."

She blinks a few times, and I can practically see the wheels turning in her mind.

And then... she laughs.

"This is amazing."

It's my turn to gape at her. "No, it's not."

She shakes her head and holds up her hand. "Okay. Firstly... It was one Mounties player, and I've known he's had a thing for you since you two started working together this season, so this isn't entirely unexpected. And you totally have a thing for him, too."

"What?"

She smirks. "You think you've been hiding it, but I saw the way you two were dancing at the club. It was so obvious, especially after he was hanging around here for breakfast every morning after your walks. The two of you have been circling each other for weeks."

I swallow. "You haven't said anything to Riley, have you?"

She scoffs. "As if I'd say anything to Riley. I love my brother, but this is definitely not something he needs to know about."

I let out a breath, my shoulders dropping from where they'd been up near my ears. "Why didn't you say anything?"

She raises an eyebrow. "Did you need me to tell you how you were feeling?"

"Clearly."

She shakes her head. "No, you didn't. You knew. You were just trying to lie to yourself so that you could ignore those feelings."

I groan and flop backwards to rest my head on the back of the couch.

She pats my knee. "But none of this explains why you're calling yourself a raging bitch."

I roll my eyes to look at her without moving my head. "I may have implied to Dean that the only reason he wanted me was because I was someone he couldn't have. Right before I asked him if he even knew anything about me."

"Ah... Okay. Bet that went well." She leans back beside me.

I return my gaze to the ceiling, focusing on the cobwebs in the corner that neither of us are tall enough to reach with the duster. "Oh, it went very, very badly."

"Did you really believe that was how he felt?"

I let out a breath. "I thought I did. Now I'm not so sure."

"What did he actually say?"

"Well, after he picked his jaw up off the airport floor, he listed all the things he knows about me, and then told me he respects my decision and would keep things professional from now on. And then the only thing he said to me after he jump started my car was that he'd see me at work."

She pats my leg. "Well... I guess that's a good thing, right? It's not like you can really have a relationship with him while you work for the team."

I shrug, still staring at the cobweb. I really need to work out how to get rid of that. I bet Dean could reach it. I'm sure he could touch the ceiling without even having to stand on his tiptoes. Bet he could do it while pinning me against the wall and fucking me hard...

Tierney pokes my leg. "Alanna?"

I sigh and turn to look at her. "I don't know."

She cocks her head to the side, studying my face. "Do you... Do you want a relationship with him?"

"I don't know."

She sighs. "You've got yourself into a real pickle, Lahney."

"Correct."

She gets to her feet and walks into the kitchen, returning with a tub of Ben and Jerry's Choc Chip Cookie Dough ice cream and two spoons. "Guess it's time to dig into the good stuff."

And we spend the next few hours on the couch eating junk food and talking about everything else possible except for a certain grumpy goalie.

Too tired to bother unpacking, it's not until the next morning that I unpack my bag and put on a load of washing before work. I haven't looked at my phone since I walked in the door yesterday, and when I dig it out of my handbag to charge it, I'm surprised to see a missed call from my brother, Charlie, from several hours ago.

Doing a quick time difference calculation, I know it's too late to call him back now, so I shoot off a text asking if everything is okay before dropping it back on the bed. When I turn back from putting my duffle bag away, my phone lights up with Charlie's name on the screen.

Sliding my finger across the screen, I hit the speaker button. "Hey. Is everything okay? Isn't it super late?"

"Yeah, it's like two, I think. I haven't actually looked at the time. I've been out with the guys."

I frown. The guys he's referring to are his rugby mates, and not the best influence on my impressionable twin brother. I'm pretty sure they only hang out with Charlie because of who our dad is, and the connections he could bring them.

"So what's up?"

"I was thinking of coming for a visit."

I feel my eyebrows fly up. "Really? Why?"

He snorts. "Way to tell me you don't want me to come, Lahns."

I sigh. "No, I want you to come. But you've never shown any interest in coming to visit me before, so it took me by surprise."

"Well, I'm showing interest now."

I can't shake the suspicion that something else is up, but I've already pissed off one man in my life this week, and I don't feel like adding another one to the list.

"So when are you thinking?"

"How about next month?"

Yeah, something is definitely up. "So soon? You know it's the hockey season, right? I can't take any time off and will have to travel while you're here."

"It's okay, I'm a big boy." I can practically hear him shrug through the phone. "I can take care of myself. Have you got somewhere I can crash, or should I book a hotel?"

"I'll have to check with Tierney, but I'm sure she'll be okay with you crashing on the couch. How long are you thinking?"

"Couple weeks?"

Unable to stop myself, I blurt out. "Charlie, what's going on? What about work? What about Tilley?"

He's quiet for a moment, and I wonder if the call has dropped out. But then I hear a ragged breath and realize he's crying.

"Charlie?"

"Tilley left me."

I gasp, covering my mouth. "What? When?"

Charlie and Tilley have been together since high school.

They'd gotten married just before I moved to Canada, and I honestly thought they'd be together forever.

"She left last week. She said she couldn't handle Dad anymore, and you know I can't just leave him..."

I groan. "Charlie. We've been through this. You're not responsible for Dad."

"I know that, Lahney," he says sharply. "I was working on a way to get him some help without it causing issues."

"So why'd Tilley leave then?"

"She said it was taking too long, and she couldn't spend the rest of her life taking care of an old drunk."

I laugh, the bitterness rolling off me in waves. "She's not wrong, Charlie."

"Not all of us can just fuck off to the other side of the world and run away from our problems, Alanna," he snaps.

I glare at the phone, wishing I could smack him right now. "Isn't that what you were just trying to do? How are you going to deal with him while you're here?"

"I've asked the guys to check in on him daily. You know, to make sure he hasn't choked on his own vomit or anything?"

My stomach clenches as memories of our childhood come flooding back. Memories I have been shoving down any time they try to take hold. Memories of coming home from school to find a house full of empty beer bottles and a drunk lying on the floor. He was never abusive, just really sad, and it was beyond painful to watch.

Charlie and Tilly bought the house next door to our childhood home, which I thought was stupid. But Charlie was always more family oriented than me. I'd just wanted to get out of there and never look back.

"Maybe it wouldn't be such a bad thing," I whisper, and Charlie sighs.

"You don't really mean that. I know you were keen to leave

us all behind, but you would hate yourself if he died that way, and you know it."

My brother has always been good at keeping me grounded. Even from half a world away, he can still remind me I'm not actually the cold-hearted bitch I try to be when it comes to our father.

"You're right. But it's not our responsibility to take care of him, Charlie. We're the kids."

"We're family. And families look out for one another."

"At the cost of our own happiness?" I ask quietly, and he doesn't reply for a long time.

"Sometimes."

I sigh. "Let me know when you book your flights and stuff."

We hang up and I flop forward onto my bed, burying my face into my pillow.

My life is already complicated enough. It's a good thing Dean and I are never going to end up being a thing, because I don't think I could handle any more complications. Not now.

Not ever.

Chapter Twenty-Seven

DO YOU WANT ME?

Dean

It's been two days since Alanna accused me of being a playboy who only wants her because she's out of reach, and my mood has not improved. When I'd walked into the gym and saw that she was the one who was setting up the various workout stations for dryland training today, I'd nearly turned and walked right back out again.

After twenty minutes of silently stewing over the shit situation we're in, I let the weights in my hands fall to the floor with a scowl and switch stations. I've been trying to avoid looking at her and had shoved my earbuds in to block out the sound of her voice. But that's done nothing to help the emotions raging through me.

Hence the slight tantrum with the dumbbells.

Lincoln has his back to me, and when the weights hit the floor with a bang, he jumps before turning to glare at me. "Jesus, man! What is with you? You're even grumpier than usual."

I shrug and pick up my towel to wipe the sweat off my face.

"Oh, and now you're not talking, either? Seriously, do you need to get laid or something?"

He has no idea how fucking close to the mark he is with that question. But there's only one woman I want to get down and dirty with, and she's currently on the other side of the room talking to Sarah. Seems like, in the space of a few days, those two have become real tight. I'd be happy for Alanna, if I didn't feel like I wasn't allowed to care.

Halfway through my first set of deadlifts, Seth wanders into the room. It looks like he hasn't shaved since I last saw him at the airport, and while that isn't completely out of the ordinary, the dazed expression on his face is new. I run a wary gaze over him as he just stands in the middle of the gym, his arms hanging loosely at his side as he stares off into space.

"Everything alright, bud?" Lincoln asks, flicking an uneasy glance my way before returning his full attention to Seth.

"Um... Kinda..." Seth runs a hand through his hair as he looks around, almost like he's just realized where he is.

I pull out my earbuds. "What's wrong?"

"Oh, now you're talking?" Lincoln asks, and I glare at him before turning back to Seth.

He lets out a long breath. "We went for Kylie's first scan."

"It was okay, right?" Lincoln is doing his best not to look too worried, but it's hard not to be when something is clearly troubling our captain.

"Yeah... I mean... If twins are okay?"

Lincoln and I stare at him for a moment, our mouths open.

"You guys are having twins?" Lincoln exclaims, jumping up from the bench he'd moved to for his next workout.

Seth gives him a weak smile. "Yeah. Twin boys."

"Holy shit, man. That's awesome." I clap him on the shoulder, a smile spreading across my face.

Feels like the first time I've had a reason to smile in a while.

"Kylie doesn't quite feel the same way," he says, the troubled expression returning to his face.

"Oh..." The smiles slips from my face. "Is she okay?"

He lets out another breath and drops down onto the bench behind him, although I'm not entirely sure he even knew it was there. "She's freaking out. Which is understandable, because she's got twin sisters and knows how much work we're in for."

"Ah, that's right. I remember meeting them at the wedding. So I guess it must run in her family, then?"

Seth laughs. "Yeah, I guess. She's upset that it's her who is having twins, when neither Emma or Dayna have had twins themselves. She keeps focusing on how much harder it's going to be, and asking why she's the one who was cursed."

"Oh... So she's really not taking it well..." I turn to look at Lincoln. "I'm assuming she hasn't told Adele, if you didn't know?"

Lincoln shakes his head. "Not unless Adele has become way better at keeping secrets than she used to be."

"So no, then?"

Lincoln grins. "Yeah, probably not."

"She's only told Tara. She rang her in a blind panic when it was the middle of the night in Brisbane."

Lincoln cringes. "Bet that went down well, since Brandi has only just started sleeping through the night," he says, referring to the baby I remember seeing at the wedding.

Although, given that was just over a year ago, I'd say the baby is now a full-blown toddler. If it has been two years since she's had a decent sleep, I can only imagine how pissed Tara would have been about a phone call in the middle of the night.

I often forget that Lincoln is also close to a few of Kylie's Australian friends back in Brisbane. He and Seth had met Kylie and Tara on a holiday a few years ago. Kylie's best friend is often the voice of reason when it comes to Kylie's more impulsive side, and it doesn't surprise me she's the only person she's told so far.

"Yeah, Tara wasn't thrilled. But when she heard Kylie crying, she went into problem-solving mode."

"Shit, she was crying?" Lincoln rakes a hand through his hair. "Should I tell Adele?"

Seth shakes his head. "Let Kylie be the one to tell her. Once she's processed it all properly, I'm sure she won't be as freaked out and will go back to being excited..." He doesn't sound sure at all.

"Did I hear you say you guys are having twins?" Sarah asks, seemingly having abandoned the conversation with Alanna.

I glance past Sarah to see Alanna watching us all. She meets my gaze briefly, but I look away, not ready to deal with all of that.

Seth nods and Sarah squeals. "Oh, that's amazing!"

I shake my head. "Seems like Kylie's not quite that pumped about it."

Sarah laughs. "Of course she's not. She's the one who's going to have to do all the work."

"I'll be there to help her," Seth protests, but Sarah waves him off.

"And while you're travelling?" She gives him a pointed look, and he sighs again, nodding dejectedly.

Lots of sighing going on right now. Not that I can blame him. Having one kid with our lifestyle is enough work for some of the WAGs. Twins are a whole other world that none of us knows how to navigate.

"Seth?" Alanna joins the conversation now, moving to touch Seth lightly on the shoulder.

He looks up at her. "Yeah?"

"You guys are totally going to be okay. I'm a twin, and my mother raised my brother and me while our dad travelled playing rugby professionally. It's not always easy, but you guys have got a great support network here."

I raise an eyebrow, but don't say anything. I'd known she had a brother, but I didn't realize they were twins. And this is the most I've ever heard her talk about her family in general.

Seth's shoulders lower slightly. "Thanks Alanna. Maybe once Kylie calms down a little, she can talk to you and get some tips?"

She nods with a smile. "Of course. Give her my number, okay?"

Seth nods back, and she flicks another glance my way before moving off towards where Michael and Riley are working through a circuit with resistance bands on the other side of the room.

It's a sign of just how distracted Seth is that he doesn't pick up on the look between us, and I send a silent thank you into the universe for that small mercy.

We eventually get back to our workouts, though it's obvious that Seth is just going through the motions. When we're finally done, Lincoln drags him off to do some much needed day drinking at Buck's. Hopefully, our captain can get his head right before our game tomorrow.

Deciding not to join them, I hit the treadmill instead, relieved that I'm finally able to run again. With my rock playlist blaring in my ears, I zone everything out around me and clock in a few kilometres. With everything that's been going on recently, I've been having trouble switching off, and it feels good to finally just run full out to burn off the nervous energy that's been coursing through me.

Once I've done an easy ten kilometres, I head to the locker room to take a shower. I hadn't realized I was the last one here until I walk back through the training room as Alanna is switching off the lights.

"Oh! Sorry, I thought everyone had left," she stammers while she stares at me with wide eyes.

"It's fine. I'm leaving," I reply, not quite able to meet her gaze as I walk towards the door that leads out to the hall.

"Dean."

I stop walking and suppress a sigh. Guess they're catching.

"Can you look at me, please?" she asks.

I clench my jaw and close my eyes for a moment before turning to face her. "Can I help you with something?"

She frowns, crossing her arms. "Is this how things are going to be between us now? You being all cold and distant?"

"I don't know what you're talking about. I mean, we hardly know each other, right?" I know I'm being a dick, but it's kind of my default setting at the moment.

"So, in other words, yes, you're going to make this as unpleasant as possible. Got it."

I scoff. "I'm just keeping things professional. You made it pretty fucking clear that's what you wanted."

She throws her hands up in the air. "No, I didn't! You're the one who said that. I just..." Her words trail off as she studies my face.

I stare her down, my jaw tense. "Go on. Finish that sentence. You just what? Think I'm a bunny chaser who was only interested in you because you're off limits?"

She groans and looks up at the ceiling. "That is not what I said. I don't even know what the hell a bunny chaser is."

"A bunny chaser is a player who sleeps with the women who are after us for status - or our money - and has no regard for their feelings. So, basically, what you accused me of wanting to do to you."

"Oh." She has the sense to at least look embarrassed.

"Yeah. Oh."

"That's not what I meant, Dean. I just... I'm scared."

I throw her an incredulous look. "Of me? Come off it, Alanna. You know I would never hurt you."

"No..." She takes a deep breath. "I'm scared of throwing away everything I've built for myself on someone that has nothing to lose if this all goes wrong."

I process her words for a moment, but am still struggling to understand what she's getting at. "Wait... What?" I take a step closer to her.

She bites her lower lip. "If something happens between us..."

I keep moving until I'm standing right in front of her and gently press my thumb against her lip to pull it out from between her teeth. "What if something happens between us?" I ask quietly, my gaze locked on hers.

She swallows. "If something happens between us and anyone else finds out... I can't lose this job, Dean. It's everything I've worked my whole life towards. Never mind the fact that my visa is tied to my employment here. If I get fired, I'll have to move back to New Zealand and will have destroyed any hope of ever working in men's sport again." Her expression can only be described as pleading.

If I was a less selfish person, I'd walk away right now. Because she's right. A relationship between us would break so many rules, and she's the one who would pay the price.

But I'm not that self-sacrificing.

"Do you want me?" I ask, my voice coming out huskier than I expected.

Her lower lip wobbles a little as she continues to search my face with those beautiful big green eyes. Just when I think I've misread what she's saying, she gives the smallest nod.

I bend to brush my lips to hers, holding myself back from devouring her like I really want to.

She whimpers and rises onto her tiptoes, wrapping her arms around my neck and pressing her chest against mine.

The kiss grows less tender the longer it goes, and I slide my arms around her waist before lifting her off her feet. She wraps her legs around my hips, hooking her ankles behind my back as she slides her tongue against mine. I back her up against the door to the training room as she moans against my lips.

"We shouldn't be doing this," I murmur before kissing my way down her neck. "I don't know if there are cameras in here."

She gasps and pushes me away, looking around the room with a panicked look in her eyes. She unhooks her legs and slides down, her feet hitting the floor with a thud.

"I can't see any, but you're right."

Disappointment hits me in the gut, but I nod, stepping back.

She bites her lip and takes my hand while she looks me in the eye. "Let's go."

I raise an eyebrow as she pulls me towards the door. "Where?"

She flicks me a heated glance over her shoulder, filled with the same amount of need coursing through my own veins. "Your place."

Well. Fuck.

Chapter Twenty-Eight

I'M PROFESSIONAL LIKE THAT

Alanna

I follow Dean back to his place, waiting for the indecision to kick in once again. But as I drive behind him into the underground parking garage beneath his apartment building, I'm more certain than ever that this is where I want to be.

He pulls his truck to the very back of a tandem car space, and I drive in behind him before killing the engine. He climbs out, and a million butterflies take flight in my stomach. Each time I look at him, the attraction I feel for him grows, and I honestly don't think I could have continued fighting this if I'd even tried.

He comes to stand beside my car and bends to open the door. "Planning on getting out, or are you just going to sit there undressing me with your eyes?" he asks with a smirk.

I roll my eyes but take his outstretched hand and allow him to help me out of the car. "I wasn't undressing you with my eyes."

The smirk grows wider. "My mistake. You were fucking me with your eyes."

I shake my head as I close the door behind me. "You're such a child."

He backs me up against the car and presses his body against mine, bracing himself against the car with one hand. "Definitely not a child." He takes my hand and presses it to his crotch. "That's all man, baby."

I groan, equal parts amused and turned on. "I think I liked you better when you were grumpy."

He grins. "I can go back to being a dick, if you'd prefer?" He pushes off the car and slides his hand down to weave his fingers through mine, the cocky grin slipping a little. "Are you one hundred percent sure about this?"

I nod. "Yes. I promise I'm done fighting this."

He pushes a loose strand of hair behind my ear. "Good. Because the only fighting from now on will be over how many orgasms I plan to give you once we're upstairs."

I laugh. "Wow, with lines like those, how did I ever resist you?"

He flashes me a toothy grin. "I've been asking myself that for weeks now."

Bantering over, I allow him to pull me towards the elevators. He tucks me into his side and presses a kiss to my temple while we wait, and I lean into his embrace. When the elevator arrives, I follow him inside and watch as he scans a keycard before hitting the button for the penthouse.

The ride up to his apartment is quiet, although he keeps me close, running his hand up and down my back while I continue to lean into him. The doors open directly into a large open plan living space with an amazing view of the city. The lights on the Calgary Tower come on just as we step out of the elevator, and I'm drawn to the floor to ceiling windows to take it all in. I know the guys make a ton of money, but I'd not given much thought to what their homes must be like. Dean is far neater than I expected, and once I tear my eyes away from the view, I look around with interest. A black leather lounge with a chaise faces a massive TV that's attached to the wall, with a glass dining table between the couch and the kitchen. The kitchen itself is large, with a grey marble bench top and white cupboards. Aside from a coffee machine, there's nothing else on the bench. It all feels very clean and modern. If I didn't know better, I'd think the apartment was used for show only and not someone's actual home. The only sign of any personality is the bookcases that line the walls on either side of the elevator doors. They are filled with books of varying colours and shapes, and I know I'll have to check them out later, remembering the in depth conversation we'd had about the books we liked on our one and only date.

He comes to stand behind me, resting his chin on the top of my head, and I lean back into his arms.

"We don't have to rush into anything tonight," he murmurs.

I turn my head to look up at him. "What do you mean?"

He kisses my forehead. "You were worried I only wanted to sleep with you, right? That this was just about the thrill of the chase?"

I shake my head. "I don't know if I ever truly believed that."

He shrugs, squeezing me tighter. "Well, I'm happy to take this at whatever pace you want. We both know you're the one with the most to lose, and I don't want you to feel like I'm pushing you into something more than you're willing to give. If you want to just have dinner and hang out on the couch, I'm good with that."

I turn my body to face him and wrap my arms around his neck. "Thank you. Maybe we can start with dinner?" He nods and goes to step back, but I keep my arms locked around his neck. "But let me be clear." I rise on to my tiptoes in an attempt to bring my face in line with his, and he laughs, bending slightly so that we're eye to eye. "I'm going to need you to fuck me tonight."

He lets out a shocked laugh before grinning down at me. "I suppose I can do that." He crushes his lips to mine.

Dean takes the night off from his dietitian approved meals and we order pho from his local Vietnamese restaurant. Realizing I'm still in my work clothes, he offers his guest bathroom for me to take a shower if I want to get comfortable.

The bathroom is huge, with a clawfoot tub in the corner and a shower that runs the full length of the wall, with shower heads at both ends. I'd not exactly grown up poor, being a professional sportsman's daughter, but this is a whole new level of luxury I've never experienced before.

I'd commented on the variety of feminine bath products when we first walked in, and he'd assured me it was for when his mother comes to visit, a nervous expression crossing his face. I can tell we're really going to have to work through the damage I caused with my comments on how many women he's been with.

Once I'm done in the shower, I pull on the soft cotton Mounties t-shirt he'd given me to wear, and it falls down to my knees, more like a dress than a t-shirt on my shorter frame. Another reminder that Dean is huge, in all the best ways.

I pad back out into the living room where he's sitting on the couch and notice he's changed into his grey sweats, although he's still wearing his black training t-shirt that hugs his biceps. For once, I allow myself to run my gaze slowly over his body, taking in every muscle on display beneath the tanned skin on his arms.

"Keep looking at me like that, Lahney, and I'll be having

you for dinner instead," he says without looking up from his phone.

I grin and move closer. "How can you tell how I'm looking at you when you're staring at your phone?" I stop in front of him.

He tosses the phone aside and pulls me forward until I have no choice but to straddle his lap."I'm a goalie. I see all kinds of things no one else notices."

I slide my hands up his arms before clasping my fingers together behind his neck. "Oh yeah? How was I looking at you, then?"

He reaches to cup my cheek, stroking it with his thumb. "Like you can't wait to see me naked again."

I smirk. "I've seen you basically naked a thousand times. That isn't anything new."

"Nope. Work doesn't count. I always keep my pants on whenever you're around. I'm professional like that." He gives me a cheeky grin.

I sit back slightly and slide my hands down slowly, gliding them over the thin cotton that covers his pecs. "True. But I'm well acquainted with what's under here."

He slides his hands up my bare legs, stopping where his shirt has ridden up to just cover my thighs. "Well, I guess I'll have to become just as familiar with what's under this shirt to even the score, won't I?"

The intercom rings, and he groans as I hop up to buzz the delivery person into the building.

"I'll go downstairs and get the food from the lobby. You wearing only that shirt is for my eyes only." He gets up and kisses my nose before grabbing his security key and hopping into the elevator.

I take a seat at the dining table and return to staring at the view. When he comes back upstairs with the carry bag containing two steaming bowls of hot soup, he grabs two spoons and takes a seat beside me.

"So how come you never told me your brother is actually your twin?" he asks as we start eating.

I shrug, fiddling with my necklace. "I don't know. I wasn't keeping it a secret or anything. I just don't really say 'my twin brother' when I tell people about him."

He chews on a piece of beef for a moment, eyeing me warily. "And your dad? I knew you'd worked with rugby players before you came to the Mounties, but I didn't realize you'd come from a sporting family."

I try not to stiffen at the mention of my father. "I just... I don't really talk about my family. Tierney doesn't even know much about them, although she's heard me talk to Charlie."

He raises an eyebrow. "So... You don't talk to your dad?" I can tell he's trying to be tactful, but I figure if we're going to do whatever the hell it is we're doing, I may as well be honest with him about my upbringing.

"Dad played for New Zealand for years. I was born into a family that was basically rugby royalty back home, because my grandfather also played for the team back in the day, as well. Everyone knew who Dad was. Who we were. And during the years he played, when he was home, it was amazing. He was a really hands on dad when he wasn't travelling, and Charlie and I worshiped the ground he walked on." I scowl down at my food. "But then he was injured. He hid it for a long time, and he and Mum fought about it a lot, because she could see he was at risk of doing permanent damage to his back because of it. Things were different back then. They always told players to just suck it up and push through the pain, so he refused to talk to the team's medical staff about it. As far as he was concerned, if he couldn't play, he might as well just die. And then it happened. One high tackle and that was it. His career was over. The drinking started not long afterwards." Dean reaches to cover my hand with his, but I don't look at him, even when he squeezes gently. "He never hit any of us, or anything like that. But I haven't seen him sober since I was thirteen. When Mum died in a car accident when we were nineteen, Charlie took it upon himself to take care of him," I say, twisting my pendant back and forth, noting the way Dean's eyes drop to the movement. "Charlie had the potential to play Rugby professionally, but he's stuck playing at the semi-pro level because there isn't as much travel involved. He and his wife bought the house next door a couple of years ago so they could keep an eye on him and still have their own space. But Charlie told me yesterday that she left him because she couldn't handle having her life revolve around an old drunk anymore, and I don't blame her. I haven't seen or spoken to my father since I went away to university, except at Charlie and Tilley's wedding. And he was too drunk to even notice I was there."

He squeezes my hand again. "I'm sorry Lahney. I had no idea."

I give him a weak smile as I look up finally. "Why would you? I never talk about him. As far as I'm concerned, the man who was my father ceased existing the moment he started drowning his sorrows in a bottle of whiskey."

He watches my fingers as I curl them around my pendant. "Do you notice how often you do that?"

I look down at my hand, then bring my gaze back to his. "Yeah... It was my mum's... I haven't taken it off since she died. I started wearing it to feel her presence still, and then it just became habit to hold it whenever I'm stressed... To feel like she's here with me."

He studies my face for a moment, his expression tinged with sadness. "Is that why you got into sports medicine? Because of your dad?"

I nod. "Yeah. I want to help athletes learn that if they work with their support teams, we can help them avoid career ending injuries. You wouldn't believe just how stubborn *some* professional athletes can be when it comes to treating injuries properly." I give him a pointed look.

He huffs a laugh, picking his spoon back up. "Message received."

We finish our soup without any more talk of dysfunctional families, and for just the briefest amount of time, I allow myself to grow comfortable in his presence. It's rare for me to let my guard down around anyone, but he seems to have found a way beneath the armour I've built around myself. And I don't even mind.

Chapter Twenty-Nine

ARE YOU BEGGING?

Dean

I try not to let Alanna see how much her story affected me. The idea of a young Alanna dealing with her childhood hero falling apart is enough to make my chest tighten, but I know she won't appreciate me feeling sorry for her.

Needing a moment to process my thoughts, I get up to clear away our empty containers. She watches me with her head cocked to the side, as though waiting for me to judge her. Instead of saying anything further, I return to her side, taking her hand and tugging her back towards the couch. We sit down, and I pull her feet into my lap, rubbing my thumb over the arch of her foot, delighted when a little moan slips from her lips. "Good?"

She nods. "Yeah, keep doing that."

I apply more pressure, massaging both her feet until she's practically purring, her moans causing me to harden beneath my sweats.

"If you keep making noises like that, I'm going to have to kiss you," I warn, my heated gaze on her face as her eyes flutter closed.

She moans again, louder this time, and I reach to scoop her up, pulling her into my lap as she grins at me.

Gripping her chin, I force her to look me in the eye. "Is this what you wanted, Lahney? You wanted to drive me crazy, so I'd devour you?"

Her breath hitches when I slide my hand up her leg, and she bites her bottom lip. "Maybe..."

I move my hand higher, my eyes widening when I find her bare. "No underwear, Alanna?" She keeps biting her lip, shaking her head, and I groan, clasping the back of her head with my other hand. "Such a naughty girl. If I'd known that when you were straddling my lap before, you'd have been screaming my name long before now."

She smirks, and I pull her face to mine, kissing her hard as I find her clit with my thumb. Once she's breathless, I guide her to lie back on the couch before pinching her nipple between my fingers. She moans again, arching her back when I slide a finger inside her, easing a second in once she starts panting. I fuck her slowly with my fingers, watching her face to gauge what she likes. Learning her body once again.

Just like the other night, it isn't long before she comes, her moans growing louder until she cries out, my name slipping from her lips.

While I can't wait to bury myself inside her, I want to make her come again. Lifting her butt so that I can slide out from under her, I ease her legs further apart and bend to kiss her clit. She jolts before moaning again, and I chuckle before sliding my shirt up her body to expose her breasts. As I pinch one nipple, I suck the other into my mouth, swirling my tongue over it.

"God, Dean," she whimpers, weaving her fingers through my hair.

I stay there for a while, moving between her breasts to make sure they both get an equal amount of my attention, revelling in every moan and gasp that escapes her lips. Eventually, I kiss my way back down her body, running my tongue through the moisture from her previous orgasm before sucking her clit into my mouth. She lifts onto her elbows, her half-closed eyes meeting mine as she grasps the back of my head, urging me to suck harder. As I oblige her silent request, her head tips back and a long moan fills the room as her back arches off the couch. I slide my fingers back inside her, pumping them in and out, faster this time, impatient to see her come apart again. Her breaths grow ragged, and she moves her hips, grinding herself against my face while she grips the back of my head tighter. I let her set the pace while I keep sucking her clit, and she goes off like a rocket, screaming my name as her other hand clings to the armrest behind her head.

I grin, lifting my head to watch her face while still moving my fingers inside her, loving the feeling of her inner walls clamping around them.

"I can't wait for it to be my cock you're squeezing so tightly," I murmur, kissing the inside of her thigh as I wait for her breaths to even out again.

"I'm going to need you to fuck me, now, Dean," she says once she's recovered her voice

"If you insist." I grin as I get up to shed my clothes, yanking the condom wrapper from the pocket of my sweatpants that I'd stashed there earlier.

Sitting back down, I roll it on before lifting her easily to straddle my lap. I don't guide her down immediately, running my tongue over her nipple for a moment.

"No more foreplay," she whispers, and I chuckle as I line myself up with her entrance.

She whimpers again as I tease her, slipping just the tip in before lifting her again. "Are you begging, Lahney?"

"God, yes! Just fuck me, Dean!" she demands, and I laugh again before pulling her down slowly.

I grit my teeth as her inner walls grip me tight, breathing through my nose to keep from embarrassing myself by coming straight away. Once she's adjusted, I rock her hips, urging her to move, and she begins to slide herself up and down along my shaft. I groan and suck one of her nipples into my mouth to give me something else to focus on other than how amazing it feels to be buried inside her.

She keeps the same steady pace as she cups my cheek, and I pull away from her breast to look her in the eye. She smiles and brushes her lips to mine, moaning when I wrap my arms around her back and thrust upwards. Taking over, I drive myself into her over and over as she clings to my shoulders, gasping and moaning against my lips. Feeling her flutter around me, I pick up the pace, determined to come with her. A few more thrusts and her cries fill the room as she buries her face in my neck. I'm right behind her, chasing my own release over the edge as she squeezes me so tight I almost see stars. My body shudders as I groan, and we cling to each other, breathing heavily.

When she finally recovers enough to sit up, she smiles, holding my face in both her hands as she holds my gaze. When she kisses me again, she pours all her emotions into it, and I tighten my hold on her, unsure I'll ever be able to let go.

I'll follow her lead with how we handle the attraction between us, but if she tells me this is it, I'm pretty sure my heart is going to shatter apart. Because this woman has taken possession of me - mind, body and soul.

Chapter Thirty

NOTHING GOING ON THERE

Alanna

It takes all my strength to pull myself away from Dean after the third time we have sex, but I know I need to go home. If we're going to keep this whole thing under wraps, then I can't have Tierney wondering where I am. Although she knows about the previous interactions, I don't think it's a good idea to tell her that we're now sneaking around.

"Are you sure you can't stay?" Dean murmurs against my lips while he kisses me goodbye.

We're leaning against my car after he'd insisted on walking me down, and I really want to say 'fuck it' and crawl back into his giant bed with him.

"I really want to. But I can't. I've never stayed out all night, and Tierney is going to get suspicious if I suddenly start now."

He brushes his thumb over my lower lip. "You've never stayed over at anyone's place?"

I shake my head as I suck his thumb between my lips.

He groans. "Not helping, Lahney."

I chuckle and pull my mouth away. "No, I haven't been with anyone since I moved here. Other than you, obviously."

His eyes widen. "Serious?"

"As a heart attack."

"How come?" The look of utter confusion on his face is cute, and I grin up at him as I shrug.

"Just never met anyone else I wanted to sleep with, I guess. And I've been so busy with work."

"Well... I guess I should be flattered you took a chance on me then." He pulls me tighter against him. "Why did you say yes to me?"

I study his face for a moment, surprised to see the uncertainty there. He is so confident that it seems strange that he's so unsure when it comes to me.

"I guess I saw something in you that I haven't in any of the guys that have hit on me in bars and stuff. I know it seems strange, given our history, but I've never been a one-night-stand type of person. I need to form a connection with someone first before I sleep with them." A look I can't decipher crosses his face, and I swallow, wondering if I've said too much. "I mean, not that I expect anything from you. This was fun."

His arms tighten around me. "Don't do that."

I frown. "Do what?"

"Try to brush aside how you're feeling because you think I will freak out."

God, he's way too intuitive.

"I just don't want to read too much into whatever this is," I mumble, looking away.

"Lahney..." He waits for me to eventually look at him again before continuing. "This isn't some fling for me. I'm all in. So the question is, what do you want?"

I let out a long breath. "I want you. I just don't know how we're going to make this work."

He nods. "We'll go slow. No one needs to know anything, and we'll just keep things professional at work."

"Okay," I say with a smile, tugging his face back down to kiss him again.

He reluctantly lets me go and I climb into my car, stretching up for one last kiss before he closes the door and taps the roof of my car. "Drive safe. Message me when you get home, okay?"

I smile and nod as I start my car, blowing him a kiss before pulling out of the car space.

The drive home is uneventful, and when I message him to let him know I made it back, he replies with a kiss-face emoji. I grin at the phone and let my head rest against the back of my seat for a moment. I know this will probably all blow up in our faces, but right now, I'm just going to enjoy whatever we're doing, and try not to get hurt in the process.

We have a home game the next day, and after morning skate, the guys head home to have their pregame naps before coming back to warm up. I usually go home when the players do for my own nap, but today I have paperwork to catch up on after being away earlier in the week. The trainer's room is deathly quiet, and once I can no longer handle it, I connect my phone to the bluetooth speaker we use during dryland training, and the silence is replaced by my favourite 90's R&B playlist.

"Ooh, good choice," Sarah says, coming into the room a few moments later, hips swaying in time with the music as she sashays across the room.

"Hey," I say with a smile.

She hops up onto the desk beside me with a smile. "What are you doing?" Her long blonde hair hangs loose down her back in waves, and she's obviously dressed for the night's game already, with full make-up and one of Ollie's merch jerseys paired with jeans and sneakers.

Most of the other WAGs turn each game into a fashion show, but I've noticed Sarah, Kylie and Adele all prefer low-key outfits, usually wearing their jerseys with comfy clothes underneath. They are definitely women after my own heart.

I wave my hand over the files beside me. "Putting all these notes into the system from our road trip. We keep handwritten notes while travelling and then draw straws over who has to put them all onto the guys digital files. I, sadly, drew the short straw this time."

We really do need to just use our laptops, but Trevor is a stickler for not changing how things are done. And since it was my suggestion, it definitely won't happen.

She grimaces. "Well, that sounds boring. You're coming for lunch."

I raise any eyebrow. "Oh, I am, am I?"

She nods. "Yep. On game days, I go out for a long lunch with the girls while the boys are at home napping, and you are now officially one of the girls."

A jolt of panic hits me, and I swallow. "Um... But I'm not a WAG." Surely she doesn't know about Dean and me... Right?

She laughs. "You don't need to be a WAG to hang out with us. Adele used to come out with us all the time for years before she hooked up with Lincoln."

I try not to make my sigh of relief obvious. "Oh, okay then. Who else is going?"

"You, me, Kylie and Adele," she says, listing off names on her fingers. "And Tamara and Tierney."

"Oh, Tierney's coming?" I ask, perking right up.

Sarah grins. "Yep, so as you can see, definitely not all WAGs."

"As long as Bethany and her hangers on aren't included, I'm fine with that."

Sarah groans. "No, they have their own little clique happening. Kylie and Adele aren't comfortable around them, either. I can pretty much promise you, when it's not an official work thing, we avoid that crowd like the plague."

I'd kind of worked that out for myself, but it's still a relief to hear that I won't be expected to make conversation with the women who have gone out of their way to look down their noses at me when I've attended work events.

"Okay cool. When are we going?"

She slides off the desk and pulls me out of my chair. "Right now. No, leave your bag," she says, shaking my head at me when I go to grab my handbag from where I've stashed it behind the desk. "Ollie's paying. Gotta have some perks to this whole hockey wife schtick." And with that, she drags me out of the room.

When we arrive at the restaurant, Adele is already at the table, chatting with Tierney. I know that Tierney has spent more time with all of them, but I've never spoken to Adele much, and find myself feeling a little nervous.

"Where's Kylie?" Sarah asks, taking a seat beside Adele, while Tamara and I take the seats across from them.

"Bathroom," Adele replies, frowning a little.

Tierney gives me a side hug from her seat beside mine. "Hey, you came!"

I nod. "Yep, Sarah kidnapped me."

"And I'll do it again," Sarah threatens with a smile before turning back to Adele. "Is everything okay with Kylie?"

Adele shrugs. "She's still freaking out. I'm hoping that Tara has more luck than Seth and me at getting her to calm down."

"Oh, is she coming over?" Sarah asks, and Adele nods.

"Yeah, Lincoln was talking to her earlier. She's coming in a few weeks. She was trying to wait for when her husband could come, too, but he's studying and has got exams coming up, so she's about to make the trek with a toddler solo. At least she'll be in business class, because Seth is paying for her flights."

I grimace. "Not sure business class would make it any easier with a toddler."

Adele shudders. "Right? My worst nightmare. Well, actually, kids in general are my worse nightmare, unless they belong to someone else and I can hand them back when they start screaming."

I laugh, stunned at her honest admission that she has no interest in having children. As someone who has never really seen herself having children, I tend to just keep that to myself, so I'm not used to having another woman declare it so openly. I think I like her.

"How about you? How's work going?" Sarah asks, and Adele grins.

"So good. We're fully booked for the next twelve months. Probably not the best time to lose Kylie, but we'll find some new guides before she finishes up."

I'd wondered what Kylie was going to do when the babies arrived, as being a tour guide doesn't seem like the easiest job to juggle with small humans around when your husband spends most of the year travelling.

"I'll still do some of the summer ones, once Seth finishes up each season," Kylie says, sliding into the seat on Adele's other side. "Otherwise, I'm on day trips only once I go back after maternity leave." She looks rather pale, and her usual smile seems forced when she nods towards Sarah and me.

"How you holding up?" Sarah asks kindly.

Kylie shrugs. "Freaking the fuck out."

"It'll be okay. You'll see. You and Seth are good at pivoting when life throws you curve balls," Adele says, squeezing her cousins hand.

"Yeah, but this time it's going to be me dealing with this massive curve ball mostly on my own, because of course, I'm going to be having fucking twins during the hockey season." She glares at the menu, and Tierney flicks me a panicked look.

Neither of us know them well enough to involve ourselves in the conversation, and I'm starting to wonder if I should have insisted on just staying at work.

"Honey, you're not going to be alone. Seth will take a few weeks off, and you've got all of us. And you know Grandma and Grandpa will basically move in if you ask."

Kylie sighs. "Let's not talk about this today. I don't want to bring everyone else down with my problems. Let's change the subject." She looks over at me, and I swallow when I realize she's going to use me as a diversion. "Seth mentioned he's noticed Dean checking you out, Alanna."

Well... that was not what I was expecting.

"Oh. Well..." I splutter, trying to work out what the hell to say to that.

"They're just friends," Tierney says quickly, and I have to keep myself from flicking her a grateful look.

Kylie smiles. "Oh, I know. I told Seth he was probably reading too much into it, but I noticed the way he was dancing with you that night we all went out. I don't think I've ever seen Dean look at any of his hook ups like that, so it was interesting. Hopefully, he hasn't made you uncomfortable, though? I know you're not allowed to hook up with the players."

I shake my head. "No, he's been fine. Nothing going on there."

Sarah laughs. "Yeah, and Alanna is very good at keeping the boys in line."

The conversation shifts to other things, and I am eventually able to unclench my jaw. Tierney gives my leg a quick squeeze under the table, and I do my best to follow the conversation, not wanting to appear antisocial. But when no one is looking, I pull my phone out of my pocket and send Dean a quick text under the table.

ALANNA

Did you know Seth thinks you've got a thing for me?

DEAN

Yeah, he's been watching me like a hawk.
Why? Did he say something to you?

ALANNA

No. I'm out at lunch with Sarah, Adele and Kylie, and Kylie mentioned it. We're going to have to be really careful.

DEAN

I promise to keep my eyes, hands and feet to myself.

ALANNA

Feet??????

DEAN

Yeah. No footsies under the table.

I snort, before remembering where I am. Tierney raises an eyebrow, but thankfully, the others are so into their conversation about property prices that they don't notice.

I want to confide in my best friend, but Dean and I had decided it was best not to tell anyone. All it would take is one person to slip up, and I can kiss my job goodbye.

But I know, eventually, the sneaking around is going to get

old. I just have no idea what we're going to do in the long run, if this turns into a full blown relationship.

Until then, we're just going to have to do a better job at hiding our feelings when we're around our friends and colleagues.

Chapter Thirty-One

NOT PLAYING FAIR

Dean

When I pull into my spot in the players underground parkade ahead of the night's game, I take a deep breath, preparing myself to put on the show of my life. I'm on the bench tonight, but I still need to warm up in case there's any reason that Mark has to come off the ice. Like if a player lands on top of him and practically tears his body in half... Oh, wait, that only happens to me.

And warming up means being stretched out by my trainer. My trainer that I fucked three times last night.

Knowing that Seth has mentioned something to Kylie has me even more on edge. I'm not a secretive person. Never had any need to be. But I don't want to give up this thing with Alanna, and I can't risk her career. So I guess I'm about to become the world's greatest actor.

I head inside, and Sarah stops me, pointing towards Tamara, who aims her phone at me.

I groan. "Not another thirst trap video, woman?"

"My job is to get butts in seats, Dean, so suck it up," Sarah says, looking less than impressed.

Whether it's at me or the fact that they are forced to pimp us out for likes, I'm not sure. The team socials have apparently been going wild lately for all these damn pregame "players in suits" videos.

"Shouldn't we be trying to draw in actual hockey fans?" I beg.

Tamara snorts. "Look, most of those women end up becoming actual hockey fans. And your face is just so pretty."

I think I liked her better when she was too scared to talk in front of me.

Sarah pushes me back towards the door. "Now, I want you to walk in with an actual smile, please. And no more grouchy comments."

I scowl as she heads back towards Tamara. Once she's safely behind the phone, Tamara points at me and I sigh, walking back down the hall once more with the fakest smile on my face.

After I pass by them, I turn back to glare at the pair of women. "I am more than my looks, ladies."

"Doesn't it suck being objectified?" Sarah says, her eyes flashing with humour. "Scurry along, grumpy goalie."

I bite back my retort, knowing that there's no point in trying to act like women haven't been dealing with this shit far longer than hockey players. But it still grates.

Lincoln is already in the locker room, his suit hanging inside his cubby. He's in his Mounties athletic shorts and shoving his feet into his slides as he downs a bottle of water.

Once he looks at my face, he laughs. "I see you're as impressed with the suit walk video as I was."

"If by impressed you mean voicing my dislike of being objectified for likes, then yes, I was as impressed as you were." I slide my jacket off and put it on the hanger.

Lincoln snorts. "Yeah, Adele has been getting super fired up every time she catches the comments on those posts."

Alanna wanders in while I'm stripping out of my suit, and I watch her flick her gaze my way, quickly schooling her facial expression to hide the lust that flashes there as I shrug my shirt off. I keep my expression neutral and struggle to continue the conversation with Lincoln, doing my best to act like her presence hasn't immediately derailed my thought process.

"Adele never struck me as the jealous type before? Why does she care what some random women on social media have to say?"

Lincoln shakes his head as he screws the lid back onto the now empty water bottle and tosses it back into his bag. "Have you not seen the comments section of these videos?"

"No. I deleted all my accounts. Now it's just the one that Tamara and Sarah manage. I hate that shit." I'd rather read a book than stare at my phone.

"Not sure how you missed the way the rookies have been getting their kicks out of the comments section, full of women asking if we're looking for wives, and more than a few guys expressing interest as well. And Adele has been fielding them on Milo's social media account, which she thinks is gross, thirsting after me on our beloved fur child's account." Lincoln is smirking, and I know he just finds it all crazy.

I used to enjoy some of the attention, but I feel like things have just exploded recently, and now it makes me uncomfortable.

"I think it's safest for me to stay away," I reply, and Alanna clears her throat.

"Yeah, as soon as people find out what I do for a living, you wouldn't believe the things they ask. Someone once saw me in the background of one of the YouTube behind-the-scenes videos Sarah posts, where you guys are all shirtless between periods. Next thing I know, these crazy women have tracked me down and, my god, the questions they asked. Someone was asking how many of the players I was fucking and if I could hook them up. I had to make all my accounts private after that."

We both gape at her as more of our teammates stream into the room, but she just shrugs. Like it's completely normal to have people asking you that about your job.

"O'Malley, you're up first for stretching, seeing as you're ready," Alanna says, nodding towards the training room.

We're both doing an excellent job at not looking each other in the eye, and I give myself a little mental pat on the back. This will be easy.

The forwards and defensemen have different warm-up exercises to the goalies, and once I'm in my shorts and sneakers, I grab my juggling balls from the shelf where I keep them in my cubby, heading out into the hall to join Mark. Neither of us speaks as we get in the zone, practicing juggling and focusing on our reflexes for half an hour with our noise cancelling headphones in place. Without saying a word, he turns to me and we throw the balls back and forth quickly.

Once Alanna pops her head out into the hall and waves me over, I leave Mark to it and join her on the mats in the training room. I go through the series of solo stretches first while she kneels beside me, and once I need help, she grabs hold of my calf, resting it against her shoulder and pushing back so I can stretch out my lower back. Being flexible has its benefits, but when it comes to stretching, it means I need to go harder to really feel the stretch properly.

I catch myself smirking as she looks down at me, and once I do a quick scan to make sure no one else is around, I run my hand up her thigh and give her ass a quick squeeze as she pushes the stretch deeper.

"That's not playing fair, Dean," she whispers, but there's heat behind her gaze as her eyes drift to my lips and her other hand just happens to rest on my upper thigh, just beside my crotch.

I flash her a cheeky grin. "Sorry. Couldn't resist. I'll be a good boy now. Although feel free to move that hand a little further to the left."

She rolls her eyes and switches between my legs. It's on the side of my injured hip, and I wince a little when it catches.

She studies my face. "Bad?"

I shake my head. "Just a twinge." She doesn't look convinced. "I promise," I add. "I meant what I said. I'll be honest if I'm hurt again, okay?"

She nods, releasing my leg from the stretch. "I'll hold you to that, big guy."

I raise an eyebrow. "Big guy, huh?"

Her eyes twinkle as she gets to her feet. "Oh yeah, it definitely fits." She winks.

I reach over my head and push myself upwards, flipping onto my feet from lying down, and she laughs as I grin down at her.

"What are you doing tonight?" I murmur.

She looks around to make sure we're still alone before rising onto her tiptoes to whisper in my ear. "Getting railed by the grumpy goalie."

I swallow as she turns away and flicks me a cheeky smile of her own over her shoulder. My eyes drift to her ass as she saunters off towards the locker room, shaking my head. This whole acting like we're not together is going to make for excellent foreplay.

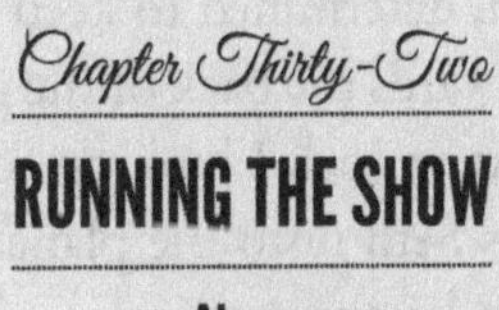

Chapter Thirty-Two

RUNNING THE SHOW

Alanna

A few weeks later, we are headed for New York for the first of four away games and Nicholas calls as I walk onto the plane. While the trainers travel with the team, the doctor doesn't, leaving us to handle minor injuries solo. Any major injuries are handled by local hospital staff, with his input given over the phone.

"Hey. So, Trevor is out with the flu," the doctor says, and I raise an eyebrow.

"Oh, wow. So is Simon joining us?"

"No. We needed him to stay and work with Max and Pieter so they aren't delayed with their recovery."

Both players are currently on the injured reserve list. Seems like we are having a run of bad luck for injured players lately.

I nod. "Okay. Joel and I can cover it all then, no problem."

"I want you running the show on this road trip."

I pause, my eyes wide as I process his words. "Me? Really?"

"You're the most qualified. The guys follow your lead and the players respect you. Unless you don't think you're up to the task?"

I shake my head quickly, aware that I am close to talking my way out of a chance to prove myself to Nicholas without Trevor getting in the way.

"No, I can handle it. Thank you for the opportunity." I school my expression, determined to keep my excitement from showing as I move towards the back of the plane.

Taking a seat next to Joel, I look up to find Dean glancing my way as he follows Seth onto the plane. A small smile plays across his lips before he turns to respond to something Seth says.

I wish I could tell him the news. Wish I could look at him without worrying about anyone catching us and growing suspicious.

"Did Nicholas tell you about Trevor?" Joel asks, pulling my attention from the goalie who had given me several orgasms last night.

Shaking off the memory, I turn to face my colleague. "Yeah."

Joel grins. "Congratulations, boss." He winks, and I raise an eyebrow.

"You don't seem surprised."

"Alanna, you and I both know that you deserve this opportunity. And it means you finally get to be behind the bench where you belong."

Excitement flutters in my belly. I hadn't even thought about that. I've only been behind the bench twice, but this time will be different. This time, it will all be up to me.

I just hope I don't let anyone down.

The next evening, I stand behind the bench with Joel at my side, a headset firmly in place over my ear while the players warm up on the ice.

The energy in the arena is electric. The Mounties are one

of the most popular teams in the league, and there are almost as many of their fans in the crowd as there are locals, and it's firing the players up more than any away game I've seen before.

Dean's in net tonight, and it's hard not to watch him as he crouches low, his eyes laser focused on his teammates as they practice taking shots. His last two games have been shutouts, and I know he's gunning for number three tonight.

With all the work we've been putting in lately, he's at the top of his game, and I'm confident he's being honest when he says the pain has lessened.

And by the time the puck drops, I'm swept up in the electricity that buzzes through the crowd, unable to believe that I finally get to be out here. It's a hell of a rush.

During the second intermission, I'm stitching up a cut on Lincoln's cheek while the rest of the team listen to Stephens discuss a series of plays he wants them working on. We're up by two points, but New York is playing dirty, and the Mounties players can't afford to grow complacent. This is the second lot of stitches I've done this game, having patched up a cut on the back of Ollie's neck earlier when a New York player's visor cut into him while they were fighting over the puck behind Dean's net.

"Make sure I still look pretty, Red," Lincoln says with a grin while I finish the third stitch.

"I'm sure you'll look just as pretty with a scar, O'Malley."

"Aw, you think I'm pretty?"

I roll my eyes and snip the thread. "Go on, you big flirt."

He chuckles and ambles off to join his teammates, completely at ease with the fact that he was bleeding profusely only moments ago. I have no doubt it stings, but these guys just roll with it, which I don't know if it's impressive or stupid. But it keeps me employed, so I can't complain.

Once I clean up my work station and remove my gloves, I move towards the training room, brushing against Dean's arm as I walk past where he's sitting near the door. I breathe in sharply when I feel his fingers brush against mine. It's the briefest of touches, over too quickly. But it's enough to get my heart racing.

"You look sexy as hell in that headset, Lahney. Like you belong out there," he murmurs quietly so that only I can hear when I pass, and I feel a tightening in my chest.

God I wish we could have more than these stolen moments.

There's two minutes left in the third period, and Dean is so close to his third shutout that you can feel the anticipation in the air. Every time New York has possession of the puck, it's like you can hear the Calgary fans draw a collective breath.

It takes all my willpower to keep my eyes off him as he hunkers down, his focus never leaving the trajectory of that little black disc as it's passed from player to player. But my job is to monitor the entire team, not just the goalie, so I force myself to remain focused, assessing for any injuries with each hit the players take.

Every check into the boards, every scramble for the puck, every raised stick - all are just one breath away from time off the ice. From a potential career ending injury. And it's my job to make sure nothing is left unnoticed.

Hockey is a fast-paced game, and I'm becoming addicted to the adrenaline. I rarely get the chance to watch like this, and I can understand the passion the fans are exhibiting the closer we get to the end of the game. The New York centre takes a shot on goal, but Dean's prepared, deflecting it with his stick, which is an impressive move. Usually goalies rely on their bodies or glove to defend the goal, as their sticks are less precise. But this just shows how good Dean is.

When the buzzer finally sounds, the players on the bench hit the ice to celebrate his third shutout in a row. His gaze finds mine before he disappears behind a wall of his teammates, and I can feel the heat burn through me. Something deep in my belly flutters, and I feel my cheeks heat while I look down at the folder in my hand. Around me, the coaching staff shake hands before filing out of the visitors bench and back down the tunnel to prepare for the usual media scrum. Forcing my legs to move, I follow behind, wishing I could throw my arms around Dean and share this victory with him.

Back in the locker room, the guys begin stripping their jerseys off while continuing to celebrate, chirping back and forth as they toss their sweaty uniforms into the laundry hampers the equipment guys have set up. One thing I don't think I'll ever get used to is the smell in a men's locker room. I've had so many women comment on how lucky I am to see these guys in various states of undress, but there is nothing sexy about the smell of twenty grown men after two hours of playing hockey.

I get to work helping various players with their cooldown routines, and the time flies by. The thrill of being in the thick of the action still hasn't worn off by the time I'm packing everything up and the guys are showering.

"Great work tonight, Alanna," Coach Stephens comments while I'm wiping down the treatment tables alongside Joel. The two of us worked better together tonight than we ever have before, and I can't help but think of the reason why.

"Thank you," I reply, unable to hide my smile at the praise.

Dean walks back into the room with a towel hanging low on his hips, catching the conversation, and I don't miss the proud smile on his face that quickly disappears when he remembers we're not alone. The rest of the team soon reappears, and I head out of the room to give them privacy while I put our treatment notes together.

"Are we celebrating tonight?" Sarah asks, sliding into the chair across from me in the visiting team's training office.

"I'm sure the guys will be up for it, based on how chirpy they all are in there right now. I doubt any of them will let Dean go without at least one celebratory drink," I reply with a grin.

"They are doing so well this season. I mean, obviously after winning last year, it's expected, but Dean is on fire. Whatever is going on with him, he's had a massive turnaround after last year's grumpy goalie nonsense."

I raise any eyebrow. "So he wasn't grumpy before last year?"

She shakes her head. "No. I mean, he was always sarcastic and stuff, and sometimes it's kind of hard to tell if he's being a dick or just joking around. But yeah, the snapping at teammates was new. Glad that's stopped. Maybe he's finally getting some again after his drought. Although I don't want to make it seem like going without sex is an excuse for a bad attitude." She takes a sip from her water bottle, completely oblivious to the fact that she's talking to the woman Dean is sleeping with.

"Well, whatever he's doing, it's obviously working for him," I reply, attempting to seem uninterested.

"Yeah. You guys have been working well together, too. Maybe he just needed to change trainers to get his mojo back."

I need to change the subject before this becomes any more awkward.

Thankfully, Coach Stephens knocks on the open doorframe, announcing it's time to head for the bus that will take us back to the hotel for dinner.

The support staff board before the players, and I end up in a seat on my own at the back. Finding the bus a little too warm, I shrug my jacket off and place it on my lap. Relieved for a moment to myself after such a busy evening, I slide my headphones on and rest my head against the back of the chair, closing my eyes.

I feel someone take a seat beside me and sigh inwardly. Hopefully whoever it is doesn't want to talk, because I'm drained.

Cracking my eye open, I'm surprised to find my seat mate is none other than the grumpy goalie who is never far from my mind.

"Hey. What are you doing?" I ask quietly.

The players generally don't sit with the support staff, with the exception of Sarah and Ollie.

"It was the last seat left," he replies with a smirk as I raise an eyebrow.

"Pretty sure that's not true."

He shrugs. "Don't know what to tell you, Lahney."

I shake my head with a sigh. "This is risky," I mutter under my breath as he places his hand on my thigh beneath my jacket.

"Only if we get caught," he replies.

He doesn't try to do anything more than squeeze my thigh gently, which is a good thing, because I'm not sure I'd have the willpower to stop him. We're surrounded by my colleagues while the rest of the team are towards the front of the bus, and it does look as though there were no other seats available, but it just seems awfully convenient. My heart races, and I can't tell if it's because of his proximity or the idea of someone finding his choice of seating suspicious.

"Are you going out to celebrate with everyone tonight?" I ask, keeping my voice steady as he traces a circle on my thigh with his finger.

"That depends on who else is going." The finger begins running back and forth along the inside seam of my leggings.

"Well, I'm sure most of the team are keen to celebrate with you." I reach beneath the jacket to wrap my hand around his fingers, squeezing as I flash him a warning look.

He chuckles and slides his hand away. "What about the training staff? Do they want to celebrate with us?"

I study him for a moment. There's a lightness to his expression, and I know he wants me to come out. Even though we can't do anything.

"Maybe. It's been a big night, and I was kind of looking forward to falling into bed."

He raises an eyebrow before leaning in closer. "And whose bed will you be falling into, Lahney?"

He says it so quietly that there is no way anyone else could have heard him, but it doesn't keep me from flicking my gaze across the aisle to where Joel is sitting next to David, the equipment manager. Joel has his phone to his ear, no doubt talking to his wife, while David is reading a book.

"We can't, Dean," I whisper back.

He grins and doesn't reply, simply sitting back in his seat before closing his eyes.

Great... Now I'm going to be thinking about being in his bed all night.

In the end, I decide not to join the others in celebrating. I wasn't lying when I said I was tired. Being in charge was more mentally draining than I'd expected, so when the team leaves to hit up some exclusive club, I head up to my room and take a shower.

We have three more games on this trip, but they are all against teams in the area, so the hotel we're in is our home for the next five nights, which is a novelty that only happens once or twice a season.

After an hour of reading, my eyes have grown so heavy that I'm not able to keep them open any longer, and I roll over to turn off the light. Just as I'm burrowing back into the comfy nest I've made myself, there's a light knock on the door. At first, I don't move, convinced it must be someone knocking on the door of the room next to mine. But when it comes again, a little louder this time, I groan and throw back the covers.

Padding to the door, I wrench it open and blink against the harsh light of hallway that pours in around the tall figure standing there. Even though I'm half asleep, my body still reacts to the sight of Dean standing before me in jeans, a dress shirt and his Mounties cap worn backwards. It honestly should be a crime how good he looks right now.

He slips inside while I'm still processing his sudden appearance, closing the door behind him with a grin.

"Hey," he says, sliding his arms around my waist as he backs me against the wall, my arms sliding around his neck automatically. "Cute PJ's."

I probably should have packed something sexier than my Minnie Mouse PJ's, but I really hadn't thought he'd see them. The idea of sneaking around on road trips might seem sexy, but I'm too scared of losing my job to entertain the idea.

"I thought you were out celebrating with everyone?" I murmur against his lips as he presses them to mine in a chaste kiss.

"I was. But I left them all to it because there was only one person I want to be with right now." He trails kisses down my throat.

"Well, that's very sweet. But I wasn't kidding when I said I was tired. I was just about to fall asleep."

He kisses his way back up to my ear. "That's okay. I just want to hold you. We never get to fall asleep together. That's all I want."

I pull back to look up at him and see the sincerity in his eyes in the dim light inside the room. The blockout curtains aren't really doing a great job, but I'm tired enough that it wasn't bothering me.

"What about in the morning? What if someone sees you leaving?"

He presses a kiss to my forehead. "I'm not sneaking out of here in the early hours, Lahney. I want to wake up next to you, even if it's just this once. We'll work that out in the morning. Please?"

Caving due to his pleading tone, I nod and he lets go of my waist, slipping a hand into mine and leading me back to bed.

I slide back between the sheets, and he strips off down to his boxers before climbing in behind me and spooning his body around mine.

It's been so long since I've fallen asleep beside someone else, but just like that first night we had together, I'm asleep within minutes, nestled safely in his warm embrace.

Chapter Thirty-Three

LIKE THE ENERGIZER BUNNY

Dean

After the best sleep I've had in months, I awake to find Alanna kissing her way down my chest, her lips feather-light as they brush against my abdominal muscles the further south she moves.

"Good morning," she whispers, lifting her eyes to meet mine when I run my fingers through her hair.

"Good morning. What are you doing?" I ask, the corners of my lips lifting as she continues to work her way down my body slowly.

"What does it look like? I'm celebrating your third shutout of the season the way you deserve." She reaches the waist band of my boxers and runs her hand over my erection through the thin fabric.

I groan, my eyes half closed as she moves her hand slowly back and forth.

"You don't have t-" I start to say, but she shushes me and slides the front of my boxers down, wrapping her hand around my cock.

When she bends to run her tongue over the tip, I jolt before melting back into the mattress as she takes me further into her mouth.

I force my eyes open to watch as she bobs her head, taking me further each time until I eventually hit the back of her throat. She barely gags, and I stare in amazement as she locks her eyes on mine while giving me the best morning blow job I've ever had. While I've gone down on her countless times now, I'm usually too eager to get inside her before she has a chance to get on her knees, and I have to force myself not to wrench her up and bury myself inside her.

"Fuck... Baby, if you don't slow down, I'm not going to be able to fuck you like I really, really need to right now," I say through gritted teeth as she swirls her tongue around me, her hand massaging my balls when she takes me all the way to the back of her throat once again.

She smiles, and I can tell she's determined to have me coming in her mouth, but I want her moaning while I'm inside her. I weave my hand into her hair and pull her head back gently.

"Naughty girl," I growl, and her eyes widen, arousal swirling in her gaze.

Sitting up abruptly, I pull her upwards and crush my mouth to hers. Once she's breathless, I reach over the side of the bed and grab my wallet to get the condom I'd slipped inside last night, knowing I'd eventually end up in her room, one way or another.

Tossing it next to my pillow, I roll her onto her back, shedding her cute as fuck pyjamas slowly while I kiss my way down her body. She sighs, running her fingers lazily through my hair when I settle between her now bare legs, kissing the inside of her right thigh as I stroke my finger lightly over her clit. A moan slips from her lips, and the hand in my hair tightens when I bend to draw her clit between my lips.

"God, Dean," she whispers, before losing the ability to speak when I pick up the pace.

I've become an expert on her body over the last few weeks, and she's coming within a minute, her back arching off the bed as she cries out while covering her mouth to muffle the sound.

I have no idea who is on either side of her room, but we definitely don't need anyone to hear her.

Before she has a chance to catch her breath, I flip her onto her stomach, sliding a pillow beneath her hips before rolling the condom on. Pressing my lips to her shoulder, I slide inside her, and she buries her face into her pillow to cover her moans.

Taking both her hands, I lace her fingers with mine as I hold them above her head and drive myself inside her, snapping my hips forward in time with each of her cries. I'm loving the affect I seem to have on her, knowing I'm driving her as crazy as she does me.

When I feel her inner walls start to flutter, I slide my hand beneath her to stroke her clit, and she bites the pillow to muffle her scream as she comes undone.

I breathe in sharply as she almost pulls me over the edge with her, pulling out before I lose control.

She's almost boneless when I lift her up, turning her so that she's straddling my lap. Giving her a chance to breathe, I run my tongue over her nipple, and once she's caught her breath again, I thrust upwards, sliding inside her once again.

"God, you're like the energizer bunny," she moans, and I chuckle as I hold her still while I drive myself upwards.

"Just have some energy to burn after last night," I tell her, as my own orgasm begins to build.

She brings her lips to mine, kissing me hungrily as she moves to meet me thrust for thrust, and pleasure shoots through me as her arms wrap around my body. Breaking the kiss, I muffle my groan against her throat, holding her close as my body shakes.

"It's going to make it extremely hard not to stay overnight now, knowing how good morning sex with you is," she murmurs into my hair, and I chuckle while I catch my breath.

"I want you in my bed all night, every night, Lahney. Just say the word, and I'll handcuff you to the headboard."

She pulls back to smirk down at me. "Didn't know you were into bondage, Mr Thomas?"

I brush my lips over hers before bringing our foreheads together. "Baby, when it comes to you, I'm into everything."

"So many pretty words," she whispers, wrapping her arms around me tighter.

God, what I wouldn't give to be able to wake up next to her like this every day.

Glancing at the clock, I groan and push her hair back behind her ear.

"We should get down to breakfast. The bus will be leaving in an hour."

She bites her lip, nodding. "Okay. You better go first. I need to take a shower."

I nod and we untangle ourselves so I can get dressed.

Bending to kiss her, I lift her chin to bring her eyes to mine. "We are sleeping in the same bed for the rest of this trip, Lahney. That is a promise."

She smiles shyly, nodding and after one final kiss, I let myself out, checking the hall to make sure it's empty before heading a few doors down to my own room, hating that I have no control over this situation and wishing we didn't have to hide away like this. Wishing I could declare to the world that I'm pretty sure I'm falling in love with Alanna Jameson.

Chapter Thirty-Four

DOUBLE SHIT

Dean

I feel like Alanna and I should receive an Academy Award each for how well we've kept our involvement under wraps from everyone around us. It's all been very professional, and not even Seth, with his damn near bloodhound skills when it comes to sniffing out shenanigans, has noticed anything different between us. She's been over every night since we threw caution to the wind, either at my apartment or in one of our hotel rooms when we've been travelling, but we still haven't had a sleepover at my apartment, and she leaves after only a few short hours. It's getting harder to say goodbye though, and I'm trying to work out how we can spend a night together at my place without having to sneak around.

But with her brother's imminent arrival, things are about to get a whole lot harder.

"Maybe we can just tell Charlie the truth?" I say the night before he's due to get in.

I'm watching the game between Winnipeg and Los Angeles while she's lying across my lap after dinner, reading through the latest research on one of the rookies injuries that he sustained during last night's game. I'd never realized just how much work went on behind the scenes for the training staff, and it just makes me respect her a whole lot more. I don't know if the male trainers put in even half the amount of effort that she does, but her dedication to the team is impressive. I've always found smart women to be a huge turn on. Although the fact that she's wearing nothing but my t-shirt and barely there underwear may also be adding to the intense attraction I'm feeling right now.

She rolls her head to the side to look at me around her tablet. "Why would we do that?"

I shrug, running my hand up and down her thigh and admiring the goosebumps that follow in it's wake. "So that he won't think it's weird when you don't come home after work straight away. Or why you're out on your nights off."

She raises up onto her elbows. "I mean... It's not like he'll say anything." She bites her lip as she studies my face. "What should I tell him?"

I grin, pulling her up so I can kiss her. "How about 'Hi Charlie, meet my boyfriend, the hottest man to ever rock my world. And by the way, he is the goalie on the hockey team I work for, so keep your mouth shut.'? I think that sounds good."

She smirks as she wraps her arms around my neck. "Boyfriend, huh?"

I raise an eyebrow. "Well, it's either boyfriend or the man who is fucking me senseless every night. Which do you think your brother would prefer to hear?"

She laughs, her head tipping back, exposing her throat, and I can't resist leaning in to kiss it. She shivers when I move my lips slowly down her throat, sliding my hand between her legs at the same time to brush her clit with my thumb over her lace underwear.

"So, what do you think? Can I come with you to pick him up from the airport?" I ask, sliding a finger inside her as I kiss my way back up to her mouth.

"Do you really want to talk about my brother while you're doing that?" she asks, gasping when I apply more pressure to her clit.

"No. So you should really say yes so I can get back to my task," I reply, leaning back slightly to look at her with a grin.

She rolls her eyes before moaning when I flick her clit. I keep working my hand slowly, determined to get an answer out of her even if I have to torture her to do it. She tries to urge me to pick up the pace by attempting to ride my hand, but I hold her still, and she groans.

"If I say yes, will you stop torturing me?"

I grin. "If you say yes, I'll go for three orgasms before I fuck you on the kitchen bench."

She raises an eyebrow. "Why the kitchen bench?"

I shrug, sliding my finger back inside her. "It's the right height for me to lay you down and fuck you while I'm standing without having to bend too much."

Her breath hitches as I curl my finger. "You've given this a lot of thought."

I bend to kiss her again. "I spend far too much time thinking about all the ways I want you, Lahney." I nip her lower lip, and she jerks in my lap. "Say yes, baby."

She groans, her head dropping back as I swipe my thumb lightly over her clit. "Fine. You can come with me and introduce yourself as my boyfriend."

I grin and apply more pressure with my thumb. "Good girl."

And then I reward her just like I promised. Because I'm nothing if not a man of my word.

The next day, Alanna and I drive to the airport together. We've got a few days off between home games, and it feels good to just hang out with her without having to think about work. We've not been game enough to go out on dates, given my high profile, so this is the closest we've gotten to being seen in public together.

We hang around the arrivals area while we wait for him, and I scan the crowd for any sign of him based on a recent photo she showed me when we got here. But instead of a tall redheaded man who looks eerily like his much shorter sister, my eyes find another redhead who is far more familiar.

And the sight of her has my heart racing.

"Shit," I mutter, and Alanna looks up at me as I pull my arm away from her shoulders.

"What is it?"

I don't answer immediately, continuing to scan the crowd and swallowing hard when I see Seth and Lincoln a few metres away. It's honestly a miracle they haven't spotted us already, but they are both focused on the woman who is moving towards them with a toddler on her hip while dragging a massive suitcase behind her.

"Double shit," I say, turning my back to my friends and hoping they don't notice me. "Tara must have come via Auckland."

Alanna's eyes widen after a moment as my words sink in. She glances around me, and I can tell the moment she catches sight of the guys, because she straightens quickly and stares up at me as she uses my body as a shield.

"What do we do?" she asks, and I can hear the panic in her voice.

I open my mouth to reply, but a voice to our right cuts in.

"Alanna!" Charlie is barrelling through the crowd towards us.

I'm too nervous to turn around and see if the guys heard him while Alanna turns on the biggest smile she can muster, staying where she is and waiting for her brother to come to us. I step back to give them space, and he wraps his arms around her, lifting her off her feet. She squeals before laughing.

I knew Charlie played rugby at a semi-pro level, but I hadn't expected him to be so built, and am surprised by how strong he is. I'm still taller than him, but I'm pretty sure he could take any of the guys on the team and come out ahead. Guess Alanna and Kylie weren't exaggerating about how strong rugby players are.

"Put me down, you big oaf." Alanna smacks her brother's arm, and he grins, lowering her back to the ground.

"Well, it's been over a year since I've seen you. I got a bit excited," he replies, and I notice his accent is thicker than his sister's.

"Well, I suppose I can overlook the manhandling just this once." Alanna grins up at him for a moment before turning to look at me. "Charlie, I want you to meet -"

"Dean?"

I close my eyes for a second, cursing under my breath before turning slowly to find Seth, Lincoln and an exhausted-looking Tara standing a few feet away. Lincoln has Tara's daughter, Brandie, in his arms, but she's trying to crawl all over him, so he is slightly distracted.

Seth isn't, though, and he's already noticed who's beside me. "What's going on?"

"Hi, Seth! What a surprise to see you here," Alanna says brightly.

Too brightly.

My girlfriend doesn't do brightly.

Seth's eyes narrow as he glances between the two of us, then looks at Charlie.

"My car broke down yesterday after work, so Dean offered to drive me to pick up my brother today," Alanna continues, reaching the point of babbling.

I want to reach out to calm her down, but that definitely won't work, so instead, I nod. "Yep. Her car is constantly breaking down lately. I had nothing else on, so figured it was the least I could do after everything she's done for me lately."

It's clear from his dark expression that Seth doesn't believe us, but Charlie sticks his hand out to introduce himself to me first, before doing the same with the guys. Then he smiles at Tara.

"I see you found your friends? Hopefully Brandie calms down a bit for you now," he says kindly, and the rest of us raise our eyebrows, glancing between the two of them.

"You guys know each other?" Alanna asks.

Charlie and Tara nod. "Charlie was unfortunate enough to be stuck sitting next to us after our flight connected in Auckland. Brandie was good for the first few hours, but then boredom set in and she turned into an unholy terror." Tara gestures towards where Brandie is attempting to fling herself out of Lincoln's arms. "Like that." Brandie lets out a shriek, glaring at Lincoln as he keeps a tight hold on her.

She seems like she is really set on trying to smash her head onto the tiled floor right now, judging by the constant escape attempts she's making.

"Well, let's get you guys home, and Lincoln and I can tire her out while you take a breather," Seth says, and I'm just relieved that his attention is no longer on Alanna and me.

I'm not entirely sure dealing with an overtired toddler is going to help Seth's cause with his wife right now, but I'm eager to get the hell out of here and away from his accusing gaze, so I clap my hands together.

"Anyway, we should go. I have a date tonight, so need to get these guys home," I say, trying not to look at Alanna as I lie through my teeth.

Seth still doesn't look convinced, but Lincoln has had

enough, shoving the toddler at our captain and dragging Tara out of there with a "See-ya!" in our direction. Seth has no choice but to follow as Brandie tries to kick her way free.

I have no doubt I'll be hearing from him once he has a chance to take a breath, though.

Not looking forward to that.

"You know you guys are acting weird, right?" Charlie asks, looking between Alanna and me.

Alanna sighs. "I'll explain in the car."

When we get to my truck, I let Alanna do the talking, and Charlie frowns at me in the rearview mirror as I back out of the car space.

"So now you're going on a date, even though you're secretly dating my sister?"

I huff a laugh. "No. I just said that because Seth clearly knew something was up, and I was trying to throw him off. I don't think it worked, though." I reach over and squeeze Alanna's hand. "Sorry babe. I should have just let you get Charlie on your own."

She sighs and squeezes back. "It's okay. Worst bloody timing, though. Of all the flights for Tara to be on."

"Tara was pretty cool. Sucks she had to deal with that on her own, but she said her husband couldn't make it this time," Charlie says.

"Yeah, he's studying and in the middle of exams apparently," I reply.

"Well, with how out-of-control Brandie was on that flight, I'm sure Seth will be too distracted to give you guys the third degree for a while."

"Maybe," I reply, just praying he's right.

Chapter Thirty-Five

THE ONLY ONE I WANT

Alanna

After we stop at Dean's for dinner, I bundle Charlie into my very much not broken-down car and start the drive home.

"So... About this whole secret relationship thing..." he says once we're alone, his tone serious.

I flick him a questioning look before returning my attention to the road, waiting for him to get out whatever is bothering him about Dean and me.

"Is he worth potentially destroying your career for?"

And there it is.

I sigh. "Believe me, I'm very aware of how dangerous this all is for my career. But I tried to fight my feelings for him, and no matter what I did, I couldn't push those feelings aside. He's incredibly difficult to ignore."

"I get that. But..." I can tell he's trying to be careful with his words, which is a surprisingly new thing when it comes to my loud and sometime obnoxious twin brother. "You've worked so hard to get where you are, and you love your job."

I nod, still keeping my eyes on the road to avoid meeting his worried gaze. "I know. And we're both incredibly careful when we're at work. We're both old enough to know how to keep things professional."

"Except two of his teammates saw you together tonight..."

The reminder makes me groan. "I know. That definitely wasn't ideal. I just have to hope that Seth is too caught up with Tara's arrival to focus too much on our terrible poker faces. I cannot believe that the first time we try to go anywhere in public together, we end up face to face with his two best friends."

"I just hope you know what you're doing, Lahney. He seems nice and all, but if this blows up, you're the one who's going to end up out in the cold, as shitty as that is."

I reach over to squeeze his knee. "Thank you for caring. But you don't have to worry about me."

He snorts. "I have been worrying about you since we came out of the womb, sister. Not going to change now."

I grin at him. "I thought I was the one worrying about you."

We drop the subject of Dean and our secret relationship and move on to discussing the state of Charlie's marriage.

"So Tilley still won't come home?" I ask.

Charlie sighs, and I see him shake his head out of the corner of my eye. "No. She's gone back to her mum's, and you know how much that woman hates me."

"I'm sure she'll change her mind soon. Does she know you're here?"

"Yeah. I keep her updated on everything and constantly tell her how much I love her. Sometimes she replies, so at least I know she hasn't blocked my number."

It breaks my heart to see my brother hurting like this, and I know reminding him that Tilley has a point when it comes to Dad won't help, so I stay silent.

We arrive at the house, and Tierney meets us at the door with a smile.

"Hey!" She throws her arms around Charlie, and I laugh at the stunned look on his face.

"Um, hi," he says once he manages to untangle himself from her hug.

"Charlie, meet Tierney. Tierney is very happy to have someone else's brother around for a change," I say, still grinning.

Tierney nods enthusiastically. "Correct. I'm hoping that when my brother sees how *not* overprotective you are, he might remember how to be a brother instead of a father."

"Okay... Cool." Charlie blinks a few times, and I can tell that he's struggling to process exactly what Tierney said.

He's not stupid, but jet lag is clearly making him a little slower on the uptake.

"How about I show you where you can take a shower? I ended up buying a mattress so that you can crash on the floor in the study nook. Figured it would give you at least a little bit more privacy than the couch."

Charlie nods gratefully, and I show him where he can dump his suitcase, before pointing across the hall to the bathroom. While he gets settled, I follow Tierney into the living room and flop down on the couch beside her.

"I feel like I haven't seen you properly in weeks," she says, picking her mug up off the coffee table.

I try to ignore the stab of guilt I feel when I see the sadness in her expression. We have grown so used to spending all our free time together that it hurts not being able to tell her what's going on. But it's just too risky, because if she says anything that might raise Riley's suspicions, we're screwed.

"Sorry. Work has just been so busy."

It's not exactly a lie, because when I took over as Dean's

primary trainer, I still kept my other players as well. So I have been busier... Just not in the way she thinks...

"I know. I still miss you, though. Will I see you more now that Charlie is here?"

I nod. "Yeah. I'll do my best to leave work on time when I'm in town. Are you sure you're okay with him staying here when I'm on the road next week, though? I can book him a hotel, otherwise?"

She shakes her head. "No, it's fine. He can watch all the bad shows with me that you don't have time for anymore." She's grinning, but it still doesn't keep me from feeling like a shitty friend.

Not for the first time, I wonder if this whole situation with Dean is worth all the secrets and lies. While I might not be the most open person, I don't lie to my loved ones, and now I'm lying to absolutely everyone about what is fast becoming the most important relationship in my life. But despite the guilt I'm feeling, I'm not ready to give him up. I'm not sure that I ever will be. Which just makes this all the more dangerous.

It's still dark out when I wake up the next morning to find my brother standing over me, and I give a little shriek.

"Jesus Christ, Charlie! What the hell?!" I yell, hand to my chest as I sit up quickly.

"Sorry! I was about to wake you up when you opened your eyes." He grins, while I try to get my heart rate back under control.

"Why are you hovering over me at-" I grab my phone to check the time, "6am?!"

I have the day off to help him get settled, and was really looking forward to a sleep in. The team has a game tonight and it's my first chance to attend a game as a spectator only. But I'd like to do that after a decent sleep, and that now appears to be wishful thinking.

"I want to go for a run."

"And you needed to wake me up to do it?" I rake a hand through my hair, still not entirely awake.

"What's going on?" Tierney appears at the door, rubbing her eyes.

"Charlie is an asshole, that's what's going on," I grumble as my brother laughs.

"I want to go for a run, and was going to wake Alanna to see if she wanted to come, too. But she woke up as I was about to wake her, and screamed blue murder."

"Fun times. I'm going back to bed," Tierney mutters, and I shake my head.

"Na-ah. If I'm going for a run in the dark, so are you," I reply, and she rolls her eyes as I turn back to Charlie. "You're lucky it hasn't snowed yet, or there would be no running happening."

He bounds off with a dopey grin while I continue to mutter to myself about annoying siblings.

Ten minutes later, the three of us are dressed and in my car with the heater on. While it may not have snowed recently, it's still freezing outside and I'm not sure why I agreed to this insanity.

"Should we ask Dean to come?" Charlie asks, and I whip my head around to look at him.

"Why would we do that?"

"How do you know Dean?" Tierney asks at the same time, her eyebrows knitted together in confusion.

"Oh..." Charlie stares at me with a panicked look on his face while I silently curse my idiot brother. "Um..."

Tierney turns to look at me, a smile slowly spreading across her lips. "How does he know Dean, Lahney?" she asks in a sing-song voice.

I groan as I throw the car into drive. "I hate you both."

Tierney claps her hands together. "I knew it! I knew something was going on with you two!"

"No you didn't," I reply, pulling out of the driveway.

"I totally did. You're never home anymore and it's been ever since you got back from that trip where you were wailing about all the orgasms he gave you."

"I did not need to know that," Charlie interjects from the backseat.

I glare at him in the rear vision mirror. "Shut up, big mouth."

They spend the rest of the drive giving me a hard time about my secret boyfriend, and once we arrive at Glenmore Reservoir, I'm ready to murder them both. Once we're out of the car, I pull Tierney aside, fixing her with a pleading look.

"You absolutely can not say anything to Riley."

She shakes her head. "I already told you that I wouldn't say anything." She sounds wounded that I'd think she wasn't trustworthy, and I feel guilty for a moment, but I squeeze her hand as I hold her gaze.

"I know. But I can't lose my job. And the more people who know, the more likely that's what will happen."

I know she's a good friend and wouldn't say anything on purpose. But there is so much on the line with with more people now knowing - or at least suspecting - something is going on, and I can feel anxiety kicking in. I love my job, despite the shit with Trevor.

Unfortunately, I'm also beginning to realize my feelings for Dean are growing stronger, too.

Just as I'm having this rather alarming realisation, a very

familiar truck pulls into the parking lot, and Tierney's grin widens.

"What a coincidence. It's your secret boyfriend."

I glare at her as Dean rolls to a stop alongside us, and Tierney's face falls when she sees her brother in the passenger seat.

"Hey! What are you guys doing here?" Riley asks, climbing out of the truck.

Dean remains quiet as he gets out of the driver's seat, eyeing Charlie warily. If only he knew that we also have Tierney to worry about now. But I can't say anything in front of Riley, so that bombshell is going to have to wait.

"Charlie's jet lag decided we should go for a run before the sun came up," I reply, before introducing Riley to my brother.

Dean sticks his hand out, introducing himself to Charlie like he didn't spend all of last night with him. My brother looks amused at the awkward position I've found myself in, smirking at me as he pretends he's never met my boyfriend before.

"Well, I guess we can all run together, then." Riley is so oblivious to everything, it's almost sad.

But I'd rather he remain oblivious than work out that something is going on between me and his teammate.

We move towards the path and start off at a slow jog. Tierney and I are both competent runners, but the guys have much longer legs, and after the first five hundred metres it's obvious they are trying to shorten their paces to stay with us while flashing looks at each other.

"Go on, I can feel you itching to see if rugby players are faster than hockey players," I say after a few minutes of this.

Charlie flashes me a grin and takes off. It takes Riley and Dean a moment to realize what's going on, but a few beats later, they are both gone too, leaving me alone with Tierney.

We slow to a walk without saying anything, and I know she wants to hammer me with questions about Dean.

Sure enough, as soon as the guys are out of sight, she starts talking.

"So... Is this serious between you guys? Or just sex?"

"He introduced himself to Charlie as my boyfriend last night, so... I guess serious."

She cocks her head to the side to study me. "Why don't you sound sure about this?"

I hesitate before answering, trying to sort through the mess of thoughts in my head. "Because although I have some pretty strong feelings for him, how can this go anywhere? It's my job that will be on the line if this gets out. But..." I let out a breath, about to be more honest with myself than I've been since this started. "I'm falling for him, T. And I don't know how to stop."

She puts her arm around me and squeezes, quiet for a few beats too long.

"I guess you need to work out if he's worth losing everything you've been working towards. Because if this gets out..." She doesn't need to finish that sentence.

Because we both know how this will end if this gets out. And it won't lead to a happily ever after.

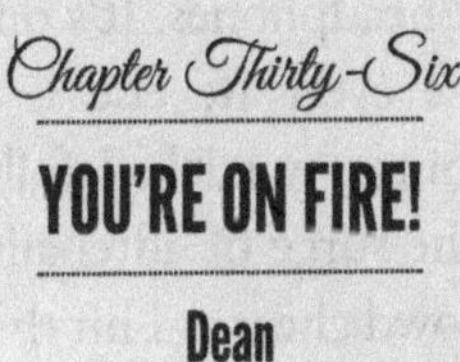

YOU'RE ON FIRE!

Dean

It feels strange to be prepping for a game without Alanna. I hadn't realized how much I'd become used to her presence until she wasn't around, and I'm not sure I like it.

I'm trying not to cling to my superstitions, but any time my routine changes, it's been a struggle not to worry that I'm going to end up injured again.

But at least I know Alanna is here, watching me. She's texted to say she would be watching from the family box with Charlie and the WAGs, so that's something, I guess. Just wish she was the one helping me stretch and go through my pregame reflex exercises.

I've avoided Seth for most of the day. It was easy enough during morning skate when I was working with Oscar and Mark. One of the joys of being the goalie is that I can switch off from the rest of the team and focus entirely on what the goalie coach has to say, which was more than welcome today when I'd seen the look on Seth's face when he arrived a few minutes before I escaped onto the ice. Now that we're all in the locker room ahead of warmup, though, it's a little harder to avoid his suspicious gaze.

Actually, maybe it's a good thing Alanna isn't here, after all.

Instead of allowing him to get inside my head, I practice my breathing techniques, closing my eyes while I listen to the music pumping through my headphones. It's only when Lincoln taps my arm that I realize everyone else is heading towards the players tunnel. Grabbing my stick, I follow behind my teammates and welcome the surge of adrenaline that races through me when I hear the crowd cheer as I hit the ice first.

I don't think I'll ever grow tired of this feeling.

With only a few minutes left in the game, the team is on fire tonight. With the score currently at four to zero against Pittsburgh, I'm closing in on my fifth shutout of the season, and I'm trying not to let the pressure get to me. Anders has taken possession of the puck and skates behind my net while he waits for Mitchell and Maxim to get into position. I keep my eyes trained on Pittsburgh's captain, Hans, when he gets a little too close to me. We used to play together in Los Angeles, and he's been hanging around a little too much for my liking. The one goal he'd made was denied due to goaltender interference, so he's particularly annoyed with me now. Even though it was all his own fault. He was always a bit of a dick, but we've not had beef before.

When Anders finds space and starts to streak down the ice, Hans takes off after him, and I allow myself to relax a little.

Anders drives to the net and takes the shot that flies past their goalie's blocker. The buzzer goes off as the crowd goes wild, and the clock stops with forty-three seconds left to go in the game.

I turn to grab my water bottle from the top of the net, squirting water into my mouth through the cage of my helmet. For once, my body isn't aching all over, and it's a relief to know that all the exercises Alanna has had me working on are finally paying off. Now I just need to make it through the next forty-three seconds and I can celebrate with my friends and secret girlfriend when we all head back to Seth and Kylie's house for a movie night.

Our fourth line takes the ice for the face-off and I crouch back down, watching the puck closely. With five goals under our belt, all we need to do is keep the puck away from Pittsburgh for the next thirty-nine seconds and run down the clock.

Of course, this is the moment when Pittsburgh's star rookie decides to finally step up his game, throwing a fierce body check and stealing the puck. I expect the refs to call a penalty, but I guess they've decided to let it play out. There's a loud chorus of boos from the crowd, but I block it out while I track the puck as the Pittsburgh forwards flick it back and forth, making their way towards my net. Our defence deflects the puck into the corner and attempt to steal it back, but Pittsburgh has upped their physicality, making one last push to break the shutout.

After another big hit from the rookie, it's obvious the refs have fallen asleep, but I can't focus on anything other than the three forwards in my zone cycling the puck behind the net. I'm determined that I'm not going to lose this shutout now with only fifteen seconds left in the game, hunkering down with my glove hand up, ready for whatever they are about to try.

With seconds to go, the rookie takes his shot, aiming for my right side. My reflexes take over and I slide down into the splits with my arm out, stopping the puck inches from the goal post just as the final buzzer goes off. The crowd erupts as my teammates hit the ice, barrelling towards me.

I'm sure they are all grinning, but I keep my head down for a minute, holding my breath as the pain courses through my lower back and hip. Lincoln and Riley help me up, but neither of them seem to notice that I'm injured.

"Fucking five shutouts, baby! You're on fire!" Lincoln screams in my ear.

I brace myself as Seth reaches the net and slaps me on the back. It shouldn't hurt like it does, but the shock reverberates down my spine, and the pain in my back almost steals my breath away.

As the rest of guys tap their helmets to mine, I concentrate on making sure I activate my core muscles like I've been working on with Alanna and just hope that I can make it back to the locker room without collapsing.

Chapter Thirty-Seven

DON'T HURT LINCOLN, HE'S TOO PRETTY!

Alanna

I'm sitting in the family box for the first time since I started working for the Mounties, and I could definitely get used to this. A large selection of food has been laid out, and we have our own bartender, meaning we don't have to venture out into the crowd between periods. Something I'm told is like a battle to the death to make it to the bathroom before the rest of the women in the crowded arena.

"Have you been to a game before?" I ask, leaning across Charlie to look at Tara.

She grins back, her eyes shining. "Yeah, when we came out two years ago, my friends and I got to see two games. We're probably a little spoiled, because we've only ever been in here, rather than down with the general public," she says, waving down at the crowd below.

Charlie is staring with an open mouth, wide-eyed, as the guys zip around in the middle of the arena. "Wow, this game is fucking fast," he says, and I can hear the awe in his voice.

"Right? Even the games without many goals are impressive," I reply, keeping my eyes trained on Seth and Lincoln when they zoom along the ice.

In the year and a half that I've worked with the team, this is the first time I've attended a game as a spectator only, and I have to admit, it's pretty thrilling.

"I still don't quite get the rules, though," Charlie admits, and I grin, turning to look at him.

"Don't tell anyone, but neither do I," I whisper back.

Tara snorts on Charlie's other side, and Kylie grins across at me from beside her. Apparently Kylie hasn't let Tara out of her sight since she arrived, and the pretty redhead is now enjoying some kid-free time while Kylie's grandparents babysit her hurricane of a child back at Seth and Kylie's place.

"None of us get the rules, other than puck-in-net means yay," Kylie says, keeping her voice low so that none of the other WAGs in the box can hear her.

This is what happens when you have a group of Aussies and Kiwis trying to work things out on their own at an ice hockey game. Sarah is busy filming content for the social media account, Tierney had to work tonight, and Adele left a few minutes ago to take Milo out to do his business, so unless we want to ask Bethany and her entourage questions, we're on our own.

And none of us want to talk to Bethany.

"Right? Like... why are they allowed to smash each other around like that?" Tara asks, gasping as Lincoln is smashed into the boards by one of the Pittsburg players. "Don't hurt Lincoln, he's too pretty!"

I snort at the indignation in her voice. The further we've gotten into the game, the more violent it's become. Even I know that at least some of the hits should have been penalties. It's like the ref has fallen asleep, or is just blind to anything the Pittsburg players are doing.

At least Dean looks to be on track for his fifth shutout of the season. I've spent far too much time during the game staring down at my boyfriend with butterflies in my stomach. Each time he's blocked Pittsburg's attempts at a goal, it's made me even hotter under the collar, and I can't wait to climb him later. If we can manage to steal some alone time.

Kylie and Seth have organized for a few of us to head back to their place for a movie night after dinner. Without me knowing how it happened, I seem to now be considered part of their inner circle. I suspect it's Sarah's doing. So there's no way we can get out of it without raising any suspicions. This whole sneaking around thing is really starting to get old.

A chorus of boos from the crowd pulls me from my musings, and I lean forward to watch as one of the Pittsburg players steals the puck from Riley after knocking him to the ground, tearing back towards their goal, where Dean is crouched with his glove up. I honestly don't know how he deals with the stress when players are flying at him like that, but he seems to be completely in control down there.

The Pittsburg player takes the shot, and Dean slides down, doing a full split with his glove hand stretched out. The buzzer goes off just as his glove comes down on the puck right in front of the net, and the crowd goes absolutely crazy.

Everyone in the family box starts celebrating, high-fiving one another while cheering loudly.

Adele reappears with Milo and it's smiles all-round as Charlie throws his arms around me, but the way that Dean is hanging his head has me concerned. He hasn't risen from the awkward split position, and it seems like he's in pain. No one else seems to notice when he only gets to his feet with the help of Lincoln and Riley, who both clap him on the back. Lincoln is yelling something, no doubt celebrating the shutout, and Seth skates up to tap his helmet against Dean's. While they are too far away for me to fully read their expressions, none of them appear to be concerned about the fact that Dean's clearly injured, which has me wondering if I imagined it.

Maybe it's just the athletic trainer in me, or the fact that it's my boyfriend down there, but there's no hiding the way he's favouring his hip as he skates off the ice a few minutes later, and I have to stop myself from rushing down there to check on him.

My eyes narrow as I focus on his hips when he steps into the players tunnel, and I can tell he's favouring his left side once again.

When he's named first star of the game, he skates back out, waving his hand at the crowd. He is definitely favouring his hip, skating slower than normal before coming to a stop in front of a child from the crowd, placing a large gold chain around her neck, with the Mounties logo glinting in the light.

He better hope he's honest with me when I finally talk to him, because there's no way that's one of his regular aches.

Chapter Thirty-Eight

PROVE IT TO ME

Dean

When no one else seems to notice that I'm moving slower than usual, I decide to just see how I go overnight. Surely I've just pulled a muscle and it'll sort itself out? I've been playing so well lately that I'm scared to say anything to any of the trainers, in case they insist I need to be put on the injured-reserve list for the next few games. And maybe Alanna will be able to come and work on it for me later tonight, if she's able to sneak out for a while.

I finally check my phone after showering to see a stream of messages from her.

ALANNA

Charlie is now officially a Mounties fan. He is very impressed with your reflexes.

I could totally get used to being in this cushy box. Although some of the WAGs scare me. Bethany actually asked me if I was lost when I walked in, even though I was with Kylie and Adele.

So close to a shutout!

Sorry, that probably jinxed you. But you won't see this til later…

But it's the last message that makes me groan.

ALANNA

You better not be hiding that injury, buddy. No one else in here noticed, but I saw how you skated off the ice.

Fabulous. I'd really hoped I'd be able to pass it off as nothing with her, but of course she noticed. That woman has the eyes of a hawk.

I message her to say I'm fine, but it's clear she doesn't believe me.

ALANNA

Nice try. I'll be waiting by your truck.

DEAN

What about Charlie?

ALANNA

He's catching a ride with Kylie and Tara to dinner. I told them I need to do some paperwork and will get a lift with someone.

DEAN

Probably not such a great idea. Seth has been super vigilant today.

ALANNA

Nice try. Get your ass down here now.

I sigh and grab my backpack, trying not to wince when the pain radiates from my back straight down my left leg. If I can just get some painkillers in me, I know I'll be fine. But there's no chance they'll work before my girlfriend gets her hands on me.

I hang back a bit to let the rest of the guys leave first, hoping that by the time I get to the parking lot, they'll all have left and I won't have to worry about smuggling Alanna into my truck.

I arrive to find her leaning against the driver's door, and am relieved to see my vehicle is the last one left.

"Hey. Did anyone see you?" I ask, bending to kiss her cheek.

She shrugs. "Riley did, but I told him I was just walking Charlie down. They left a few minutes ago, and I pretended to head back upstairs." She runs her eyes over me. "Where does it hurt?"

I sigh. "I'm fine, really."

She scowls. "Don't do that."

I try for a charming smile. "Do what?"

The scowl deepens. "Lie to me about your injury. Did you tell Simon when you came off the ice?"

"There was nothing to tell Simon. I'm fine. I just need some Advil and will be good to go," I say, reaching out to tug her closer. She resists, and I let my arms fall back to my sides. "Lahney, I promise, I'm fine."

"Alright then. Fuck me in your truck right now."

I stare at her. "What?"

"If you're so fine, then you'll be able to fuck me in your truck without it hurting. Prove it to me."

I can tell she is waiting for me to call her bluff. There's no way she'd actually want me to fuck her in my truck at work.

But she's forgetting that I'm as stubborn as she is, so I open the door and wave my hand towards the backseat. "After you, then."

She grits her teeth, but climbs in and turns quickly to watch me. I school my expression to hide a wince when I lift my leg to climb in after her, but she catches it. Because of course she does.

"Dean, for fuck's sake! You are hurt. Why are you trying to lie about this?" She climbs back out to glare at me.

"Because I'm fine," I say, starting to feel like a broken record. "Hockey players hurt after games, Alanna. It's part of the game." She jabs her finger into my hip, and I yelp as my leg buckles slightly. "Fucking hell! What'd you do that for?"

"Because that's not a normal reaction to just being a bit sore after a game, and you know it."

I bite back an angry response, not wanting to fight with her about this.

Taking a deep breath, I just shake my head. "Can we please just go and have dinner?"

She continues to glare at me, and I wonder if she's actually going to start yelling. But after a moment, she just sighs and walks around to the passenger side, shaking her head.

"You've got tonight. If that is still playing up tomorrow, you and I are going to have some serious words. And don't even think about trying to sweet talk me right now, because I'm pissed at you."

Well, this is going to be a fun evening.

At dinner, Alanna sits across from me, deep in conversation with Charlie, Kylie and Tara. Seems as though Tara has roped Alanna and Charlie into helping her convince Kylie that she actually *can* manage juggling twins. I'm just relieved not to have Alanna glaring at me, but I wonder if we're going to end up arguing about my non-injury later tonight.

"Did you realize your shutout tonight has you top of the leaderboard?" Seth asks as he digs into his dinner.

"Yeah, Coach mentioned it when I spoke to him earlier. I've been so focused on staying on top of all my aches that I kind of forgot about my stats over the last few games."

Lincoln raises an eyebrow as he watches me from across the table. He's sitting next to Alanna with Adele on his other side, but Adele is preoccupied, chatting to Sarah.

"That's not like you. You're usually all over your stats."

I shrug, because I don't really have an answer to that. I've become so distracted with Alanna and keeping our relationship under wraps that I'm starting to realize it's pulling my focus from where it should be. I've been in relationships before and know I'm more than capable of keeping my head in the game. But this is the first time I've been forced to keep a relationship a secret, and it's starting to mess with my head more than I realized.

The guys continue chatting around me but I simply focus on getting through dinner. I'm already regretting agreeing to go back to Seth's place later, but he's trying to keep Kylie happy, and it's not worth pissing him off right now. He still hasn't said anything to me directly about Alanna and it's best to just keep on his good side.

Once everyone has finished eating, we head back to the James-Davidson house. Ollie, Sarah and Riley join us as well, so it's a fairly full house when we arrive, with various cars parked in the driveway and on the street out the front. Lincoln and Adele only live down the road, so they get changed at home before joining us, but the other guys and I change out of our suits here before we all pile into the media room. Despite the fact that Alanna is still pissed at me, I wish I was able to pull her into my lap like my teammates do with their partners.

As the night drags on, the pain in my hip grows steadily worse, and I slip off to the bathroom to down some Advil without an audience. When I come back out, I find Alanna in the hall, leaning against the wall opposite the door.

"Hey," I say warily, my eyes zeroing in on the line between her brows.

The one that only appears when she's frustrated as fuck with me.

"It's still hurting, isn't it?" she asks, keeping her voice low.

I sigh, scrubbing my hand over my face. There's no point denying it now, so I nod.

"You need to get Nicholas to look at it tomorrow morning."

I shake my head. "He'll just bench me, and I can't be off the ice again, Lahney."

She glares at me. "Are you seriously saying that you expect me to just say nothing? This is serious, Dean."

"It's just a strained muscle. I don't need to go running off to the team doctor for every single little ache in my body. I'll ice it tonight, just like always, and it'll be fine in a few days."

She throws her hands up in the air. "I swear to god, this is like arguing with a fucking brick wall."

"What's going on?" Seth asks, and we both turn quickly to see him standing at the end of the hall with his arms crossed.

"Nothing," I reply.

But Alanna has clearly had enough. "He hurt his hip again at the end of the game and is being a stubborn asshole about it," she says, turning to look at Seth.

I gape at the side of her head. "Are you kidding me right now? You just ratted me out to my captain, Alanna."

She turns back to glare at me again. "Well, someone had to be the grown-up in this relationship, and it clearly wasn't going to be you."

"Un-fucking-believable," I say, before realizing she's just admitted we're in a relationship in front of Seth.

I look towards my friend who is watching all of this with a stoney expression, and I don't know whether to laugh or cry.

"I'm going home. I'll see you at work tomorrow, and you

better be prepared to tell Nicholas, or I'll be doing it for you," Alanna says, pushing past me and storming back towards the media room, where the movie is still playing loudly.

I hear her tell Charlie they are leaving and ask Riley to give her ride home, and I know I've fucked up royally. I also know better than to run after her right now. So instead, I face off against my captain and wait for him to unload.

"Relationship, huh?" he asks, still watching me with his arms crossed.

No point in lying about it now. "Yeah," I reply, letting my head fall back against the closed bathroom door.

"How long has this been going on?" His voice is scarily calm, and I almost wish he was yelling right now.

"About two months."

He groans. "Christ, Dean. You know it's against the rules. She'll lose her job if anyone finds out. And for what? Is this just some fling?"

"Fuck no," I snap. "I'm in love with her."

"Who are you in love with?" Lincoln asks, appearing behind Seth. "Why are we all hanging out in the hall in front of the bathroom?"

"Dean and Alanna are in a relationship, apparently," Seth replies, and I sigh.

"Let's just tell everyone, shall we?"

Lincoln gapes at me. "What the fuck? Are you trying to get her fired?"

I throw my hands up, straightening again to face off against both of them. "No, I'm trying to do the exact opposite of that, which is why we've been keeping it to ourselves."

Seth shakes his head. "There's no way this is going to end positively, for either of you."

"Thanks for the vote of confidence, captain," I spit out.

He raises an eyebrow. "Dean. How do you think this is

going to go? She is the only female trainer on the team and she's just starting out in her career here. She's risking that for you. And now you're being a stubborn dick and trying to hide injuries?"

"You're hiding injuries, too? What the fuck, man?" Lincoln interjects, and at this point, everyone else may as well just join the conversation, because he sure as shit isn't keeping his voice down.

"You need to sort this out. I'm pulling rank. You are seeing Nicholas in the morning to get assessed. And work something out with Alanna, because you owe it to her for putting her job on the line. We'll keep the whole relationship thing to ourselves for now, but the second it causes a problem, I have no choice but to say something," Seth says.

I clench my teeth, but keep myself from retorting, and they exchange a look before Seth returns to the others and Lincoln waves his hand towards the closed door behind me. I step aside so he can head into the bathroom, and once he closes the door, I return to the media room to grab my backpack.

"I'm gonna head home. See you guys later." I wave at everyone without meeting Seth's eye, catching the way Kylie is looking between us with her head tilted to the side.

No doubt things are about to get a whole lot worse, but right now, I just need to get the fuck out of here.

I leave without another word, and when I get home, I collapse onto my bed and spend the next few hours staring at the ceiling, trying to work out what the hell I'm doing.

Chapter Thirty-Nine

GOING TO END IT

Alanna

I can't believe I opened my stupid mouth in front of Seth.

I'd been so angry with Dean that the words slipped out before I could stop myself. The second Seth's eyebrows had raised, I knew I'd screwed up.

Watching Dean hide his injury is bringing a lot of memories of my childhood to the surface. While I know he's nothing like my father, I can't shake the feeling that this is the start of things spiralling out of control, and I wonder how I'm going to handle this.

The next morning, I'm a jittery mess the whole drive to work, terrified of what I'm about to walk into.

Am I about to be fired? Is Trevor going to be sitting behind his desk with a smug smile on his face, telling anyone who will listen how he knew women didn't belong in this role, because we can't keep our legs closed around the players?

How could I be so stupid? I let my personal relationship with Dean cloud my judgement.

When I park my car, I sit for a moment, listening to the engine tick as it cools while preparing myself for what will inevitably happen when I walk inside. Guess I better message

Tierney and tell her she'll be looking for a new roommate, because I'm about to be deported.

I've never been prone to catastrophizing before, but apparently I now just go straight for the worst case scenario.

Steeling myself, I finally get out of the car and head inside. I'm still too angry with Dean to check in and see if he has arrived yet, so when I walk into the training room and find him sitting on a treatment table, talking to Nicholas, I'm surprised. I'd been so sure he was going to be a stubborn idiot and refuse to be honest with the team doctor, but I guess my tantrum last night sank in.

"You were icing it last night and it's still playing up this morning?" Nicholas says, neither man looking my way as I enter the room.

Dean nods, wincing. "Yeah. I felt something pop last night and was hoping it would ease up with stretching overnight, but it's not getting any better."

Nicholas glances towards me as I come to a stop at the end of the treatment table. Dean still keeps his focus on the doctor, though.

"We should get an ultrasound done, to check for any tearing. We'll need to rest it again, unfortunately. We can't risk you playing while you're still tender."

The muscle in Dean's jaw tenses, and he nods tightly. "Okay."

Nicholas nods. "I'll go and get the referral sorted out for the imaging appointment. All going well, you should only be out for a game or two. And you're in good hands with Alanna here. Your recovery last time was quicker than I expected, so you two make quite the team."

Dean finally looks over at me, though I can't quite decipher the look on his face. "Yeah... I guess we do."

Nicholas nods again and walks into his office, closing the door behind him as he raises his phone to his ear.

Nerves swirl in my stomach as I run my eyes over Dean's face. His expression is closed off, and I wonder what he's seeing in my own expression.

Why did I have to fall so hard for this man? I knew this was going to end up turning to shit, but I didn't listen, and now look where we are.

"Hi," he says finally.

I guess one of us had to speak first.

"Hi. So it's still hurting?" He nods, and I let out a breath. "What did Seth say last night?"

"Oh, you mean when you dropped the bomb about our relationship and then took off? He had quite a lot to say."

Yeah, he's pissed.

"Is he going to tell anyone?" I ask, deciding not to react to the jab.

He sighs. "Not yet. But he will if this ends up causing problems for the team. Lincoln walked in on the lecture, so he knows now, too." I close my eyes, taking a calming breath as I mentally curse myself again. "Guess it doesn't really matter anyway," Dean continues, and I open my eyes to study him.

"What's that supposed to mean?"

"Well, you're going to end it anyway, so it's not like he has to worry about it affecting anyone else on the team."

I realize now that the expression on his face is *hurt*. And he's trying to hide that hurt behind his bravado. Wanting to be the one to say the words first.

I look back over at Nicholas' office to make sure he's still preoccupied.

Confident he won't overhear us, I turn back to him, allowing my expression to soften. "Why do you think I'm going to end it?"

His blue eyes widen. "Aren't you? You were pissed last night. Pissed enough that it made you slip up and admit our relationship in front of Seth, which you would never have done if you'd been thinking properly."

I let out a long breath. "I don't know... You're right, I wasn't thinking clearly last night, and I've been cursing my stupidity ever since I left. I fired up, which is what I do when I'm frustrated. And the reason I was frustrated is that I care so much, and went against my own better judgement. If you were any other player..." I let the words hang in the air, knowing I don't need to finish that sentence.

If he'd been any of the other guys, I would have immediately been on the phone with Nicholas. Instead, I'd allowed our relationship to get in the way and risked it all - my career, his career...

All because I've gone and fallen in love with this aggravating man.

"Dean?" We both look over to see Nicholas sticking his head out of the door. "They are expecting you."

Dean nods and slides off the table, wincing when his feet hit the ground. "Thanks, Doc." He turns to me. "I'll talk to you later."

There's no way we can continue this discussion now, and we both know it. So I simply nod, schooling my expression to remain neutral as he walks away. Wishing I knew what the hell to do.

Chapter Forty

DO YOU NEED ME TO BE AN ASSHOLE?

Dean

I've spent the afternoon lying on my couch, alternating between a heat pack and an ice pack on my hip while feeling sorry for myself. As soon as Nicholas confirmed that the muscle is just a strain, he'd ordered me home to rest for a few days. Although it's not a serious injury, it means at least another week off the ice yet again. Which sucks enough on its own, but I haven't heard from Alanna all day, and we still have to finish our conversation. Seemed like a pretty big deal to me, so not hearing from her has just made my dark thoughts even darker.

Glancing at the clock, I see that it's almost seven.

Surely she's home by now?

I try calling, and when there's no answer, I take matters into my own hands. Grabbing my car keys and the walking stick Alanna forced on me last time, I head down to my truck.

I've never just shown up at her place before, and it occurs to me as I'm pulling up out the front that I have no plan other than demanding my girlfriend talk to me.

Probably not the most solid of plans... But my gut is churning as the fear that our relationship is about to end before it really had a chance to begin takes hold.

I limp up the path to her house and knock, praying Tierney isn't home yet.

A moment later, the door is flung open, and Tierney appears, her eyebrows raised as she looks at me.

"Hey! What are you doing here?" she asks, glancing back over her shoulder.

She seems distracted, but I can't tell if that's a good thing or not.

"Um, I'm here to talk to Alanna," I reply, trying to think of a valid reason why I'd be showing up at her door unexpectedly, and coming up with nothing.

Tierney turns back to study me closely, her gaze trailing down to the walking stick at my side, then back up to my face.

"You fucked up, didn't you?"

Thrown by her question, I gape at her for a moment. Alanna appears beside her, opening the door wider to let me in.

Tierney glares at me for a moment before flouncing off, leaving me wondering what the hell just happened.

"Tierney knows," Alanna says, watching my face as I stare after her best friend.

At this point, the list of people who *don't* know seems far shorter than the people in the know about our relationship.

"Oh," I reply, not sure what to say as I take in her defeated expression.

"Yeah. Come on." She turns and signals for me to follow her, leading the way into her bedroom.

It's the first time I've been inside her bedroom, though I strongly suspect that this conversation isn't going to lead to us falling into her bed together.

She closes the door behind me and moves across the room to lean against her desk. She doesn't seem quite able to meet my gaze, and the sinking feeling in my stomach grows stronger.

Neither of us speaks for a few moments, and the air feels thick with all the words we've not yet said.

"Did Nicholas tell you-"

Alanna cuts me off as I finally speak. "Yeah, he mentioned it was a strain. So only a week off the ice this time."

I clear my throat, not quite sure I agree with the 'only' part of that sentence. Any time off the ice is too much for me.

When she still doesn't move closer, I lean against the closed door and study her face.

She's always had a pretty good poker face, but I can see the cracks in her mask right now, and the slight tremble of her lower lip gives her feelings away. My eyes lock on the way she's gripping her mother's necklace.

She hasn't done that in months, and I know this is it.

"You are ending this, aren't you?" I ask finally, doing my best to keep my emotions in check.

She draws in a deep breath, finally looking me in the eye for the first time since I walked in the door.

"I have to. This has all gotten out of hand. Seth, Lincoln and Tierney all know, and it's only a matter of time before someone lets it slip in front of the wrong people. I have worked so hard to get where I am, and no matter how I feel about you... about us... I can't throw my career away. And your determination to try and hide your injuries..." she trails off, brushing aside a tear as she looks away again.

I want to go to her and pull her into my arms. To hold her close one more time before what we have is ripped apart. But I know I've broken us.

"I told you when we started this that the second you said it needed to end, I'd respect that. And I will." I clear my throat, attempting to push the lump in my throat down. "But I just need to say something first." I pause, waiting for her to look at me again. When she finally does, the tears in her eyes threaten to break me, but I force the words out. "I don't regret a single moment between us. I don't regret falling in love with you. And if you weren't my trainer, I'd be fighting like hell to keep this from falling apart, because this is the first time I have ever felt like I could see a future with someone. And if things were different..."

Her lower lip trembles uncontrollably now, and she doesn't bother to wipe the next tear away.

"Why did I have to fall in love with you? Why did you have to make this even harder?" her voice cracks, and I cross the room in two steps, ignoring the pain in my hip to give in to my need to wrap my arms around her.

I hate that the first time we say those words out loud is when we're about to let each other go.

She buries her face into my chest, and I feel the damp from her tears spread through the thin material of my shirt.

"Do you need me to be an asshole?" I murmur into her hair.

"Yes," she half cries, half laughs, her words muffled against my chest. "I need you to be the grumpy goalie I know you can be."

I chuckle, ignoring the tears pricking my own eyes. "I can arrange that. How about I start tomorrow?"

She snorts, and I think I love her even more in this moment than I ever have before. "Sounds good." She pulls back to look up at me. "I'm sorry, Dean."

I bring my hands up to cup both her cheeks. "Don't be. I'm not. You made me a better person, Alanna Jameson. And I won't ever forget that. And I promise, from now on, I'll never put you in a position to have to choose between protecting me or doing your job." I press a kiss to her forehead before stepping back, letting my hands drop to my sides.

"I'll see you at work," I murmur, before doing the hardest thing I've ever done.

I turn and walk away.

I can't find it in myself to go home. Home is empty and quiet. I used to crave the solitude of my apartment. But now, it's just a reminder that Alanna will never be there again. And I'm not ready to face that.

So instead of going home, I open the group chat that I rarely participate in and send an SOS, then drive to Buck's.

I've only been sitting there for five minutes when Lincoln and Seth arrive. Riley, Michael, Anders and Ollie aren't far behind, all looking a little confused as they slide into the over crowded booth.

"So... SOS? Is this about your hip? What's going on?" Riley asks, his eyebrow raised.

"No. Well. Kind of," I reply, not missing the stoney expression on Seth's face as he sits back in his seat with his arms crossed.

"Okay..."

I chug my beer before taking a deep breath, wondering if I'm about to regret this. But these guys are my closest friends, and I need to talk to someone about all of this before my head, and heart, explode.

"So... some of you already know this, but... Alanna and I were in a relationship."

Riley's eyebrows fly upwards as Michael's mouth drops open.

"Trainer Alanna?" Anders asks, as Ollie shakes his head beside him.

"What do you mean 'were' in a relationship?" Lincoln asks, causing four heads to swivel in his direction, while Seth remains silent.

"You knew about this?" Riley asks, looking pissed.

Whether it's because of the relationship, or being kept in the dark, I'm not quite sure.

"For like twenty-four hours," Lincoln protests, holding his hands up.

Riley turns back to me. "Explain. Because I swear to god, if she lost her job because of you-"

"We broke up because we can't risk her job, so cool it with the big brother routine, alright. We both knew the risk, and once these guys found out-" I jab my thumb towards Lincoln and Seth. "We knew it was only a matter of time before it got back to the higher ups. And I love her too much to let her lose everything she's worked for over me."

"We were never going to say anything," Lincoln protests, and I look at Seth.

"Not unless it was going to fuck up things for the team, right?" I say, hearing the bitterness in my tone.

Of everyone on the team, Seth is probably the one I'm the closest to, and I can't deny how much it had stung seeing his disappointment last night. Even if I knew he was right.

"I would never have done anything to jeopardize her job, Dean. She's too damn good at what she does. But you had to see that it was a shit position you'd put me in? I'm supposed to keep this team together and working like a family," Seth says, and I can tell it's been weighing on him.

He looks torn between frustration and sympathy for the shitty situation I've found myself in.

"Well, I need the family part at the moment, because even though I know that breaking up is the right thing for us to do, I feel like absolute shit right now. And you know it takes a lot for me to admit that."

The six of them stare at me in stunned silence.

It's no secret I hide behind my sarcasm and surly attitude, and I'm pretty sure they all thought I didn't know how to cope with emotions. Because I've done such a good job of playing up to the grumpy goalie reputation. But right now, I don't want to be the grumpy goalie... I just need to be a guy, realizing his world is falling apart. And I'm smart enough to know I have friends who will keep me from spiralling while that happens.

Anders is the first to come to his senses, clapping me on the shoulder. "Then family is what you'll get." He raises a hand to get Buck's attention, and within minutes, a round of beers appears, and we're talking about the game last night while pretending that I didn't just drop a bomb that has the potential to rip the team apart.

When it's time for most of them to return to their wives and girlfriends, I'm left sitting with Riley and Michael.

"So... You guys decided to end it, huh?" Riley asks, sitting back in his seat to study me as I nod, peeling the label from my beer bottle.

"Yeah. I mean, it was mostly her call, but I knew it was the right one. There's no way we can make this work while we're both working for the same team."

Michael shakes his head. "Surely there has to be a way you guys can stay together? I mean, you've been on fire this season. And Alanna is professional. No one had any clue about this, so that should be proof enough you guys won't let it affect the team?"

I give a dark chuckle, shaking my head. "Pretty sure Tristan won't see it that way." While he's not an asshole like Alistair was, our new general manager is still pretty set on following the rules. "And Trevor would love any excuse to fire her. He's been a complete dick to her ever since she arrived."

Riley sighs, scratching the back of his neck. "Honestly... I know you don't want to hear it, but... I agree. I don't think there's anything you guys can do. And I've come to view her as another sister, so I think you're doing the right thing. For both of you."

"I know. But it's going to take me some time to be okay with it. I love her, man. And I don't know how to turn those feelings off." I lift my eyes to look to the ceiling, determined not to give in to the tears threatening to overcome me.

Riley nods. "I know. Break ups suck, and I'm sure that it's worse when the thing keeping you apart is something neither of you can control. But you'll eventually get used to it. And be able to move on."

Michael and I look at him with raised eyebrows.

"You sound like you're speaking from experience," Michael says.

Riley shakes his head with a sad smile. "I had a whole life before I came here, man. But this isn't about me. Just know that, eventually, you'll be okay."

Realizing that I really don't know a whole lot about Riley's life before he came to the Mounties, other than his history with raising Tierney, I have to wonder just how much he understands about my situation.

But I sure hope he's right.

Chapter Forty-One

EVEN IF HE IS AN ATHLETE

Alanna

"Lahney? Are you awake?" Tierney's head appears through the crack at my door, light streaming in behind her into my pitch black bedroom.

"Yeah," I reply, struggling to find the energy to respond.

She pushes the door open further, revealing the rest of her body, showing she's dressed for work.

Like I should be.

"Are you getting up?" she asks, cocking her head to the side while she studies me with eyes full of sympathy.

"No. I live here now." I roll over to face the wall, sighing when I feel the bed dip behind me.

A moment later, her arm comes over me as she wraps me in a hug.

"I'm so sorry, honey. I know this is hard."

Hard is an understatement. I haven't slept at all since Dean left two nights ago, and I'm pretty sure I have no liquid left in my body after I cried it all out.

"Do you want me to call in to work? Tell them you're sick?" she asks quietly, stroking my hair.

Thankfully the break up lined up with my two rostered

days off, so I've been able to hide in my room and cry. But I can't do that today.

I shake my head. "I can't. The whole reason we broke up was to protect my job. I can't very well call in sick because I'm too chicken to see him."

"At least take the day. Lie on the couch with your brother and eat all the ice cream."

"Oh god, I hadn't even thought about Charlie. I'm meant to be showing him around town over the next few days."

"Leave your brother to me. I'll keep him entertained while you wallow. Riley and I can show him around, seeing as he's actually home for a week. They apparently hit it off when they were all trying to prove who was the fastest the other morning."

I choke out a laugh and push myself upwards. "Thanks, T. You're a good friend."

"No, I'm an amazing friend." She grins at me before heading out of the room, leaving me to drag my sorry self into the bathroom, where I diligently avoid looking in the mirror, not ready to deal with the mess I know I'd find looking back at me.

Half an hour into running the team through a series of work outs for dryland training, it must be obvious to a few of the guys that I'm just phoning it in.

"You doing okay, Red?" Lincoln asks, sliding an arm around my shoulders between sets and giving a little squeeze.

Based on the fact that he's basically whispering, I have to guess that he knows about the break up, because Lincoln isn't exactly known for being discreet.

Dean probably told him so he'd back off and stop worrying that our relationship was going to affect the team morale.

"I'm fine," I mutter, shrugging his arm off my shoulders when Trevor walks into the room.

"Yeah... I believe you." Lincoln flashes me a sad smile before moving back towards the weight rack.

Seth steps up beside me, taking his best friend's place.

And of course, if Lincoln knows, Seth definitely knows.

"You know he's also not doing great, right?" Seth asks, keeping his voice low.

"I don't know if that makes me feel better or worse," I reply, keeping my eyes trained on where Riley is holding a plank in the corner.

"I didn't tell you to make you feel either way. Just thought you should know that you're not alone in feeling crap." He pats my shoulder and follows after Lincoln.

And, because the universe hates me, it's at this moment that Dean walks into the room.

He looks as crap as I feel. It's obvious he hasn't shaved since I last saw him, and the lines of fatigue on his face tell me he hasn't slept much either.

Simon has been working with him on his rehab on my days off, but now that I'm back, it's my responsibility again. My chest tightens when I realize I'm going to have to touch him when I'm working on his hip later.

He flicks a glance my way but doesn't say anything as he walks past, heading for the stationary bike. I open my mouth to tell him not to use it today, in case it causes more issues with his hip, but I clamp my mouth shut. He know his own body, and he won't do anything to jeopardize his return to the ice.

Lincoln pauses midway through his set of bicep curls, flicking his gaze between myself and Dean with a grimace. Seth smacks his arm when he stays still for too long, and he quickly goes back to what he was doing, but it was long enough for it to be obvious that the tension between Dean and myself is at risk of causing problems, just like I'd worried.

I just need to make it through the rest of the day and then I can get some space.

And hopefully some clarity.

When I pull my car into the driveway, I find Charlie sitting on the porch steps, dressed in jeans and a jacket with his beanie pulled down over his ears.

"Are you going out?" I ask him while I climb the few steps leading to the front door.

He gets to his feet and comes to stand beside me, and I have to crane my neck to look up at him. I often forget just how tall my brother is, but as he stands beside me now, I realize he's just as tall as Dean.

The thought sends a jolt of pain through my chest.

"Um, yeah... About that..."

"About what?" I ask, wary of his guilty tone.

"Riley is coming to get me... With Dean. They've offered to take me out for a few drinks at their local while they are in town."

I swallow hard.

"Oh... That's cool that you've made friends with them."

He wraps his arms around me, pulling me into a solid hug.

One thing about my brother I've always taken for granted is that he is an excellent hugger, and I let myself sink into his embrace, willing myself not to cry.

"I'm sorry you guys broke up, Lahns. He's a good guy, and I could see how much he loves you. Exactly the kind of guy I thought you'd end up with one day. Even if he is an athlete," he adds, and I let out a half hearted laugh as he squeezes me gently.

"And I saw his face when he left the other night. It's obvious this is killing him just as much as you."

I bury my face into his chest. "Everyone keeps telling me that, but I don't know what to do with this information? It just makes me feel shittier."

"Take it from someone who's wife left him and barely talks to him anymore, it means that he still loves you and if things were different with your jobs, you'd still be together. So I guess you just need to work out if you want to get over him... Or find a way you guys can make this work."

Sure... Because neither of those things seem impossible...

I nod, unable to talk without falling apart.

"I'll leave you to it, then." I head inside, unable to handle seeing Dean again after leaving him at work.

When I walk into the living room, I stop.

"Um... Hi," I murmur, surprised to find Sarah, Kylie and Adele sitting with Tierney.

All four women are looking at me with varying levels of sympathy, and my stomach plummets.

"What's going on?" I ask cautiously, letting my backpack drop to the ground beside me.

"We heard you might need a friend," Sarah answers, exchanging a wary glance with Adele and Kylie.

"Oh... Why?"

"Dean kind of told the boys about you guys being a couple... and that now you're not," Kylie replies quietly.

I think my brain is glitching as I process the fact that our secret is imploding.

"Don't worry, we're all sworn to secrecy. He just told Lincoln, Seth, Ollie, Riley, Michael and Anders," Sarah says quickly, and my eyes widen.

"He did what?!" I practically screech, gripping my necklace

tightly as my gaze hops from one woman to another. "If you guys know, that means Anders must have told Bethany! There's no way she won't twist this to her advantage." I can't keep the panic from my voice.

I'm going to get deported and this will all have been for nothing!

"Anders won't tell Bethany," Sarah jumps up, coming to stand in front of me and takes my hands. "Breathe, okay? Just breathe. Anders doesn't tell Bethany anything. He's aware of what the team think of her and her friends, and he promised Dean it wouldn't get back to any of them."

I blink back tears. "Why did he tell all of them?" I whisper.

God I hate how vulnerable I sound right now.

Sarah squeezes my hands as she looks at me with a sad smile. "Because he needed his family. Just like you need yours. That's why the guys told us after seeing you at training today. They wanted to make sure you had support, too. Especially if you're even half as cut up about this as he is. Dean never let's people in, so for him to go to the guys..."

She doesn't need to finish that sentence. It would have taken everything for him to go to the guys and pour his heart out.

Guilt stabs my chest, and I can feel the tenuous hold on my emotions begin to crack.

Sarah must sense that I'm about to crumble, stepping forward to wrap her arms around me as I choke back a sob.

Other than Tierney, I've never been one to have many girlfriends. Knowing that these three women have come here to simply support me is more than I know what to do with. The tears start to flow as the others come to our side and wrap us in a giant hug while I allow myself to draw comfort from their presence.

Because I'm beginning to realize I can't deal with this on my own.

They stay with us for a few hours, not forcing me to talk as we dig into tubs of Ben & Jerry's and watch reality TV that requires zero thinking.

I hadn't realized how much I needed this, and it gives me a boost I hadn't expected. But once they leave and Tierney goes to bed, the sadness reappears, and I cry myself to sleep once again.

Three days later, on Dean's first night back on the ice, I force myself to go to work after calling in sick for the last few days, something I've not done in all my time working for the team. We have a game against Edmonton tonight, and these games always end up being fairly brutal, as the two teams are staunch rivals, and I can't allow myself to take any more time off. They even refer to games between the two teams as The Battle of Alberta, so the training staff always prepare for a busy night of stitches and checking for concussions.

Arriving at the arena, I head for the elevator leading from the staff carpark up to the ground floor. The players carpark is above ours, and my heart leaps into my throat when the doors open and Dean is standing there, dressed in his game day suit. The black suit and dress shirt is one I haven't seen before, and it takes me a moment to realize I'm holding my breath as I take him in. The all black look works for him, and with the addition of the backwards Mounties cap, my body is screaming at me to wrap myself around him.

Despite how good he looks, the pained expression on his face tells me he was as unprepared for my presence as I was for his.

We look at each other for what feels like an eternity before he gets in and moves to the back of the elevator to stand behind me. I keep my eyes forward as the doors close and we remain silent as the elevator continues upwards. The tension in the small space is thick, and I don't move when he steps forward, his chest pressing against my back. He reaches around me to hit the emergency stop button, then bends to skim his nose along my neck as I close my eyes and let my head drift to the side, giving him better access.

I know I should stop him, but I've missed him so much that I can't help but lean back into his body when he pulls me closer.

"I miss you," he whispers in my ear, and I can feel tears prick the corners of my eyes.

"I miss you," I whisper back, letting his hands roam over my body for this one, stolen moment.

With a groan, he reaches around to grip my chin and turns my face towards his. His lips crush against mine in a short, fierce kiss that's over too soon.

Then he's hitting the emergency stop button again, and the doors open a few seconds later. I step out like my body isn't screaming for him and head for the training room, not meeting Sarah's gaze as she stands in the hall with Tamara, waiting to take the usual content shots of the players arriving in their suits. I can feel my cheeks burning, and I know she can tell something happened when she clears her throat.

"Dean," she says, her tone a mixture of sympathy and warning, and I know he must look as guilty as I do.

But I refuse to look back.

Once I reach the training room, I busy myself working alongside Joel and Simon, getting the room ready for the players to warm up ahead of hitting the ice.

Riley walks in, taking a seat on the treatment table I direct him towards, and I lower my head when Dean appears at the door, having changed into his workout gear. But I'm not fast enough to miss the flash of pain that I know is mirrored in my own eyes.

I take a deep breath and turn back to taping Riley's shoulder, ignoring the pain in my chest once more. And praying it will eventually get easier.

Chapter Forty-Two

HAVEN'T SEEN YOU AROUND MUCH

Dean

My first night back on the ice looks set to be a pretty shitty return. I've already let three goals by me that I know I could have saved if my reflexes were faster, but I've barely slept in the last week, and it's showing. I truly thought I'd be able to handle being around Alanna, but seeing her tonight is just a reminder that we're no longer together. I couldn't keep myself from kissing her in that one, all too brief moment in the elevator, and now I've just gone and split my heart open all over again.

This is why dating a coworker is forbidden.

Despite Riley's words that night, it really doesn't feel like it's getting any easier. I'm sure he meant it would take longer than a week, but I've never been known for my patience.

By the time we're halfway through the third period, the scores are tied, four all, and I lock my body into position, determined not to let any more pucks by me. Alanna is behind the bench tonight, the first time since she covered for Trevor in New York, and it kind of feels like the universe is working against me right now. But when Edmonton's captain is streaking down the ice towards me on a two on one, I block out the sight of her watching, the crowd holding its collective breaths, and of the rest of my teammates. It's just him and me.

He fakes taking a shot, but this isn't the first time I've come up against him, and I anticipate it when he passes it over to the winger who one times the shot. I bring my glove up, sliding to my right, letting out a sigh of relief when I feel it hit the glove.

Relieved that I'm able to get my head into the game finally, I refuse to look towards the bench, knowing that if I catch sight of Alanna's face, I won't be able to keep it up. If I can't get my emotions under control, I'm going to have to talk to my agent about a trade, because this shit is getting ridiculous.

When the buzzer goes off, the relief subsides and I skate back to the bench, ready to hear the strategy the coaching staff have put together for the overtime period. Could have done without going into overtime for my first day back on the ice. I refuse to listen to the way my body is screaming at me, because it just means I'm going to be spending time on the table later while Alanna works on my aching back and hip.

The thought causes me to glance over as she talks to Lincoln while he rotates his arm and points at his shoulder.

I force myself to look away, gritting my teeth.

Definitely can't think about Alanna touching me right now.

Halfway through overtime Edmonton scores, and I kneel on the ice with my head bowed, completely exhausted.

The crowd lets their displeasure be known as we skate off the ice, and I can't shake the feeling that my performance tonight is the reason we lost. It doesn't matter that we still got a point for overtime. I blew it, plain and simple. And it's all because I can't get out of my head when it comes to the woman currently responsible for keeping me on the ice.

I clomp into the locker room and begin stripping off my jersey and pads before ripping off my skates.

"Take a breath, man. I can feel your inner monologue from here," Lincoln says, clapping a hand down on my shoulder as he walks past, aiming for the treatment room.

When I'm down to my compression shorts, I force myself to take a few calming breaths before heading for the treatment room myself. Lincoln is still with Alanna, and Simon waves me over to his table. Raising an eyebrow, I head towards him.

"Hey, O'Malley is going to be awhile, so Alanna asked me to help you out."

I look over at Alanna, who has her head down while she works on Lincoln's shoulder. I'm certain she is avoiding looking at me, and the gnawing sensation in my stomach grows stronger.

I guess we found a way to avoid each other further.

At dinner, I take a seat with Anders and Michael, avoiding the table where Alanna sits with Seth, Lincoln, Kylie and Tara, who is apparently flying home tomorrow. Guess she's calmed Kylie down, because the bubbly brunette seems to have returned to her usual self and is joking around with Lincoln about something while stroking her stomach. She is definitely looking pregnant now, and I wonder how Seth is handling the pressure of becoming a father soon.

Bethany slides into the seat next to Anders, and I suppress a groan when Anastasia takes the seat next to me. I'd forgotten that Bethany had her entourage with her tonight and really wish I'd sat with Riley, Ollie and Sarah instead. Although I'm avoiding Sarah on account of her glaring daggers at me when I followed Alanna out of the elevator earlier.

"Hey stranger. Haven't seen you around much lately," Anastasia says, placing her hand on my thigh under the table.

I shift away as I take a bite of my chicken, hoping she gets the hint.

Unfortunately she doesn't. Instead, she trails her hand up and down my inner thigh, and I jerk away, shooting her a warning glance while I keep chewing.

Anders notices the exchange and attempts to draw Anastasia into the conversation he's having with Bethany, grimacing in my direction. I swear to god, one day I'm going to ask him what the hell he was thinking marrying into this group of women. He certainly doesn't seem like he's too thrilled with the way Bethany is acting right now, scowling when she wraps herself around him while he's trying to eat. He's at work, for fuck's sake, and some of the players have their kids here, and they definitely don't need to see the way she's basically humping his leg. Something must have happened in the family box that made her feel like she needs the attention on her. My guess is that it's to do with the attention Kylie is getting with being pregnant. I've heard Bethany making snide remarks along the lines of 'you'd think no one had ever been pregnant before'. Wouldn't surprise me if she starts begging Anders for a baby any day now.

I spend the next five minutes wolfing my dinner down, needing to put as much distance as I can between myself and the busty blonde beside me - who doesn't know the meaning of personal space - before I snap.

Pushing away from the table, I head for the bar, handing my empty plate to a passing server with a nod of thanks. I hadn't noticed Charlie was also here, and I shake his hand when he sidles up next to me.

"Hey. How you holding up?" he asks as I order a soda.

"Just peachy," I reply, not bothering to hide the sarcasm.

We've spent a bit of time together in the last week, although I've refused to ask him how his sister is doing. I haven't been able to stomach the idea that she's handling the break up better than me.

Anastasia uses that moment to try her luck again, coming to my other side as I turn away from the bar, sliding her hand over my chest while smiling up at me.

"What do you say we head back to your place? I can help you feel better after everything tonight," she says, her voice low and husky.

She truly is tenacious, I'll give her that.

Charlie raises an eyebrow as he glances down at her hand on my chest, before shooting me a glare, but I shake my head.

"No, thanks. I'm fine," I reply, stepping away from her and almost stepping on Alanna.

I hadn't noticed her walk up, and am thrown off momentarily.

"We're leaving," Alanna tells Charlie, grabbing his hand, glaring at me as she pulls her brother away.

I want to protest my innocence, but don't have a chance as she disappears outside with Charlie in tow.

All I can do is hope Charlie understood enough to be able to tell her I hadn't done anything with Anastasia.

Chapter Forty-Three

CONVINCE YOU TO STAY

Alanna

"I swear, Lahns, he wasn't doing anything with that woman. He was telling her to back off when you stormed up and made a scene," Charlie protests when I come to a stop outside the door.

"I didn't make a scene," I snap, knowing my anger is misplaced but not sure how to turn it off.

"You definitely did. If you're trying to keep your feelings from blowing up your career, then you really need to work on that." Charlie fixes me with a knowing look.

Frustration threatens to overwhelm me. Because I know he's right. Breaking up with Dean was meant to make things easier. But instead, everything feels so much harder. I knew I was being a coward when I asked Simon to take care of him tonight, but I couldn't handle being close to him again. It was hard enough helping him warm up, but it was obvious he was aching after the game and needed more attention. Which would have meant having my hands all over his body, and I just can't do it. Not anymore. Not when every moment is a reminder of what we had. Of how much I love him but can't have him.

I don't bother responding to Charlie while I march off in

the direction of the parking lot, and he knows better than to say anything else.

After the silent car ride home, I unlock the door and abandon Charlie to go to my room. Closing the door behind me, I lean against it and let the tears I've been fighting off start to flow.

This is what my life is going to be like now. Of course Dean is going to move on. And so he should. But the idea of watching him with someone else is more than I can take, and with a sob, I slide to the floor and bury my face against my knees. Knowing I have some tough decisions to make.

The next morning, after yet another sleepless night spent crying into my pillow, I drag myself to work. Charlie is due to fly home in two days and I feel like I've ruined his entire trip with my drama. This can't continue, and I don't want it to.

Instead of heading for the gym, I make my way up to the office suites that overlook the arena.

Taking a steadying breath, I knock on the open door of the HR office, and Felicity looks up, surprise etched into her expression when she see's me.

"Alanna? I wasn't expecting you, was I?" She reaches for her mouse, staring at her computer briefly before shaking her head. "Nope, definitely no appointment noted there. Is everything okay?"

While we've always been on friendly terms, we've never socialized outside of work functions, so my presence is most likely concerning her right now.

"I... uh... I wanted to chat to you about something, if that's okay?"

She scans my face, her eyebrows slowly knitting together as she takes in my expression.

"Sure. Come on in." She waves her hand towards the chair on the other side of her desk, and I close the door behind me before taking a seat. "What's up?"

Swallowing, it takes me a moment to gather the courage to say what I have been rehearsing all morning.

"I want to hand in my resignation."

Her eyebrows fly upwards and her mouth opens, although it takes a moment for her to utter a sound. "What? Why?"

"Some personal reasons, but I can't stay here."

"Is this because of Trevor?"

It's my turn to raise my eyebrows. "What makes you ask that?"

She sighs while she rubs her temples. "Let's just say, it wouldn't be the first time his name has been mentioned when someone resigns from that department."

"While he's not the reason, he certainly hasn't helped."

She stares at me as she bites her lower lip, and I can tell I've really thrown her with my request.

"What can we do to convince you to stay? You're such a good fit for the team, and I've heard nothing but good things about your work with the players."

I shake my head, balling my shaking hands into fists in my lap. "Unfortunately, there isn't anything. I think I just need to go home."

"Home? New Zealand home?"

I nod.

"Alanna, did something happen?" she asks, lowering her voice, even though there's no one else within earshot.

"No. But it's what I need to do."

She looks as though she doesn't quite believe me, and I know she's going to continue to push me to stay, so I get to my feet. "I just wanted to tell you in person before I emailed it through. I have a few weeks of leave owing to me, and my brother goes home in a few days. I'd like to go with him."

Her eyes look like they are ready to fall clean out of her head, but I don't give her a chance to say anything more as I nod and leave her office.

Going downstairs, I enter the trainers office and look around as a tightening sensation in my chest causes a lump to form in my throat.

It's hard to believe how much I'm going to miss this place. I'd come to feel like this place... this team... was my home. But now it's just a painful reminder that I found the kind of love everyone raves about with the one person I can never have.

While the place is still empty, I pull my work laptop from my backpack and set it down on the desk. Typing out my official resignation, effective immediately, I hit send on the email to Felicity, then close the laptop and leave it on the desk. Stashing my freshly washed uniforms on a shelf, I grab my backpack and walk out.

Determined not to look back.

"What do you mean you're leaving?" Tierney asks, gaping at me from where she sits beside Charlie on the couch.

They'd both been happily watching some reality show that I'm pretty sure Tierney has gotten my brother addicted to, but when I dropped the news, Tierney's eyes had immediately filled with tears, just adding to the guilt I'm already feeling.

"I can't stay, T. It's killing me, and it's going to hurt so much more when Dean does start seeing other people." Charlie opens his mouth to protest, but I raise my hand. "I know nothing was happening with that woman last night, but one day that won't be the case. And I can't handle the idea of watching him move on."

"But..." Tierney is clearly struggling to find something to say to keep me from leaving, but the words don't seem to be coming.

Whether it's from shock, or because she's realized I'm right, I'm not sure.

"Are you really sure about this?" Charlie asks, shaking his head.

I nod before turning on my heel and heading for my room.

To start packing my life up once again.

The next morning, I'm woken by the sound of my phone ringing. I must have forgotten to turn it on silent when I collapsed into bed last night.

Groaning, I grab for it blindly, answering before checking the caller ID.

"Hello?" I mumble, my voice thick.

"Hello? Alanna?" Nicholas's voice rings out, and I blink, surprised.

"Um. Hi?"

"Did I wake you?" he asks, and I stupidly nod before remembering he can't see me.

"Yeah, sorry. I'm a bit out of it." I sit up, forcing myself to focus. "Is everything okay?"

"I've just been told you've resigned?" he says, thankfully getting straight to the point.

"Oh... Yeah." I don't really know what else to say to that.

"Listen, can we catch up for coffee later this morning? There's something I need to speak to you about."

"Um..." I bite my lip, looking around at the boxes I'd half packed yesterday that are scattered around the room. I hadn't realized just how much stuff I'd gathered over the last eighteen months, and had planned to donate most of it today once I'd finished sorting it all out.

"I promise it will be worth your time," Nicholas urges, and my curiosity gets the better of me.

"Okay."

He lets out a breath. "Good. Is ten okay?"

"Sure."

He rattles off the address of a coffee shop and we hang up, leaving me to stare at the phone and wonder what he can possibly have to say to me that is so important.

Two hours later, I take a seat across the table from the doctor, nerves swirling in my belly.

Is he going to yell at me?

I have no idea why that's my first thought, but I guess the guilt of my sudden resignation is getting the better of me.

"I had a chat with Colin last night."

My eyebrows raise as I study the older man, thrown off guard. "Oh..."

Why the hell is he talking to me about the head trainer for the Cowboys?

"I don't know if you're aware, but he has put in for early retirement and is currently looking for his replacement. His health has taken a turn, otherwise he would be waiting until the end of the season. When we both received the news of your resignation, he mentioned he'd been surprised he hadn't received an application from you."

I stare at him, my mouth hanging open as my brain struggles to process his words.

"I had no idea. But... Why would he think I'd apply?"

A server appears with my coffee, and I take it with a shaking hand, needing caffeine to steady my frazzled nerves.

He smiles, watching as I take a mouthful of coffee. "It's no secret that your talents were wasted at the Mounties, under the current structure. As you know, I'm the doctor for the Cowboys as well, and I agree with Colin that you would be perfect for the role."

"Surely there are other, more qualified applicants?" I ask, unsure why I'm trying to talk him out of his opinion of me.

"We both know that if you hand that application over, Alanna, the job is yours. Colin and I were both instrumental in hiring you. As soon as Ted mentioned you, we knew we had to get you here in one capacity or another. Colin was always planning on putting you forward as his replacement one day. And now that the job has been left entirely up to him..." I stare at him, processing everything he has just said. He must take my silence as me being insulted, because he immediately shakes his head. "This is definitely a step up for you. Head trainer of an AHL team is still higher up the food chain than an assistant trainer in the NHL. It also leaves you open to the possibility of moving into Trevor's role once he eventually moves on."

I don't miss the reference to Trevor moving on, or the expression on his face when he says it.

I blink a few times, letting his words sink in.

"I...I'm just trying to work out why no one has said any of this to me before now," I say, sitting back in my seat and levelling Nicholas with a frustrated gaze.

He sighs, his expression apologetic. "Colin wasn't sure how much longer he'd be working with the Cowboys and didn't want to have the position dangling over you in case, for some reason, he didn't end up having a say in who would be replacing him. We've seen that happen before, and the team members were left disgruntled and frustrated. We didn't want you to feel trapped here, waiting for your time to come."

That makes sense. I've seen that happen, too. And they're

right. It would have left me feeling frustrated, waiting for something better to happen whilst dealing with Trevor's constant bullshit.

"Aren't any of Colin's team going for the role? I don't want to have to deal with a team of men under me who resent a woman being parachuted over the top of them."

Nicholas grins. "That's the other exciting opportunity for you. Once this season is over, all their contracts are up. So if they want to stay employed, they'll need to just deal with it. But it gives you the chance to build your own team. I'm sure you're aware that most players would prefer to be working with female trainers. We both know, in most cases, female trainers are more nurturing, and the players find it easier to be honest about their aches and pains with a woman. The female trainers are often more in tune with the psychological aspect of player injuries, as well."

Absolutely nothing he's saying is news to me. In my previous role, I was one of two female athletic training staff, and we would always have the players coming to us when they had trouble communicating with the male staff, who were simply treating the injury itself and not the issues that the players were dealing with while processing the possibility that the next injury might be the one that ended their career.

Nicholas continues talking. "I've watched how you've worked with Dean. It's obvious that he's concerned that being off the ice will mean he's no longer the preferred goalie. But it was only you who was able to see that and work with him on both the mental side of it as well as his physical limitations. I've been working with that man for nearly a decade, and I've watched him grow more sullen since Mark came on board. Simon and Trevor have both noticed as well. And yet neither of those men even tried to put the work in to help him understand that pushing himself through injuries would be setting him back. A few months of you being upfront with him, and he's actually listening, and putting the work in to work on injury prevention exercises, rather than just pushing through the pain. You got through to him. Not Simon. Certainly not Trevor. You."

I process the words as I take in his earnest expression.

Eventually, I let out a breath. "So what you're saying is, if I apply for this position, it's pretty much mine?" Nicholas nods. "Thank you. You've given me a lot to think about."

And he certainly has.

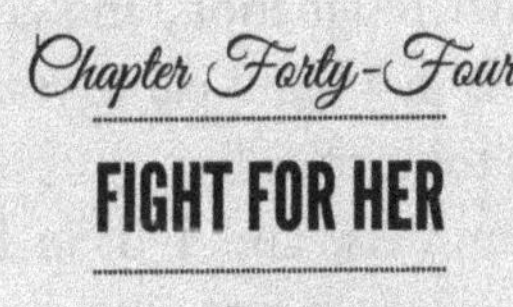

Chapter Forty-Four

FIGHT FOR HER

Dean

I arrive at work in time for morning skate in a shitty mood. Not that anyone will be surprised, because I've been a surly asshole for the last week and a half now.

We had a day off yesterday, and I spent the day on the couch, unable to find the motivation to do anything more than glare at the TV. I've never been a big fan of watching a lot of TV, but I couldn't focus on a book, and I really didn't want to see anyone.

"Hey," Lincoln says, stopping in front of me as I drop onto the bench in front of my locker.

I grunt in response, hoping he'll get the hint to leave me alone, but he stays there, his arms crossed as he looks down at me with an uncharacteristically pissed off look on his face.

"I just had some interesting news that you need to hear. Because you really fucked up."

I raise an eyebrow. "What the hell does that mean?"

"Alanna quit."

I shoot to my feet, forcing him to take a step back. "What?!"

He runs a hand through his hair, his expression shifting as he studies my face. While he'd looked ready to take me to task moments ago, it's obvious he now just feels sorry for me. Something that would normally aggravate me, but I'm too agitated now to care.

"She handed in her resignation, and according to Tierney, who messaged the girls in a blind panic yesterday, she's moving back to New Zealand tomorrow."

My stomach plummets, and I drop back to the bench, unable to focus as he continues talking.

She can't quit. The whole reason we broke up was so she wouldn't lose her job. Why is she leaving?

"Dean? Did you hear what I just said?" Lincoln asks, dragging me from my thoughts.

"No. Sorry, what?"

He sighs, looking to Seth, who I've only just noticed has stepped up beside him.

"You gotta go stop her from leaving."

I stare at him. "How do you suggest I do that? She's obviously leaving because of me, so the last thing she will want is me showing up at her door, begging her to stay."

Lincoln throws his hands up. "Honestly, how is it that I was accused of being the clueless one?" He points at Seth, who blinks at him in surprise. "You were so set on refusing to beg Kylie to stay that you let her move back to fucking Australia and I had to orchestrate a whole big thing to get her back here." He turns his glare back to me. "And now you're being a moron and are determined to let Alanna move back to New Zealand without even trying to fight for her?"

"Hey. You broke up with Adele because you thought she was too good for you last year," Seth protests, and I nod.

"We're not talking about my stupidity here. And I at least did the whole grand gesture thing without either of you stepping in," Lincoln says.

Seth mumbles something under his breath that sounds a lot

like "bullshit" but Lincoln ignores him, waving Riley, Ollie and Anders over to join in on the whole 'tell Dean he's an idiot' conversation.

"Man, Lincoln is right. You need to go and at least try to talk to her. There's nothing for her in New Zealand, aside from her brother, who I'm pretty sure will not agree with her decision," Riley says, and I know he's right.

When we went out for drinks last week, Charlie confirmed that their childhood wasn't great and he regrets the decisions he's made that led to his wife leaving him. I know he thinks Alanna did the right thing in getting out when she did.

To back up his statement, Riley pulls out his phone and dials Charlie, who answers on the first ring.

"Hey man, what's up?"

"Hey. We've just found out about Alanna," Riley says, flicking his gaze to me as I stare at his phone.

"Oh good. What are we going to do about this? Because she can't come back with me."

Riley chuckles as he watches my face. "Yeah, that's what we just said. Dean seems to think that seeing him will just make it worse, but Lincoln says it's grand gesture time."

"Lincoln's right. So, what's Dean going to do to convince my stubborn-ass sister that she's about to make the biggest mistake of her life?"

"Leave it with me," Lincoln replies for me, and I glare at him. "I have a plan."

Riley hangs up, and they all turn to look at Lincoln, like he has all the answers.

"Excuse me, but I can handle this without any of your help," I interject, and five sets of eyes turn to look at me with the same incredulous expression. "I'm not completely useless, you know?"

"Oh yeah? Then what's your plan?" Ollie asks, crossing his arms.

"She's not the only one who can quit."

And I walk out of the locker room before any of them manage to find their voices again.

When I knock on the door of Alanna and Tierney's house, my nerves are completely shot.

In those few minutes where everyone was discussing how to get Alanna to stay, I realized that she means more to me than hockey. And if it takes me retiring for her to stay with the team, then that's what I'm going to do. It's not like I need the money, having amassed enough savings to keep me comfortable for the rest of my life. But I don't want to spend the rest of my life without her, and she has too much talent to go back to working in a sport that doesn't offer the opportunities that the NHL does.

Charlie answers the door, shaking his head when he see's me.

"She's not here, man. She went to meet someone, and then texted to say she needed some time to get her head right. No idea where she is. You wanna wait for her?"

I let out a frustrated breath. I guess I could wait, but sitting around has never been my strongest suit. I'm a man of action, and I'm pretty sure I'm going to lose my mind while I wait.

Then I realize I know where she'll be.

"I have a hunch about where she is. If I'm wrong, I'll be back. Message me if she shows up first, though?"

He nods, and I jog back to my truck.

. . .

When I pull into our usual parking lot at Glenmore Reservoir, I spy Alanna's car immediately. I park next to it, relief flooding through my veins. It just confirms that I know her as well as I've told her I do.

Jogging along the path, it's not long before I find her sitting on a frozen bench, gripping a takeaway cup between her gloved hands with her toque pulled down around her ears. I slow to a walk when I get closer, and she looks up in surprise when I stop beside her.

"What are you doing here?" she murmurs, and I can't decipher the look on her face.

I take a seat beside her, shoving my hands in the pockets of my jacket, wishing it wasn't so fucking cold. When I'd dressed this morning, I hadn't anticipated being outside for long, and I am not dressed anywhere near warm enough to be sitting on a bench that may as well be made of ice.

Thank god it's not snowing, at least.

"I heard you quit," I say.

She sighs, turning back to look out at the half frozen reservoir. "Yeah... I did."

"Well, you can't quit."

She turns to look at me again, fixing me with a frustrated glare. "You don't get a say in it."

I hold her gaze as I shrug. "Tough. Because like it or not, what you do matters to me. And you can't quit, because I'm quitting."

She scoffs, shaking her head. "Yeah, okay. That's hilarious."

"I'm glad you think so. Because it's the truth."

"Don't be ridiculous, Dean. You can't quit. You signed a contract for another two years, for one. And you would lose your mind if you weren't playing. Look how much it screwed you up when you were injured and had to watch Mark and Connor play instead of you."

I shrug again. "That was before I realized that hockey means nothing to me if it means no longer having you in my life." She gapes at me, speechless for possibly the first time since she walked into my life. So I keep talking. "I love you. And if you quit and move back to New Zealand, I'm just going to follow you. Because I'm serious... It all means nothing if you aren't with me."

She's quiet a little longer, her eyes scanning my face, and I notice tears forming. "You're serious, aren't you?" she whispers.

I slide closer and take her hand in mine. "As a heart attack."

She looks down at our hands as I lace my fingers through hers, before looking back up at my face. "You're insane. You know that?"

I grin. "Only when it comes to you." She huffs out a laugh before swallowing hard. "Say you'll stay? We'll work something out. Hell, I'll go to Tristan right now and demand he decline your resignation and I'll go play for the Cowboys."

She laughs, shaking her head. "There's no need for that."

The hope I'd been clinging to begins to fade as it dawns on me that she's still going to leave.

"Please, baby," I whisper, squeezing her hand.

She shakes her head again. "There's no need, because we'd end up in the same situation again."

Confused, I raise an eyebrow, trying to work out what the hell she means.

"How would we possibly end up in the same situation? The Cowboys have completely different training staff."

She smiles softly. "I know they do. Because I'm in charge of them all."

I stare at her, stunned, as I try to process her words. "You... What?"

She laughs now, squeezing my hand while my brain continues to glitch. "I spent the morning with Nicholas and

Colin. And I signed my contract an hour ago. Colin's retiring and hired me to take over as the head trainer for the Cowboys. HR is handling the transfer of my visa and helping me apply for permanent residency."

Her words finally sink in, and I can't help the grin that spreads across my face.

"Are you serious?"

"As a heart attack," she replies.

I want to kiss her, but I still don't know what this means for our relationship. If we even have a relationship.

"What does this mean for us?" I ask carefully, praying the hope I'm feeling isn't for nothing.

"I guess it depends on if you move to New Zealand."

Laughing, I tug her into my lap. "You're a brat, you know that?"

She grins, biting her lower lip. "Maybe."

I slide my finger under her chin to tilt her face up to mine. "I'm going to kiss you now."

"It's about time."

Wrapping my arms around her, I crush my lips to hers, no longer aware of the cold as she moans, unable to believe that after all these months, we finally have a chance at a future together.

She presses herself closer as she slides her fingers through my hair, and all I want is to bury myself inside her.

"Did I mention how much I love you?" I murmur against her lips, unable to pull myself away.

"You may have said it a few times," she replies before pulling away enough to look me in the eye. "You know I love you, too, right?

"Yeah? I think I need to hear it a few more times," I tell her with a grin, pulling her back in to kiss her again.

"Take me home and make love to me, and I'll tell you all night long."

"If you insist."

Chapter Forty-Five

A GREAT DAY FOR THE JAMESON FAMILY

Alanna

As much as I want Dean to take me to bed, reality kicks in when we walk back to the parking lot and Coach Stephens calls Dean to tell him off for skipping morning skate.

"And what's this bullshit about you quitting?!" he yells through the phone, and I smother a laugh behind my hand while Dean rubs the back of his neck and stares at me, panic written across his face.

"I'm not quitting, I don't know where you heard that. But I had an emergency I had to take care of. I'm coming back in right now."

"You better, you pain in the ass." Stephens hangs up and Dean lets out a breath.

"Jesus. I forgot about the game." He pulls me back in to kiss me. "I'm sorry. I better go back and deal with all of that."

I nod, smiling against his lips. "It's okay. I get it. And I should probably go tell Tierney that she doesn't have to look for a new roommate."

"Good idea." He rests his forehead against mine. "Come to the game?" I bite my lip as I consider whether it's a good idea to immediately announce our relationship to the world. He studies my face for a moment, a smile playing across his lips. "We don't need to say anything to people yet. But the ones who matter all know, and we can work out the right time to make it public."

Loving that he can read me so well, I smile and kiss him again.

"Okay. I'll be there."

"Good." With a final kiss, we reluctantly get into our respective cars and head our separate ways.

When I get home, Charlie and Tierney are waiting on the steps, both rugged up under blankets.

"You know it's nice and warm inside, right?" I ask as I get out of the car.

"Shut up. Did Dean find you?" Tierney asks, jumping to her feet.

I smile. "He did."

She crosses her arms beneath her blanket and taps her foot. It would be intimidating if she wasn't wearing her bunny slippers and looking like a cute little burrito. "Well?!"

I laugh. "I'm staying."

"Thank god," she says, throwing off her blanket and racing towards me to wrap me in a hug.

Charlie watches us both with a bemused expression.

"So what are you going to do?"

I lead the way inside, having had enough of the cold, and when I tell them both the news, they can barely contain their excitement.

"I can't believe he was going to quit hockey?! That's so romantic. Who would've thought the grumpy goalie had it in him?" Tierney seems to be dangerously close to swooning right now, while Charlie just chuckles.

"Well, I'm glad it all worked out for you. And I have some news, too."

I cock my head expectantly as he shoves his hands in his pockets.

"Tilley and I have been talking a bit the last few days. I guess watching you deal with all your shit gave me some perspective. When I get back, we're going to put the house on the market and move away from Dad. You were right. It's time he was the adult in this relationship and I won't let my marriage be destroyed because he can't deal with reality."

Relief floods through me, and I step forward to give him a hug.

"Well, it's a great day in the Jameson family," Tierney says, before pulling a bottle of champagne out of the fridge and popping the cork.

"Did you just happen to have that lying around?" I ask, impressed.

"Well, it was going to be either celebrating or drowning my sorrows. Either way, it was required."

Laughing, we pour three glasses and toast to new beginnings.

That night, I settle into a seat between Kylie and Tierney in the family box. I've told Adele, Kylie and Sarah my news, and we've all quietly celebrated together. It'll be a little while before we go public with the relationship, but at least we no longer need to hide it from our friends.

Charlie opted to stay home and pack ahead of his early flight tomorrow, also wanting to talk to his wife again.

I haven't had a chance to see Dean since we left the reservoir, and it's going to be torture having to wait several more hours before we get a chance to fall into bed together, but it'll be worth the wait.

When the team hits the ice to warm up, I don't bother to

hide the way I'm watching the goalie, my stomach fluttering when he starts deflecting pucks as his teammates practice their shots. He really is a sight to behold, and knowing that he's mine does all sorts of things to my emotions.

"I'm so glad you're sticking around," Kylie says, smiling as I pull my gaze away from my boyfriend. "I wasn't ready to be the only southerner again. And I need all the help I can get in a few months when these little interlopers decide to enter the world." She rubs her belly, and I'm pleased to see her smiling about the prospect of being a mother once again.

"So Tara was successful in helping you see this isn't so bad, huh?"

She grins, shrugging. "Well, you also helped. Seeing how well you and Charlie turned out when you had a similar start in life to what these guys will, that certainly made me feel better."

I haven't told any of them about Dad, but I'm glad to see that knowing that my mother was able to raise the two of us while he was travelling so much playing sport has helped Kylie realize she can do this.

"Well, I'll definitely be around for baby cuddles," I tell her, and she squeezes my arm before turning back to watch Seth shoot a few pucks at Dean, who catches them with ease.

"You know who else is pregnant?" Sarah murmurs, leaning over Tierney to talk to Kylie and me.

"Who?" Tierney asks, always keen to hear the gossip.

Sarah jerks her head in the direction of Bethany, who's sitting in her usual spot on the other side of the room, the queen of her little entourage.

I gasp. "You're kidding?"

Sarah shakes her head with a grimace.

"Of all the women who should never have children..." Tierney says quietly, and we all nod in silent agreement.

"Poor Anders... I can just imagine how painful she's going to be now."

Sarah shrugs, sitting back in her seat. "He obviously sees something in her that we don't... Maybe she's different when they're alone together..."

I'd love it if that were true, but I doubt it. She doesn't seem like she's capable of having layers.

The game starts, and all conversation about pregnancy ends as we get swept up in the action. It really is so different being able to watch the games from up here, without having to think about the work going on in the background, and I realize this is going to be my life from now on. While I won't be able to go to the away games anymore, whenever the Cowboys are in town, I'll be right here, cheering the Mounties on, and I can't wait.

EPILOGUE

Alanna

"Babe, have you seen my towel?" Dean sticks his head around the bedroom door as I change into my bikini.

"It was hanging on the back of one of the chairs on the deck when I last saw it," I reply, smirking when he freezes to stare at me.

He shakes his head quickly, then walks up to kiss me hungrily.

"On second thought, fuck the beach, let's stay right here." He pulls at the string on the back of my bikini that I've just spent ages trying to tie behind my back.

I swat his hands away with a laugh. "Nope. Your parents are waiting for us, and I am not explaining to your mother that we're late because you couldn't keep your hands off me."

He sighs, giving me a petulant look as I step around him and smack his butt on the way out the door.

It's been a completely different experience with the Cowboys. Trevor had been absolutely fuming when he found out they'd essentially headhunted me, and has been unimpressed about the fact that we are equals now. When Joel and

Simon jumped ship to come work with me next season, I'm pretty sure he had an aneurysm, which had been fun to watch.

Dean and I began slowly attending events together over the last few months, and no one, other than Trevor, has said anything. I'm sure words would be had if the truth of how long we've been together came out, but none of our inner-circle have uttered a word, and I'm sure no one will be surprised when I move into his apartment after we get back from our holiday.

Tierney took the news well, deciding to move in with Riley to save on rent now that he's bought a house in the same gated community as Seth, Kylie, Lincoln and Adele. At least she'll be living in the pool house so will still have her own space.

The Mounties season ended in the second round of the play-offs, which was disappointing, but they played their hearts out to the end. The Cowboys season ended a week later, and two days after, we were on a plane, headed for Europe.

We arrived in Nice two days ago for a holiday with Dean's parents, travelling around the Riviera on a private yacht one of his dad's billionaire friends owns. We've already spent the last week in Rome, and he was in his element showing me around the city that he loves so much. And it's sexy as hell listening to him speak fluent Italian. If I wasn't already gone for this man, that would do it.

Next week, we'll be heading to Paris to meet Charlie and Tilley as they backpack around Europe. When they sold their house, they decided to spend some of the money travelling for a while, and I'm pleased to see they seem happier than ever. Apparently Dad checked himself into rehab, but I'll wait to see if he sticks with it before I get my hopes up.

Kylie and Seth welcomed their twin boys a few months ago, and it's been interesting watching them navigate life as parents of twins. But little Harvey and Everett have stolen the hearts of everyone, including my boyfriend, who has started dropping hints about starting a little hockey team of our own. It won't be happening any time soon while I concentrate on my career, but I'm more than happy to keep practicing making them in the mean time.

Climbing up on deck with Dean a step behind, I smile as his mother waves at us to join them on the boat that will take us to the beach on the little private island we've moored near.

Dean grabs my hand and waves them off. "We'll swim to shore!" he calls, and she shakes her head with a smile before turning back to his Dad, and he starts the engine.

"What if I don't want to swim to shore?" I ask, raising an eyebrow as I smirk up at him.

He pulls me in close, and I raise onto the tips of my toes to wrap my arms around his neck.

"Come on, brat. Last one in has to do a naked striptease tonight." He quickly kisses the tip of my nose, then lets me go and races to the front.

Gasping at the audacity, I run after him, diving over the side before he finishes climbing over the rail.

Guess he forgot I'm just as competitive as he is.

And as he swims after me, I laugh and allow him to pull me back in for another kiss, knowing that we'll both be doing the naked striptease tonight.

Because I can't ever imagine not wanting this man.

IF YOU HAVE A MOMENT

Thank you for reading! I hope you enjoyed Melt The Ice. Next up is Riley's story, coming later in 2026.

Please take a moment to leave a rating or review on the platform you purchased from or Goodreads. Every review helps in an incredible way.

If you enjoyed this book and would like to stay up to date with all new releases and behind-the-scenes shenanigans, please sign up for my newsletter - https://allisonaandrews.substack.com/

ACKNOWLEDGMENTS

As always, this book wouldn't have existed without the help of so many people.

To my husband, Andrew - thank you for supporting me through this amazing author journey, and for editing all the hockey scenes to make sure they are accurate. I'm glad I could help you live out your dream of cheering for a winning team.

To my daughter, Evelyn - thank you for being my biggest supporter and helping Mummy behind the scenes. One day, you'll be my paid helper!

To my amazing friends, Shannon and Jammi-Lee, and sister, Mel - thank you for your unwavering support behind the scenes with beta reading, editing and attending events with me. It's been one hell of a ride and I can't wait to continue sharing these moments with you all.

To Jell - thank you so much for being my chaos co-ordinator and being the best PA an author could ask for. I couldn't have done even half the things I do without you.

To my beta readers Tess, Roxxanne, Renee and Mo - thank you for your amazing feedback and allaying my fears that this book wasn't going to work! I'm so glad you enjoyed it.

And to my street team, Mounties Mayhem - thank you for the unhinged chats and your unwavering support throughout this incredible journey!

www.ingramcontent.com/pod-product-compliance
Lightning Source LLC
Chambersburg PA
CBHW011549190726
48287CB00010B/2799

* 9 7 8 1 7 6 3 6 6 2 0 9 4 *